Boyd County Public Library

VILLAGE SINS

Further Titles by Anne Worboys from Severn House

ALICE

VILLAGE SINS

Anne Worboys

This first world edition published in Great Britain 1994 by
SEVERN HOUSE PUBLISHERS LTD of
9–15 High Street, Sutton, Surrey SM1 1DF.
First published in the USA 1994 by
SEVERN HOUSE PUBLISHERS INC., of
425 Park Avenue, New York, NY 10022.

Copyright © 1994 by Anne Worboys

All rights reserved.
The moral rights of the author have been asserted.

British Library Cataloguing in Publication Data
Worboys, Anne
  Village Sins
  I. Title
  823.914 [F]

ISBN 0-7278-4628-0

All situations in this publication are fictitious and
any resemblance to living persons is purely coincidental.

Typeset by Hewer Text Composition Services, Edinburgh.
Printed and bound in Great Britain by
Redwood Books Trowbridge, Wiltshire.

Chapter 1

Ms Beryl Lisamore, assistant head of the Halfpenny Dun village primary school, put her bicycle away in the garage, locked it, and went up the path that wound through ornamental shrubs and bushes planted as a screen for the back windows of her hideaway. Though Badger Cottage fronted on to the high street, the lead lights in the front windows gave nothing away. On sunny days they reflected brilliantly into the eyes of the curious, and in mist and rain became black satin in metal frames. Badger Cottage was as protective a covering as any badger's sett. Here Beryl hid from her past and nurtured the wounds inflicted by life, precariously safe from the curious, though good-humoured gaze of the village.

It was from here, by means of her parrot and her little portable computer, that she sent her tiny barbed arrows out into the community, for experience had taught her that if one wished to interfere, and sometimes, with the very best intentions, Beryl did, one had to go about the matter deviously and with stealth, for in the business of closing ranks this little Kent village could teach an army a thing or two.

Nurtured by suspicion and self-pity, carrying wounds that failed to heal, Beryl thought of herself as one of life's victims. Only a captive bird had a corner of her heart. The two men who had come close to her, one when she was a schoolgirl, were both scheming philanderers and she had found herself no more a match for the second than for the first.

Beryl's past was normal enough in the context of late-twentieth-century behaviour, her misfortunes attributable to naivity rather than sin. Had she belonged to a lighthearted, goodhearted family she may well have come through comparatively unscathed, but having been born to parents who were by nature unforgiving, she did not learn forgiveness.

"Hello," said a strident voice as she put her key into the lock. "Oh shit!" The church bells ringing out across the village drowned the rest. Thursday was the evening for bell-ringing practice in the old Norman church at the opposite end of the high street.

"Hello, Quixote," said Beryl looking up, smiling at her beautiful African grey with its snow-white forehead, red lores and wing patches. Quixote peered down at her from a branch of wysteria vine that trailed picturesquely across the back wall of the cottage.

"Keep him inside," people advised her when she complained, fraudulently, that little boys had come into the garden and taught the parrot obscenities. Quixote liked to have his cage in the fresh air, she would reply with a convincing air of distress. Beryl, the non-interventionalist, had a very good reason for teaching the parrot to swear.

She turned the key in the back door and entered a long, narrow room, a late thirties addition to the seventeenth-century cottage. There were wide windows here that faced south-west and caught the sun for most of the day. Here she kept her computer and small printer, her work-table, her books and her telephone, for it was the heart of her home. The sofa was old, shabby and comfortable, the chairs nondescript. Rush matting covered the floor.

She put down her briefcase then went back for the cage. "You little bugger, you," said Quixote without malevolence, as she reached for the wire hook.

"Bugger you, too," replied Ms Lisamore laughing as she lifted the cage down. Turning towards the door, she thought she saw a movement and a flash of white behind the holly. The hand holding the cage jerked. "Watchit!" shrieked the parrot. He was not humanly intelligent. He had been taught to say Watchit when his cage rocked.

"Who's there?" Beryl asked, her voice squeaky high, her mind galloping. Archie Young, editor of the church magazine, delivering the monthly *Parish News*? Geoff Tate, Hon. Sec. of the Halfpenny Dun Horticultural Society bringing her long-overdue entry form for Saturday's show?

An exceedingly pretty girl stepped out onto the path. Her blonde hair was straight, her eyes a startling blue. She wore a pair of skin-tight jeans and a T-shirt emblazoned with a full frontal view of an elephant with the words Save Wild Life wobbling across her unharnessed breasts. Scarlet-painted toenails peeped out from thonged sandals. She moved like a model on the catwalk, long legs swinging from the hips. Her delicate features wore a mixture of disdain, disgust, and something arresting though indefinable. Beryl Lisamore stared at her, alerted by a fragile memory.

"I know you teach him those awful words," said the girl. There was a puzzling note of despair in her voice. "I've been here before. Aren't you going to invite me in?" she asked, and without waiting for a reply, stepped over the threshold.

With her eyes glassily on the back of the girl's T-shirt that depicted the rump of the elephant waving its tail, Beryl followed, tripped over the step and let the cage drop.

"Watchit!" shrieked the bird again, dancing angrily on its perch, then added, "Bugger you, too."

The visitor dropped down among the litter of newspapers and biscuit crumbs on the sofa and burst into tears.

Emerging from the shock of discovery, Beryl saw there were two options open to her. She could order the girl out of the house, and risk her exploding the myth of the parrot's vile vocabulary; or she could calm her down and try to discover what the visit, and the emotional anger, was about.

She chose the latter.

Chapter 2

"I've never heard such rubbish in the whole of my life! I haven't got a daughter. I've never even been married." Beryl was outraged.

"You don't have to be married to produce children. I found your name in an envelope in my adopted father's desk. My father who adopted me," the girl explained. "I certainly didn't adopt him," she said, resentfully pointing up the fact that her destiny had been out of her hands. "My name is Lisa King. It was a bit obvious – Lisa, Lisamore. There aren't many Lisamores in the telephone books. You were easy enough to trace."

"Shit!" said the parrot.

The girl turned her head and regarded the bird with despair, then lifted her eyes to Beryl's. "I could *kill* you," she said, her voice breaking. "That's how I feel. All my life I've dreamt about you. I wanted you to be perfect. And now to find . . ." Unable, after all, to interpret the disappointment, she repeated pathetically, "I could kill you."

"Kill," repeated Quixote, experimentally.

Beryl picked up the cage from the floor. "How d'you think I'm going to blot that word out of his repertoire?" she asked unfairly, and carried the parrot from the room. She returned with head held high, eyes sightless with fright. "If you would like a cup of tea or coffee, I'll be only too pleased to give you one," she offered. "Then I must ask you to go. I'm sorry you should have been upset like this but I do assure you, you've made a mistake. There must be plenty of Lisamores in the country. You'll find your mother, I'm sure." She added, flicking back with one hand the untidy wisps of dark hair that had blown awry as she cycled from the school, "Look at me, my dear. Look at this face, totally devoid of bone structure. Imagine a plain Jane like me producing you."

"I realise now who you are," she said, though she had recognised the girl, with stunning shock, several moments earlier. Everyone knew Goldie Montrose, the schoolgirl wonder who had been spotted by a film director dreamily and unselfconsciously dancing in the theatre foyer at Stratford after a performance of *As You Like It*, while waiting for the school coach to pick the party up. Two years later, in her first film, lavishly publicised, she had tugged at the nation's heartstrings as no actress had done since Elizabeth Taylor, fifty years earlier, appeared in *National Velvet*.

"I heard you'd taken Wayside Cottage." Beryl tried to smile kindly, but the smile was stiff and full of fear. "Everyone wants to meet you, but word has gone round that you've come for a rest and want to be left alone."

"I came to meet you," burst out the girl emotionally. "And you do look a little bit like me. Just a little bit. If you were blonde, or I were dark—"

"I quite understand that you're highly strung, talented people often are." Beryl stemmed the outburst with classroom expertise. "Imaginative, too. But you mustn't work off your fantasies on strangers."

The girl said, pleading like a puppy, "There's a picture of my father on a table in the little front sitting room. I know he's my father because I'm the dead spit of him. I'm not like you, but I am the dead spit of him." Her eyes went to the antique necklace Beryl wore, a flamboyant and unlikely piece of jewellery to be owned, much less worn, by a country teacher cycling to and from school. "It's been cut out of a newspaper. Why have you got a newspaper picture in a frame? Why haven't you got a proper one?"

Before Beryl could answer she added another question. "Is he famous?"

"You've been in my house! You've not only been spying on me in the garden, you've broken into my house!" Beryl diverted the question with an explosion of indignation.

"It's easy enough. And not such a sin, considering I am your daughter. Don't you know your side door has a loose bolt? It'll slide back if you shake the catch from the outside."

"I've a good mind to report you to the police."

Goldie Montrose stiffened. The curtain of hair that had crept forward on either side of her face slid silkily back. With a delicate, very feminine movement, she tucked a strand behind her left ear. "You won't call the police because you'd have to explain, and then the story would get round the village. And since you're so ashamed," her voice broke, "you won't want that." She wiped a tear away. "Why don't you bring the photo out?"

"There is no photo."

"I'll show you." The girl edged eagerly forward on the sofa.

"Do." Beryl spoke with soft derision. Indicating that Lisa should follow, she went to the door that led to the interior of the cottage. They passed the kitchen, then a small branch passage furnished with an iron-banded oak chest on which the parrot's cage now stood. On their right, the stairwell had been boxed in to make a cupboard where the vacuum cleaner, brushes and pans were kept. Ahead, two more doors opened into the hall, one from either side. Beryl led the way into the room on the right, then stepped over to the window that fronted on to the high street and drew the curtains, as she always did, before turning on the light.

Goldie Montrose went straight to a polished mahogany table that stood beneath the window. She stared at it, her face crumpling. "Yes, of course," she said in a defeated voice. "When you put the parrot away, you got rid of the photo."

Beryl managed an exasperated sigh. "It's seven o'clock," she said, "and I've had a long day. If you don't mind—" She indicated that they should return to the sunroom.

"I don't know anything about the adoption." Lisa stood her ground pursuing her unwelcome thesis, rendering the gesture futile, "except that it was private. Done through a doctor. But he's dead. My adopted parents—"

"Adoptive," said Beryl.

They stared at each other.

"—called King." Lisa recovered first from the strange moment of shock and stillness created by Beryl's automatic schoolmistressy intervention. "They told me he's dead. Was he your doctor?" In the waiting silence, Beryl moved back into the hall.

"You've obviously been under some kind of strain." Beryl, managing to sound kind and at the same time, brisk, turned to face the girl. "If you go round spreading this ridiculous accusation—"

"What will you do?" The pretty head lifted. The blue eyes took on a challenging look.

"I have a life to live here, and a reputation to uphold. The film business ought to have taught you that dirt sticks."

"Dirt!" repeated Goldie Montrose reproachfully. "It's me you're calling dirt."

"Oh, come."

"Your reputation, if they know about your kinky ways with parrots, isn't worth much now," the girl said resentfully.

Angered by the insult, Beryl said, "I had better give you a good strong coffee," in the tone of one who thought a good strong coffee would make a silly girl into a sensible one. She marched into the kitchen. As she poured some water from the tap into the kettle and plugged in the cord she was aware of Lisa at the door, hesitating forlornly on her way back to the garden room, then going on. The kettle began to make noises. She spooned some Nescafé into a mug, poured the water in and with an unsteady hand, added cold milk. With the sugar bowl in one hand and the mug in the other, she emerged.

The bird had flown

Ben Finlay, assistant milkman, leaned his bicycle up against the holly hedge and lifted the carton of cream from his basket just as Goldie Montrose emerged from Miss Lisamore's back gate. Wow! He stared after her, eyes popping. Romy Childs, the crystal woman who lived at Cobblers, the only other cottage in Old Wood Lane, said she had made the actress's acquaintance and had been told she didn't want to meet anyone else in Halfpenny Dun. But it wasn't true. Here she was, calling on Miss Lisamore! He strode eagerly up the garden path. Finding the back door open he poked his head inside and called.

Beryl came like a cannonball from the interior of the cottage.

"Here's your cream," said Ben uncertainly, thrown by the startled aggression in her face. "Sorry about this morning," he added, offering goodwill with his endearing grin. "It weren't my fault. More'n more people want cream these days. I run out."

She took the cream and left him on the doorstep without a word of thanks.

"You all right?" But she had already slammed the inner door behind her.

She didn't have to be so sodding rude, he thought as he trailed disconsolately back along the path and out into Old Wood Lane. It wasn't his fault about the cream. It wouldn't have hurt her to tell him about Goldie Montrose. He leaned on his bike, staring into the garden. The laurel bush, their laurel bush, came within focus. Moved by a need for consolation, he looked swiftly up and down the lane to make sure no one was about, then slipped back through the gate, parted the drooping branches and crawled under cover. Ollie would kill him for this, he told himself fearfully as he shuffled around among last years' dead leaves and brought out a half bottle of gin. Ollie was the ringleader of the gang.

He unscrewed the cap and lifted the bottle to his lips. The neat spirit burnt his throat and tears sprang to his eyes. There was never any tonic or ginger ale. A half of whisky, gin or vodka, because of its shape, was easily hidden in a shirt, or a pocket in their jeans, but the boys knew better than to walk through the village bearing circular-bodied soft-drink bottles.

There was not much excitement in Ben Finlay's life. He was up at four in the morning delivering milk, had a sleep after lunch, then spent the rest of the day kicking his heels in the high street, listening to his Sony. The village bobby sometimes asked him to turn the volume down, but Ollie had told him there was no rule against playing music in a public place. PC Edwards was only throwing his weight around, Ollie said. Ben would always turn the volume down for old ladies. He liked them. Liked all his customers. He was rattled at having fallen foul of Miss Lisamore.

He took another mouthful. Better go, now. What was that? Footsteps, coming down from the cottage towards the gate? He stayed still as a mouse and the steps receded. Golly gumdrops, he'd better get out. As he pushed the bottle back under the leaves he thought he heard the footsteps again. What was Miss Lisamore up to? Had she seen him? Was she waiting out there to go for him? He panicked. Reggie had brought this on him. Last week, in spite of the protests of the rest of the gang, Reggie had insisted on tossing a couple of empties out on to the lawn under the back windows.

"That'll excite the old fart," he said gleefully. "She'll think there's been rapists in, and they've missed her." Reggie hated Miss Lisamore for the humiliations he had suffered at her hands. She was hard on bright pupils who wouldn't work. Reggie could have gone on to higher education, she said, but he only wanted to be a bricklayer.

Ben heard a click. Miss Lisamore must have gone through the gate. She would see his bike! He waited, crouched on hands and knees, breathless with fear. There was a rattle, then a bump. Stealthily, he parted the leaves and watched with horror as she triumphantly wheeled his precious bike up the path.

The brighter miscreants, Ollie, Reg or Joe, would have hurled the bottles over the hedge into the allotments next door and bare-facedly denied all knowledge of the one she found on the lawn, at the same time indignantly accusing her of stealing the bike while they had a pee in the bushes. (That would have amused them, to say 'pee' to her.)

Ben, who was neither resourceful nor inventive, accepted that he had been caught red-handed. He fell back on the leaves, limp with despair, then jerked forward again as one of the bottles struck him in the back. He pulled it out and laid it down beside him while he thought about what he might do. No ideas came. After a while, to relieve his misery, he removed the cap of the bottle and took a sip. Whisky. He made a face. Should he fetch the boys? Would Ollie be brave enough to tackle her? No, he wouldn't do anything to help because Ben had broken that pact they made. No one was to come here alone. Ollie would be angry. He might even land a punch. What a fix! Feeling desperate, Ben took another sip, shuddered and sipped again.

His mind grew cloudy. The whisky didn't taste as good as the gin. He put the bottle back among the leaves and brought out another. That wasn't gin, either. What was it? He choked as it went down. That was vodka. He'd rather have the gin. He dug out the first bottle. By that time he couldn't taste anything.

Chapter 3

Confiscating Ben Finlay's bicycle gave Beryl a much needed boost of confidence. Odd how events juxtaposed themselves, she thought. It was only yesterday, trimming the laurel, that she had discovered the suspiciously flattened leaves and investigating, seen the tell-tale neck of a bottle. So mild-mannered Ben was one of the hooligans who used her shrubbery for their little orgies! She was surprised.

She wheeled the bicycle into the prison custody of her narrow hallway, leaned it up against the wall and paused to consider. Her profession had taught her there could be a violent side to mild-mannered boys who were not very bright. Should she have called Ben out and told him to get off the premises taking his bottles with him? Yes, she thought apprehensively, but now it was too late.

She took the precaution of locking the back door, then went to examine the bolt that the girl had so craftily displaced. Most of the picturesque old cottages in Halfpenny Dun lacked damp courses. Extremes of weather could disturb the line of a wall. Where a new building might crack, the old ones sagged, and with luck returned to normal in another season, though not always precisely on line. In the end, everything finished up on the skew.

The door was shut, latched with a decorative iron bar more commonly seen on stable doors of the period, so there was no question of its swinging open, but once the inside bolt had slid aside anyone could gain entrance by the simple expedient of turning the metal ring that acted as a latch. An intruder would not be seen from the road, for the holly hedge that ran the length of the property in Old Wood Lane was six feet tall and stood only a few feet from the house wall. How many nights, she wondered, looking back with nerves jumping, had she slept with this door unbolted? She had had no cause to examine it, and a casual glance along the passage would have given nothing away, for there was no window, and the iron bolt was dark against the oak.

Goldie Montrose, to her knowledge, had been at Wayside Cottage for a week. Had she spent the whole week spying on her, roaming in her garden, and in the house?

Agonising over her stupidity and her bad luck, she lifted the parrot's cage to the floor and proceeded to drag the chest the length of the little passageway where she jammed it hard against the door. Then she went down on her knees in the sitting room and reached under the sofa for the photograph of Paul Street. Why hadn't she thrown it away? Why had she cut it out in the first place? What a fool she was! She did not consider herself a sentimental fool. A lonely fool was more the truth of it. Even bad memories were sometimes better than none.

Last week, when the picture had appeared again in the morning paper and she read the accompanying article with its disturbing disclosures, she had sat for a long time gazing at it, feeling not only a sense of vindication, but enormous satisfaction that all these years later Paul Street had been caught.

Mr Street, as the fifteen-year-old Beryl called him even when, knickerless, she lay with him among the bushes on the riverbank below the school – had been retained by her parents in the summer of 1969 to coach her in French. When he suggested they walk down to the river it did not occur to her to refuse. She could recite French verbs in the open air quite as well as in the classroom.

What he did to her was wrong, she knew that, but he

was her teacher, and she was a little afraid of him. Besides, it was rather nice. The niceness ended abruptly one day when she complained that he was leaning too hard on her breasts.

"Sore?" he echoed, speaking sharply, lifting himself on one elbow and looking down into her face with what seemed at the time like anger, but which the older Beryl knew to be panic. "What do you mean?"

"It doesn't matter," she muttered, frightened at the change in him, recognising as he clambered swiftly to his feet and adjusted his flies, only that she had done wrong to complain. "It's girls like you who get us chaps into trouble. Get up," he ordered her. "Put your clothes on," as though it had been her idea to take them off.

She remembered standing abjectly before him in her blue regulation shirt and grey skirt, clutching her Grammar. "I wasn't blaming you," she said miserably, but he left her, anyway, striding fast across the meadow towards the school. Beryl crept miserably home.

By the time her mother began asking sharp questions Mr Street had gone on his way, with his wife and baby, to a school in Yorkshire.

"You've been sick three times, Beryl, and always in the morning."

"I must have eaten something."

"What have you been up to, young woman?" That was her father, by nature harsh and suspicious. They were not a loving family. Beryl looked into his face and quailed, remembering how Mr Street had said it was her fault.

"Nothing," she insisted.

Her parents whisked her off to Paris to work as an au pair, telling friends and neighbours they had decided she should complete her education abroad. Her mother travelled there to be with her for the birth. The adoptive parents collected the child there. It was neatly executed and they were surprised, afterwards, to find that back at home an astonishing number of people knew. The shame, the humiliation the parents suffered, though mainly in their own minds, resulted in the break-up of the family.

Beryl looked down now at the photo that had appeared in the paper when Paul Street was given the headship of a famous public school in Wiltshire. Yes, she thought bitterly, before consigning the dangerous likeness to the kitchen bin, you would have a daughter like that.

Feeling emotionally violent, she took a knife to push the frame down among the detritus of last night's supper. She did not think about Goldie Montrose being her child. She had not held her. There had been no love. It had not been allowed. An amalgam of hurt had lain for twenty-eight years behind a defensive shield.

She carried the cage back to the garden room and set it down on the coffee table. Shivering, she clutched her upper arms, seeing in the arrival of the child the loss of respect she had earned as assistant headmistress of the village school. Inevitably, there would be classroom sniggers; whispering behind hands; dinner-party gossip in the grander houses. She could even, if fate chose to play its most diabolical hand and Goldie Montrose discovered her father's identity, be named in the tabloids as his earlier victim. She thought actresses would do anything for publicity. Her imagination ran riot. Could she be called as witness if he came to trial? Appalling headlines flashed across her vision. MOTHER OF GOLDIE MONTROSE SUBPOENA'D. TESTIMONY THAT STREET WAS SEDUCING SCHOOLGIRLS TWENTY-NINE YEARS AGO.

"Shit!" shrieked the parrot, pointing up those problems that were, regrettably, of her own making.

"The trouble you've caused me!" she shrieked back, unhinged with fright. Quixote ruffled his feathers and readjusted his claws on the perch.

I shall have to leave Halfpenny Dun, Beryl said to herself. There had been enough unhappiness, enough embarrassment and insults. She could endure no more.

But where would she go? Australia? Canada? And how would she pay for the running? The mortgage on Badger Cottage kept her poor. She crossed the room and stood looking down at her computer, thinking of her brother Noel, he who was so privileged, and so unfairly well heeled.

After the Lisamore parents' divorce, Noel had gone to live with their father. Preposterously laying at his daughter's feet the blame for the expense of maintaining two domiciles, Humphrey Lisamore said – would she ever forget the hardness of heart, the total lack of compassion? – "You, Beryl, can support yourself, now."

She had not had to, for her mother opted to go back to secretarial work so that Beryl could finish her education. Brother and sister thereafter saw virtually nothing of each other, for the father was determined to keep them apart, and the mother grew more and more unwilling to face the unpleasantness that accrued whenever she wanted to see her son. Besides, she had been told Noel did not want to see her, and certainly as he grew older he made no attempt to get in touch.

Four years ago brother and sister met on the occasion of Mrs Lisamore's funeral. Beryl talked to Noel's wife Joan, whom she and her mother had not been allowed to know. Joan seemed friendly enough. She spoke to Beryl about the church shop for which she was responsible; Noel's excellent prospects; his community work, yet she showed no desire to extend this abundant goodwill to her husband's sister. Beryl, already stunned by the knowledge that she was now utterly alone in the world, came away from the funeral in despair, convinced that this would be their last contact.

Three years ago the headmistress of the village school asked if the Humphrey Lisamore listed under Deaths in the *Daily Telegraph* was related to her. Beryl, unwilling to allow Miss Cara Hagan to violate her privacy, replied No, then went to the village shop and bought a copy of the paper. She toyed with the idea of attending the funeral. "2pm St James's Church, Hartney", the notice said. He was her father, after all. She agonised for four days then decided against. She would be hurt by her brother's indifference. He had, after all, chosen not to inform her. She wondered if that had been her father's wish.

At a certain level she accepted what had happened yet, as two o'clock approached on the day of the funeral, the very real disappointment and loneliness she kept hidden became an unbearable pain. She asked to be excused her work. She was not feeling well, she said. In Badger Cottage she collapsed on her bed weeping bitterly as she faced up to the fact that her brother's silence meant the lonely years would never end.

Some time later, out of sheer curiosity, she would have said had she been asked, she obtained a copy of Humphrey Lisamore's will and was amazed to see how much money he had left. Noel was his sole legatee.

She could not accept that she was nothing to her father, even beyond the grave. He had loved her once, before she committed the unforgiveable sin of embarrassing him. She remained his daughter. She wrote to Noel, suggesting that as he had no children and a good job he might see his way clear to help her with the mortgage on Badger Cottage. It was not that she particularly needed the money. In time her debts would be paid. She wanted something she could not easily have explained. To put him right in the eyes of God? To relieve his conscience, for surely he must have one? To give him an opportunity to get to know her?

She was deeply distressed when he ignored the letter.

"Kill you," said the parrot, eyeing her experimentally.

Beryl's mind returned to the bicycle in the hall. "You stupid old bird," she muttered. "I've a good mind to sell you to a pet shop," yet she was aware, even as she made the threat, that the only real amusement, comfort and companionship in her life came from Quixote.

"Listen to the whispers," Romy Childs the crystal

woman who lived farther up Old Wood Lane was fond of saying. "Listen to the whispers, Beryl."

The whisper at the back of her mind was a wicked one, and Beryl was not a wicked woman, but she was now at the end of her tether. This brother of hers, she thought, had a lot to lose.

From his wife's chatter at the funeral she knew about his rise in the Civil Service. In the event that his working life continued along its present smooth lines he would no doubt, for that was the nature of Civil Service life, end up with an OBE. She knew who his superiors were, even the name of his secretary, for by pure chance last summer, when on holiday in Greece, she had stayed at the same pension as a junior member of his department.

"Lisamore." He had repeated her name, his eyes curious, and dark. "I've only ever met one Lisamore," he said. "He's in the Civil Service. Head of my department. I wonder if you're related."

"I have no relations," she had lied, not wanting to expose her sorry story, but the following day he had approached her on the beach and throwing his towel down beside her on the sand asked, "Mind if I join you? Glenys has gone off with that chap with the beard. I need a mother figure for comfort."

She had laughed, while protesting that considering he must be all of twenty-five, she would rather be seen as an aunt.

In the event, he had not wanted to tell her his troubles. "You are Noel Lisamore's sister," he said, settling down beside her, and before she could collect her wits, added, "It's the chin. Something about the chin."

"Does it matter?"

He had not replied and she thought he was satisfied, but a few moments later he offered, "Your brother's heavily into good works, isn't he?"

"I don't know," she admitted.

"You're not on good terms?"

"We're not in touch."

He looked at her curiously. "Shall I tell you about him?"

The temptation was too great to resist. Laurie, for that was the young man's name, supplied her with some interesting information. Her brother held several voluntary positions in his village and in the county. He lived in a large, desirable, detached house, which was not surprising considering how much money their father had left him. He was not only a member of his Parochial Church Council, but had recently been elected to the General Synod. What did God think of that? she wondered cynically.

At sunset, as she sat alone at an open-air restaurant with the sea breaking on the sands below, Laurie came to join her once again. Glenys, it appeared, had packed her bag and left with the bearded lothario for Corfu. "Mind if I join you?" he asked again, and she had welcomed him, for she had not found a companion with whom to share meals. Beryl did not mind holidaying alone but she hated eating by herself, silent amid the laughing, chattering diners.

They ate moussaka and drank a bottle of Retsina, but it was not the happy meal Beryl anticipated. Laurie was glum. "I've already had four or five brandies," he admitted, "in an attempt to drown my sorrows and my conscience."

"Conscience?" she echoed.

He took a piece of paper from his pocket and pushed it towards her. "A trouble shared is a trouble halved," he said.

On the paper was a car registration number and its make, followed by a date and time. "What's this?"

He told her, briefly, the stunning facts. There had been an office celebration at a restaurant in Soho. Her brother had left first. Walking towards his flat in Bloomsbury, crossing Soho Square, Laurie had seen Noel come out of his parking space too fast, swerve, hit a man, leap out to look at the body, glance around, jump back into his car and drive off fast. "The man was dead," said Laurie.

"And you . . . What did you do?"

"Nothing. I was the only witness. And he is my boss." He reached across the table for her handbag and pushed the piece of paper in.

Beryl was shaken. "Why are you telling me this?"

"Because my conscience is killing me. And I've already said, a trouble shared is supposed to be a trouble halved."

There had been little more conversation. Laurie ordered more brandy and Beryl, thinking he was either going to be sick or pass out, left him. Back home she decided she must not allow a casual contact with a troubled stranger on a foreign beach to affect her life. She was still trying to forget when she discovered how much money her father had left. A kind of madness – she recognised it as such – born of rejection and loneliness, came over her. She considered blackmailing Noel, not for a share of the money, simply as a weapon to bludgeon her way into his life. She felt she could swallow the insult of the inheritance. She could see no reason why he would not like her if he knew her. She would like him simply because he was her brother. His wife Joan had been amiable enough when they met at the funeral. It was not Joan, she was certain, who kept them apart.

Beryl lay awake at nights considering the wording of the letter, telling herself one moment that such a plan could not possibly work, the next, that it might. A few weeks ago she finally plucked up the courage to write a brief note, saying that she would like to discuss with him, in private, an incident that had occurred in Soho Square. He did not reply. Beryl wept.

Now, fingers on the keys, contemplating the change in her circumstances, she decided to try again. This time she did not use tact, for his friendship was no longer an issue. She blatantly threatened him with exposure, said she had witnesses, and demanded half of his inheritance to keep quiet.

As she tapped out the letter a change come over her. The familiar self-pity hardened into vengeance. On another level she was frightened by this new Beryl whom she scarcely knew. Real wickedness was not something she understood. She did not run the letter off. After supper, she thought, she would check it again. Then sleep on it. The temperature in the room had dropped. Leaving the machine running, she went to get a jacket. Passing Ben's bicycle in the hall, she was reminded of that other problem. She went on up the stairs, thinking about it.

What about cycling round the green in the morning and dumping the bike at the police station? She could say she had searched the shrubbery with a torch, and a boy, or man, leapt out and ran away. Ben, forced to reclaim his property, might well inform on the others. Beryl was pleased with the idea. She felt she might, after all, escape retribution.

She opened the window and took some calming breaths. A great golden moon lit up the lawn, outlining dark shapes that in the daytime became magnolia, hibiscus, rhodedendron and azalea bushes, green friends to ensure her privacy. On the village side, the southern side, a tall beech hedge, leafy brown in winter, leafy green in summer, shut her garden off from old Tom Sharples' allotment, the first in the row that lay in neat oblongs between Pieman's Lane where some of the grander houses in the village stood, and the stream bordering the high street. She could see quite clearly right over to The Red House, property of Brian and Letitia Grey whose back door, by the freak chance of two conifers coming down in the hurricane of 1987, was visible through the gap.

The weather report, though seldom worth taking seriously, had promised sunshine at the weekend. On Saturday the Halfpenny Dun Village Horticultural Society would hold its annual show in a marquee generously donated by Lord Oaks, the local grandee. The village was alive with excitement. Tomorrow evening, volunteers would erect the canvas in the grounds of his Georgian mansion, and on Saturday morning there would be a great bustle in the village as the residents transported their competition entries, flower arrangements, cakes, jams and prize vegetables to the judging.

A man was making his way along the path that ran between the allotments and the back gardens of the properties in Pieman's Lane. Beryl frowned, blinked, then looked again for there was something familiar about that walk, and the upright, tall figure. As the man crossed in front of what she knew to be a paling fence, misty-white in the moonlight, he came clearly into focus, stopped, bent down, disappeared, then reappeared on the other side, climbing up the slope towards the back of the Greys' house.

Beryl's first instinct was to telephone a quick warning to Mrs Grey whose husband had gone, in fact often went, to Japan, on business. She had swung away from the window when recognition dawned and she spun back, eyes wide with astonishment. If that wasn't Anthony Rowsell, she thought, she would eat her hat. Letitia's back door must have opened, for one moment Anthony was silhouetted against the wall of the house, the next he had disappeared. Moments later, there were two figures dimly etched behind the window of an upstairs bedroom. Then the curtains swung across.

Anthony, having it off with Letitia Grey, the highly respected organiser of Meals-on-wheels and chairwoman of the Women's Institute! Beryl could not believe her eyes.

Five or six years ago she had made Anthony's acquaintance while browsing round his antique shop in Castle Manton. Perversely attracted by her untouchability, for metaphorically speaking Beryl had kept her legs crossed for the intervening years, Anthony saw her as a challenge.

He enjoyed the walks and talks with her and the meals she cooked for him. He liked her admiration, for she was overwhelmed by the attention of such a handsome and eligible bachelor, and Anthony was a vain man. He took her to restaurants. When she innocently admired an antique necklace in a glass case in his showroom, scarabs and uncut desert stones, he gave it to her, yet still she remained invincible. Anthony, seriously impatient, lacking the sensitivity to recognise a bruised ego and nurtured suffering, slyly produced his second string, an apparently genuine offer of marriage.

Beryl capitulated.

It was a tragedy that within weeks of the consummation of their friendship, Susan Lambert came to teach at the school, and one day Anthony, intoxicated by the discovery that she was only child and heir to a man with a heart condition, a manor house, and three thousand acres of rich farming country in Buckinghamshire, forgot Beryl's telephone number and passed her in the street as though she had become invisible.

According to Common Room gossip, Susan was that outdated novelty, a virgin. With the easy good humour of one who is conscious of her value, she let it be known she intended to keep her virginity intact until after marriage. Beryl, unaware of the acres, the manor house and the heart condition, waited innocently for her lover to recognise defeat and return to her bed. She suffered humiliation beyond bearing when he did not come.

Susan of the iron knickers kept her man.

Beryl kept the necklace and wore it defiantly. She told people it was a keepsake. She hinted at a romantic past. It looked incongruous worn in the classroom with her simple clothes, but she wore it all the same. Continuously provoked by seeing it around her neck, Anthony deeply regretted his generosity.

Recently, Beryl had invited him, as an influential member of the County Council, to help her get double yellow lines painted in the road outside her cottage or, alternatively, No Parking signs. Cars parked there, in her opinion, constituted a traffic hazard for drivers emerging from Old Wood Lane had a restricted view of the high street. She had spoken often to the culprits, mainly local people who were merely going to the Post Office Stores opposite, but they refused to take her protests seriously. "I'll be back in a tick," they would say, smiling sheepishly, and running across the road.

Anthony did not lay the matter before the Council. In his opinion, he said, the small amount of traffic involved did not justify the expense. He felt no need to please this person of no importance with whom he had momentarily dallied on his way up the social and community ladder. It was a humiliation that Beryl felt underlined her lack of status.

Now the new Beryl, hyped up by her brush with Goldie Montrose, fearful of retribution for taking Ben's bicycle, bitter about the fact that she had to resort to blackmail in order to get help from her brother, recognised in this new turn of events that fate was making her a genuine offer of revenge.

She had nothing personal against Letitia, who was only one of the well-heeled ladies of Halfpenny Dun who did not invite her to their dinner parties, but she was not averse to seeing a glossy bird knocked off her perch, any glossy bird on whom fate had lavished the best life could offer while kicking her in the teeth. As for seeing Anthony lose his heiress wife and know the same kind of humiliation that she had suffered . . .

Beryl, who had never tasted real power in her life, experienced a breathless surge of hope. Had her luck really changed at last? Here was a heaven-sent opportunity to acquire her double yellow lines.

In her wardrobe there was a navy-blue linen coat that would be inconspicuous in the dark. She put it on and made her way downstairs.

Chapter 4

"Beryl!" There was a moment of astonished silence. Then, "What the devil are you doing here?"

"Waiting for you," said Beryl. "I saw you go in. Two and a half hours ago." She added, quietly triumphant, "Precisely two and a half hours."

Anthony stood quite still in the moonlight looking down, first at her, then at the palings he had removed from the fence, as though at a loss to know what to do with either.

"Shall we patch it up? A woman on her own doesn't want prowlers." Beryl added provocatively, "I'll have a word with Brian when he returns. He's handy with a hammer and nails." She bent and lifted one paling, then another, neatly inserting them in the fence.

He made no move to help her.

"Cat got your tongue, lover boy?" She straightened, looking up at him, holding the third paling against her bosom while she taunted him. He snatched at it, wanting to hit her with it, but she had it in a firm grip.

He pulled and she lost her balance, falling heavily against the fence. "Sorry," he said, not feeling sorry at all, thinking it served her right. "Are you okay?"

She brushed down her coat, lifted her chin, and angrily resumed the upper hand. "Caught in the act, Anthony."

"What a suspicious woman you are," he said, his voice light and careless. "As a matter of fact, I have been visiting Letitia. I had to deliver some stuff for the show."

"Come off it. I know precisely what you've been doing. Fucking her," said Beryl, all the insult and misery she had suffered over the years coming together to explode in a word she had never before contemplated using, reducing Anthony's little affaire to its most obscene, "in the lefthand back bedroom of Brian's house." Not The Red House. Not the Grey's house. Brian's house. His name, in these circumstances, had a potency that fed her newfound ego. She turned, leading the way along the track that would bring them into Old Wood Lane, confident that Anthony would follow. "Sensitive of you not to use the marital bed," she flung over her shoulder.

"Beryl—" He was breathless with shock.

"Let's talk about the No Parking signs," she suggested. An alien voice that was, a dangerous voice. He felt he did not know this Beryl. She scarcely knew herself.

"Are you blackmailing me?" He made a tremendous effort to sound amused, but the words came out thin, and scared.

"Tut, tut." Her voice exploded with power.

He was sorry he had made himself vulnerable. He thought about the wife he valued, not just for the Buckinghamshire estate she would bring him shortly when her father died, but for herself, and the two little children he greatly loved. "The Council isn't sympathetic—" he began but she broke in,

"I was counting on you to get their sympathy. You can be so very persuasive, Anthony. You can get anything you want, if you really want it. We both know that."

He accepted that she was referring to her seduction and felt himself to be on rocky ground. "I have tried. Honestly, Beryl, I have tried."

"No, you haven't. I've seen the Minutes of the Council meetings." Carried away by her own outrageous behaviour, Beryl lied without conscience. "You haven't done a thing."

Anthony vexedly accepted she had seen the Minutes. He knew it was possible. He wouldn't put anything past that little blonde typist who came to meetings in bum-length skirts and tarty boots. Beryl turned, and in the moonlight he could see her smile. It froze him to the bone.

"Such a lot of fuss over a tiny matter," he said, thoughtlessly attacking her pride.

"Tiny it may appear to you," she snapped, "but it's very important to me to get that corner made safe. Are you waiting for half a dozen little boys on bikes to be killed before you move? If even one car is parked in front of my cottage there's absolutely no view to the right when a vehicle exits from the lane."

He felt her concern for little boys on bikes was less than her concern to let the village know she had not been ignored. He saw her as an unimportant little schoolmistress in a tiny country school. His courage returned. She wouldn't dare put tales round the village about him.

"I was going to write to the Council again, but I'm sure I can safely leave the matter in your hands, now," she said. Beryl hadn't been so excited about anything as far back as she could remember.

"Beryl."

The path had widened. They were approaching Old Wood Lane. He came abreast of her and put a hand on her arm. She sensed a change in his manner. His fingers felt hard, unfriendly. Anthony had found a way out. Too late, she saw the folly of threatening a strong man who had a lot to lose. Beryl became aware of the lateness of the hour, the darkness of the narrow track, and tasted fear.

As they turned into the lane only a few yards from her back gate he said, "Let's go in, shall we? Let's have a little talk. A coffee, perhaps?"

"I wasn't counting on giving you a coffee." She tried to jerk her arm free, but he clamped it against his side. "Anthony!" Her voice rose. "Let me go or I shall scream."

"I could deal very swiftly with a scream, and you wouldn't like the way I did it." He was the old Anthony, now. The one who knew what to do. He kicked open the gate and hustled her up the path.

"Unlock it," he said as they reached the door.

"Let me go." She viciously kicked his shins. He kicked her back. As she bent over, moaning, he took the key from her coat pocket and inserted it in the lock. The light switch, he knew well enough, was inside the door of the garden room but the curtains on the long row of windows had not been drawn. His fingers hesitated on the switch. Better not.

Jerking brutally at her arm, he half-lifted her, half-forced her across the dark room and barging confidently into the passage, came up against Ben Finlay's bicycle. There was an unearthly clatter, a shriek, and they sprawled together among frail wire spokes and cold metal.

Everyone knew about Sammy Smeed's nocturnal habits, but since he had done no one any harm, the villagers left him alone. His mother locked both the front and back doors of Foundry Cottage at night, but it was not possible to lock the windows. It was difficult enough to close them. Elsie Smeed was vociferous in her complaints, offered at random in the village pub and over the Post Office counter, that Lord Oaks wouldn't spend a penny on the wysteria-clad, brick and tile-hung cottage in the high street, but nobody took any notice, for it was well known that he exacted a mere peppercorn rent. The late Dick Smeed, a good farmworker in his day, had met an unfortunate end when earning a bit extra as a beater during pheasant shoots on the estate. (No one's fault but his own, the local magistrate, who had half a gun in Lord Oaks' shoot, and was therefore a witness to the tragedy, had pronounced regretfully at the inquest.)

Elsie knew her son slipped out because several times he had been found mooching around a garden and been escorted home by the owner. Everyone in the village, accustomed to his empty, staring eyes and passive good-will, said he was harmless as a fly. This evening, having heard his mother discussing with the butcher the fact that Goldie Montrose had taken Wayside Cottage, he loped off down Old Wood Lane, hoping to get a glimpse of her through a window.

Wayside Cottage, originally built by the first Lord Oaks as accommodation for estate workers, was one of half a dozen draughty and damp cottages the present encumbent had modernised after the demise of tenant employees. Because of their beauty, their proximity on a fast train service to London, and no doubt their Grade Two status, they commanded high rents in the short term.

Sammy opened the little wooden gate and trotted eagerly up the path. Noticing that the curtains on one of the windows were only partially drawn, he crossed the small square of lawn and squinted through the glass. There she was, the lovely thing, looking even more beautiful than when he had seen her in films. But what was this? Tears pouring down her cheeks! Sammy's simple heart swelled with sympathy. Poor Goldie! He felt a tremendous urge to go in and comfort her.

He scratched timidly at the window. Through the gap in the curtains he saw her leap up from the sofa, then a high, tremulous voice came through the letter box behind him, "Who's there?"

He scurried over to the porch and called through the slit, "It's only me. Sammy."

"Sammy who?" Before he could reply the voice added sharply, "What do you want?"

"Nuffin," Sam replied in his nicest, kindest voice. "Can I come in?"

"Go away."

Sammy returned to the window. The light went off in the front room, but in the faint glow from the television screen he saw the curtain move. He raised a finger to cover the wart on the side of his nose, then put his face close to the glass so that she would see him, only fifteen years old, and friendly. The pretty face appeared. "Go away," she mouthed. "Go a-way."

Accustomed to brush-offs, Sammy reluctantly obeyed.

At the gate he paused, looking towards Cobblers, the only other cottage in Old Wood Lane, where Romy Childs, the crystal woman, lived. Sometimes, when he was wandering by, she would invite him in and talk to him about her crystals. She told him he was one of nature's innocents, a gift to the world in the new age of enlightenment. He carried a crystal she had given him in a pocket in his jeans, and slept with it under his pillow, smoothing it with his fingers, liking the silky feel of it. She said it would keep him spiritually attuned. His mother told him he had better not repeat that, or people would think he was barmy, so he didn't. But he refused to throw the crystal away, thinking of it, as the white witch suggested, as a friend.

Romy was an ersatz gypsy. There were those who thought her a humbug. The gullible and credulous consulted her in secret. It was true she could bamboozle and humour, but she never betrayed. People were welcome to come to her for help, but not for gain. Romanys, she let it be known, were straight as a forest birch, and that was how she thought of herself, as a forest creature; an educated nymph with a disingenuous knowledge of other worlds, and her feet firmly planted on terra firma. She earned a considerable income and had acquired a certain status from syndicated columns on astrology, the spiritual powers of rocks and crystals, and the paranormal.

She did indeed have Romany ancestors on her father's side, hence the name, but one of them had married, a long time ago, into an English family from which she was descended and the Romany blood was thin. Her immediate relations, accountants and shopkeepers, were acutely embarrassed by this throwback who dabbled in fortune-telling and called herself a white witch. They kept in friendly touch by telephone, but forebore to maintain closer contact.

Cobblers was in darkness. Not a sliver of light showed through the curtains. Sammy wandered round the garden. Even the ducks on the pond were asleep with their heads beneath their wings. He sat for a while on a garden seat, watching the moonlight on the water, and then he resumed his wanderings, back along Old Wood Lane, dark now where the chestnut saplings, beech and holly crept close, smelling of night greenness and musty earth.

An owl hooted. Sammy stopped to listen. If he stood quite still sometimes a badger would come shuffling backwards across the road carrying fresh bracken for its bedding. Tonight there were undergrowth rustlings, but no sign of life. Sammy wandered on. At the rear entrance to Miss Lisamore's cottage he hesitated, one hand resting on her gate. The lawn was bright with moonlight, the bushes dark. He was about to go in when he heard a sound of footsteps on the path and Anthony Rowsell appeared.

"Hello, Mr Rowsell," he said, beaming, gazing up at the great man, opening the gate for him.

"Jesus wept!" said Anthony, putting the back of one hand to his forehead and closing his eyes.

"What's the matter, Mr Rowsell?" asked Sammy, concerned.

Anthony came slowly forward and looking down into the boy's empty face took him by the arm. "You're a good boy, Sammy," he began, unsteadily. "We're friends, aren't we?"

Sammy, astonished, could only nod in agreement.

"You won't tell anyone you've seen me, will you?"

Sammy obligingly shook his head.

"It'll be our secret?"

The boy nodded eagerly.

A car turned into the lane and crept forward. For one appalling moment Anthony thought the driver had recognised him and was going to pull over. He turned sharply away from the headlights and put a hand up to shield his face. "Cross your heart?" he asked the boy, his voice abrupt, his nerve going.

Sammy nodded, anxious, as always, to please.

"Say it, Sam," snapped Anthony. The car crept slowly on. With part of his mind, Anthony registered that the driver had neither changed gear nor accelerated.

"Cross my heart, Mr Rowsell." He gazed up at his hero, slack-mouthed, with earnest little boot button eyes.

Anthony brought his hand down from his face and looked up the road, watching until the receding tail lights went out of sight. "On second thoughts," he said, turning back, sounding smiley, like a friend, "I'll tell you what I've been doing. I wouldn't tell anyone else, mind you. But I know I can trust you. Hmn?"

Greatly flattered, Sammy beamed foolishly.

"I have to check on refuse for the Council," said Anthony, pathetically inventive. "I can only do it at night when people are asleep, because they're funny about their refuse. That's why I don't want you to tell." He laid a hand on the boy's shoulder. "It has to be done, Sam, so I do it when people are in bed."

Sammy nodded, bright-eyed, doubly flattered now to find himself in receipt of Mr Rowsell's confidence.

"But you won't tell anyone."

"No."

There was another car coming. Or the same one returning? Anthony panicked. "Mum's the word," he said. "Our secret." He gave Sammy another pat, squeezed his shoulder warmly, and hurried off towards the high street.

Sammy, glowing, watched him go. He put a hand to his shoulder where Mr Rowsell's fingers had rested. He could still feel the pressure, and the warmth, through the old, hand-knitted jumper he wore. Who would have thought Mr Rowsell would share secrets with the likes of him? Dazed by the brilliance of the encounter, Sammy wandered after him. At the high street, Mr Rowsell having disappeared, he turned left and went into the bus shelter. From here he could gaze upon the security lights at the Post Office opposite. Cars sped intermittently by but he scarcely saw them for he was thinking of Mr Rowsell and the secret they shared.

Sam could dream for hours on a hard bench, so long as there was something to look at, and never know how much time had passed. After a while a motor bike roaring past disturbed him. He stood up and wandered on. At the gate of Foundry Cottage, he paused. Had Mr Rowsell come here, also, to check on his mother's rubbish? There was plenty of it lying around in the back garden.

Sammy knew Miss Lisamore put hers in the black plastic bags supplied by the Council and left them in the lane on Thursdays to be picked up by the refuse truck, but his mother didn't always bother. Wasn't today Thursday? It occurred to Sammy that Miss Lisamore's rubbish should have been picked up at midday. He swung the gate back and forth, puzzling. How could there be refuse in Miss Lisamore's garden on a Thursday evening? He decided to go back to Badger Cottage and see if he could find out what Mr Rowsell was talking about.

There was no rubbish in the garden, no plastic sacks. Not on the path, anyway, and it was too dark to look around the bushes. Noticing that the back door was open, he stepped over the threshold, fumbled for a switch and flooded the room with light. He had often wandered in the garden of Badger Cottage in the daytime when Miss Lisamore was out, and peered through the windows, but he had never actually been inside because the doors were always locked. Now, he looked round with interest.

A typewriter! His eyes lit up. He crossed to the table. There was a pretty green light on the keyboard. He poked experimentally at one of the keys. The green light disappeared, and to his delight, the dark screen was transformed to a beautiful shade of blue. Sammy gazed on the miracle. This wasn't a typewriter. Was it a computer – desk top, or lap top, or some such, that Ollie Mitchell talked about?

Tentatively, he hit another key and to his delight words appeared all over the screen. He hit another key, and another. Then, as though the machine had grown tired of playing games, it made a buzzing sound and all the writing disappeared. Sammy gazed in consternation at the blank screen. Then the buzzing stopped, and a list of names appeared. He pressed all the keys, one after another, hit them with his fist, poked them with his finger. Nothing changed.

"Bugger you," said a hoarse voice.

He jumped nearly out of his skin. It was not Miss Lisamore's voice. Then he saw the parrot's cage. "Oh, you." He crossed the room. Quixote looked up at him, head on one side, beady-eyed. "You shouldn't swear," he told the bird earnestly. "An' you shouldn't listen to people who swear." Quixote turned indifferently away. Sam felt angry with Miss Lisamore for teaching the parrot those words. She said it was Bobby Wake and Hunter Ashenden who taught the bird, but he knew it was her, and she ought to be punished for telling lies. He knew where Bobby and Hunter were, and what they were doing when she said they were here for he had seen them that night he had gone to the churchyard with a bit of steak to cure his wart. Sammy's grandmother had cured a wart by sitting on a tombstone at dead of night and holding half a pound of steak on it. Sammy hadn't had half a pound. More like half an ounce. It was all the butcher would give him. No wonder the wart hadn't gone away.

He had seen a light in the vestry that night, and thinking the choir was still there, went in. Luckily, he had been very quiet and the vicar hadn't seen him. But he had seen something.

Sammy leered obscenely and went back to the machine.

Chapter 5

"Quiet!" Cara Hagan, six-feet tall headmistress of the Halfpenny Dun village school, could cope with bedlam without raising her voice. "Quiet!" The children jerked upright, backs straight, innocent faces raised. "Where is Miss Lisamore?"

"We don't know, Miss," chorused the angels.

"Take out your reading books. Thank you. Now get on. I'll send someone in. And not another word." She hurried down the corridor, long feet at ten to and ten past the hour, bending her knees just a little in the belief that it minimised her height. Angela Rutherford looked up as she entered the office, blinking myopically through an artfully arranged fringe that mainly concealed her eyes.

"Angela dear, try Beryl at home."

Obediently, the school secretary lifted the receiver and dialled. Push-button phones did not feature on the priority list of the Halfpenny Dun Parent Teacher Association. Puerp, puerp. Puerp, puerp. "There's no answer, Miss Hagan," she said when the bell had rung half a dozen times.

The Head made imperious lifting movements with her upturned hands. "Get on your bicycle, dear. Hurry. Go and see if she's ill."

It was a mere hop and a jump from the south corner of the green to the high street end of Old Wood Lane, but Miss Hagan knew if Angela walked she would most certainly, today of all days, be waylaid by villagers overburdened by the problems and potential delights of

Saturday's show. Arrived at the cottage, Angela left her machine leaning against the street wall and rang the bell. There was no answer. She walked round the back. The outer door stood open. She stepped into the garden room. Surely, if Beryl was sick in bed, she said to herself, the house would be locked. She opened the inner door and ventured into the passage, saw a man's bicycle leaning against the door to the stair cupboard, and stifled a nervous giggle. Now, what to do! She went with hesitant steps to the foot of the narrow staircase and looked back at the bike, saw the bent front mudguard, the rusty, broken spokes, and relaxed thinking a Lothario was unlikely to turn up on such a wreck.

"Beryl!" she called. There was no reply. She went up the stairs.

There were three doors opening on to the landing. From the top step she could see inside the room on the right. The bed was neatly made up. "Beryl?" She crossed the landing. The dressing table with its jars and brushes, the familiar clothes visible through the open wardrobe door, proclaimed this was Beryl's room, but she was not here. Angela looked in the room on the opposite side of the landing. Nothing. The third door led to a bathroom.

Was that a voice? With enormous relief, Angela ran downstairs calling, "Beryl!" The cottage was eerily silent. She stood very still with one hand on the bannister, head raised, eyes flickering round the hall, listening. It was a voice she had heard, of that she was certain. Faintly unnerved, she went with quick footsteps to the front door and opened it. The sun flooded in, driving the eeriness out.

Mrs Smeed, Sammy's mother, was making for the Post Office. She saw Angela, transferred both shopping baskets to her left hand, and waved. Angela waved back and told herself not to be silly. The heavy door, made of slabs of oak, swung shut, hitting her in the back. She blocked it open with a brass door stop. Now she had an escape route, and if there was an intruder lurking somewhere, Mrs Smeed would hear her yell. Tentatively, step-by-step, she ventured down the passage, nerves tight as a rope.

"And about time. And about time."

Angela jumped, then relaxed. That damn bird!

"About time," repeated Quixote.

"Pack it in, parrot. You frightened the hell out of me." She stood on the doorstep looking round the room, frowning.

"Shit!" said the bird.

"The things you say!" Angela giggled nervously. Then through the window she saw Ben Finlay staggering up the path holding a hand to either side of his head. She went to the door. "Ben! What's the matter?" She gazed at him in consternation.

He came towards her, groaning.

"Can I 'ave a drink of water?"

"What's happened to you, Ben?"

"Gimme a drink of water. Gimme. Oh-h-h." She backed away and he teetered over the doorstep, saw the sofa and collapsed on it. She brought water from the kitchen. He reached out blindly, drank it at a gulp, then announced, "I'm goin' ter be sick."

"Don't be sick in here," she shrieked. She dragged him to his feet and pushed him through the door, then swiftly turned her back, clapping her hands to her ears in a vain effort to block out the retching. The little computer came within her line of vision, lid raised, standby light glowing. Beryl must be here. At least she couldn't be far away. She wouldn't leave the house without turning the machine off.

"Kill you," said the parrot, meditatively.

Angela froze.

Ben staggered back into the room wiping his mouth with a dirty handkerchief. "Can I 'ave some more water?"

She hurriedly refilled the glass. "Hadn't you better drink it outside?" He backed to the doorway. "What are you doing here?" she asked.

"I must've passed out," he replied sheepishly.

"So it's you who has been drinking in the garden and leaving bottles lying around! You! What on earth do you do that for, Ben?" Angela registered disapproval.

"It's not just me," he replied defensively, by-passing her question. "It was Ollie's idea."

"So, where are the others?" She peered apprehensively through the window, across the narrow strip of lawn and into holly, camellia, azalea, forsythia. Her mind skittered over imagined scenes of drunken violence, with Beryl the victim.

"Oh, my head," groaned the milkman, staggering sideways, holding it tenderly between his hands.

"Serves you right. Does the bike in the hall belong to you?"

Something surfaced in Ben's brain. "In the hall?"

"Have a look." Angela indicated the door behind her. Ben went through to the hall, Angela apprehensively following. The light flooding in from the open door caught a pink stone, quite half an inch across, that lay on the polished boards. Angela went forward to pick it up and saw, a little distance away, a green scarab set in silver. Surely this was part of Beryl's famous necklace! She held them in the palm of her hand, frowning.

Ben raised his head, howling like a dog. "She's broken me bike! Look what she's done!" Then he began to retch again.

"Get out!" shrieked Angela, dropping the stones, waving her arms, shooing him back through the garden room as she might a flock of sheep. "Get out! Get out!" She slammed the door behind him, then ran through to the front and kicked the doorstop away so that the door swung shut behind her. Grasping the handlebars of her bike, she pushed it through the gate and peddled fast down the high street.

* * *

PC Ellis, sole arbiter of the law in Halfpenny Dun, sat at his desk pleasurably breathing in the heady bouquet of warm oven scents engendered by Denise's baking for tomorrow's show. He was thirty years old, six feet two inches in his socks, with short fair hair, mild eyes and a gentle manner. No high-flyer, Charlie Ellis. He had already been marked out for a lifetime of rural duty. Charlie's type fitted into country villages as comfortably as a foot in a sheepskin slipper. He was decent and popular, he had married a local girl and his own parents had lately moved into the village to be near their grandchildren.

Out in the hall Phillip, aged three, and Sandra, two, fought a noisy battle over a toy car. Denise, his wife, was shouting.

"Can't hear what you're saying." Charlie continued to work on his papers.

Denise came and stood in the doorway, hands on hips, a pretty, untidy girl with patches of flour in her curly perm. "I said, since you're not on duty, couldn't you at least do something about the kids so I can get on with my work?" she asked crossly, then confident of his co-operation, stamped back to the kitchen.

Reluctantly, he hauled himself to his feet, confiscated the car, shoved it into his pocket, picked up the boy and carrying him on his hip, followed her. "I've got a lot to do, too, Denise," he protested mildly.

"And what d'you think I've got to do," she flared from her stand behind the scrubbed wood table, indicating basins and wooden spoons, packets of castor sugar, mysterious bundles in greaseproof paper, shortcrust rolls lined up row upon row on a tray. "If I don't get my list in to the committee by seven o'clock tonight I'll have to pay double entrance fee, and go through all the hassle – for heavens' sake, give Phillip back his car. No wonder he's screaming."

PC Ellis obediently fumbled with the car. The wheels had caught in his pocket lining. "Why are you making all those sausage rolls?" he reproved her gently. "They only ask for six. You only had to put in six."

Denise's voice leaped and danced, "So 'oo doesn't want a sausage roll? And oo's goin' to say, 'You make all that for the show and we don't get a bite?' So you don't want any?" Provocative and unreasonable, she snatched up a wide-bladed spatula and held the extras threateningly over the waiting bin.

"I'll look after the kids," said Charlie soothingly.

There was a moment of dead silence. Denise turned and stared in consternation at the washing machine, quiet as a threat. "It's broken down again!" she wailed. "And all the kids' clothes are in it! And the man won't come for days. They never will. This is the final straw."

"Don't panic. If it's a block in the outlet pipe, I can probably fix it." Still supporting the child on his hip, Charlie headed for the back door. "Hang on a moment and I'll get a spanner and bucket out of the shed."

"And while you're there, bring in that bowl with the driftwood. When I finish this lot I got to do me flower arrangement. How I'll get it all done I do not know." Denise raised her hands heavenwards and more flour from her fingertips drifted down to powder her curls.

There was a sound of clinking bottles coming from the front of the house. She took off, across the kitchen and out of the door. "There you are, George! At last! You're terrible late. We're right out. What's 'appened? Where's Ben?"

The milkman was in no mood to accept reproach. "I'm doin' the round by meself. Ben 'asn't turned up."

"It's one of them days," said Denise, who never used an original phrase when she could call on one that had been well tried and tested.

In the office, the telephone rang. Clutching four bottles to her bosom, Denise raced back. "I'll say you're out," she shouted as she heard Charlie's footsteps crossing the kitchen.

"Not when I'm on call you won't." Gently but firmly he pushed past her.

"You're not on duty." But the fire had gone out of her for she knew his heart was in his job.

Phillip had begun to howl again. "Gimme my car. You got my car."

"They'll get me on the radio, anyway," said Charlie apologetically, tugging at the toy car in his pocket. He lowered the child to the floor.

Denise, who was the perfect policeman's wife for about 364 days of the year, put the bottles in the refrigerator. PC Ellis bent down and gently cuffed the boy's ear. "Shut up, you, while I answer the phone."

"Gimme my car."

He succeeded in jerking it out of his pocket, heard the lining tear, realised remorsefully that he had given his overworked wife yet another job, and went into the office. As he picked up the telephone the screaming stopped.

Denise, listening apprehensively, heard him say, "I'll come at once."

"You're not on duty! Charlie, you're not on duty," she beseeched him as he appeared in the doorway. "Look, I got the kids and the washing machine, and all this . . ." She flung out an arm, indicating the disarray, staring defeat in the face.

"Now, Denise. I've got to go. The school's worried about Miss Lisamore. She's disappeared."

"Miss Lisamore," repeated his young wife bitterly. "Who's goin' to run away with 'er?" Collapsing on to a kitchen chair, she burst into tears.

Constable Ellis, parking unforgiveably outside the high street entrance to Badger Cottage, was in time to see Ben Finlay emerging with his old bicycle from the front door. He climbed out of his Ford Cortina. Ben dragged the machine down the flagstone path and leant it up against the street wall, then attempted to drag the mudguard back into place. Having been weakened by rust, it broke off several inches from the end. Ellis opened the gate and went through. Ben glanced up, started guiltily, grabbed the handlebars and swung the machine round. The broken spokes clattered and rattled on the stones.

"So what's this?" asked Charlie mildly. "What's going on, Ben?"

"Nuffun'."

Charlie slipped his fingers beneath his peaked cap and scratched his head. "What were you doin' 'ere?" Charlie didn't bother with h's and g's when dealing with the village boys. "Why aren't you on the round, 'elping George?"

"I slept in," Ben muttered. "Then I had to collect me bike."

"What was your bike doin' 'ere?"

"Miss Lisamore took it." He saw the expression of disbelief on the constable's face, flushed guiltily, and added, "Borrowed it, like."

Charlie swallowed his incredulity, "That old thing!" and asked merely, "Where is she?"

"I dunno. Why should I know? Miss Rutherford from the school come lookin' for her. She let me in to get me bike."

The constable glanced down at the front wheel. It looked as though someone had jumped on it. "If I were you, I'd tie up those spokes, before you go out on the road."

Ben lifted it by the handlebars and returned to the wall. Charlie went through the front door and stood, hands in pockets, looking round the small hall.

There was not much to see. Three hunting prints, an old chair he wouldn't give house room to – must be as old as the house, he thought critically, and a table with a crack down the centre. Amazing what people collected. He and Denise went in for modern. Paint and plastic. Bright, and easy to keep clean.

The warm sunlight embraced the rich patina of dark-oak

floorboards laid down two centuries ago. He could imagine the wind coming up through those cracks. "Br-r-r!" It was enough to make a bloke feel cold just thinking about it. He crossed to the door on the left, and opened it. The room was dark because the curtains had not been drawn. He switched on the light, pulled the curtains back then switched the light off again. With the lead light windows closed it was a gloomy little room. A few chairs, a small sofa, fireplace. He noticed two mugs containing coffee dregs, and a sugar basin, standing on a table by the window.

He went out leaving the door open. Across the hall was a dining room containing a narrow refectory table and three Windsor wheelback chairs; a dark-oak sideboard; a porcelain bowl decorated with Chinese characters. On the wall above, two wild-flower prints. This room, also, had an unlived-in air. He went down the short passage. The kitchen door was open. At a cursory glance he took in an old gas cooker, an old-fashioned white sink, a wooden bench. He entered the narrow room at the back of the cottage, untidy, friendly, bright with sunshine.

"Hello old chap," he said, spotting the parrot.

"Let's have a cuppa tea." Quixote stared beadily at him through the bars of the cage.

Charlie grinned. He had heard about Miss Lisamore's bird and the naughty children. "So what's going on?" He went to the open computer, noted the green standby light, and rubbed his chin thoughtfully. There had to be someone here, or the computer wouldn't be switched on. He went back into the hall, then up the stairs. He looked in the two bedrooms, one after the other, opened the wardrobe doors, glanced in at the bathroom, then climbed the narrow wooden stairs to the attic rooms.

Nothing.

He descended to the hall. The light gleamed on something bright just inside the door. He bent and picked up the scarab that Angela had dropped in her anxiety to escape.

And next to it, on a chain several inches long, a pink stone. Looking round he spotted another stone by the door. And another. He picked them all up and stood holding them in the palm of his hand, looking down at them, feeling uneasy. In front of him there was a cupboard door in a wall of tongued and grooved pine that boxed in the staircase.

He stepped forward and opened it. The body, robbed of its support, rolled forward and stopped at his feet.

Chapter 6

Annie Finlay had failed to turn up for work at Spring House in the high street, so there was no one to keep an eye on the Tate baby while Helen coped with the school run. She telephoned Letitia Grey, asking her to step in. Five children were late for school. Returning in her Volvo 240 Estate with the two gun dogs in the back, Letitia saw Ben wheeling his bike down the high street. She pulled up to enquire if his mother was ill, but Ben rushed past, head down.

Drawing up outside Badger Cottage, she laughed aloud to see Charlie Ellis's Ford Cortina parked directly in front of the gate. So much for Beryl Lisamore's efforts to throw her weight around! Letitia felt lighthearted and frivolous this morning as a result of last night's slip from grace, so dangerously close upon Brian's return. Danger for Letitia was the meat and drink of fornication.

A glance in the rear vision mirror told her Ben had got away. She shrugged and was about to turn on the ignition again when she was arrested by Charlie's unmistakable Kentish tones floating to her from the open door of the cottage. Opposite, a group of women were rubber-necking over the magazine display in the window of the Post Office Stores. What was going on? Letitia strained her ears, but all she could hear now was the busy rattle and crack of the walkie-talkie. She decided to buy a few stamps and find out.

Consciously elegant in designer denims, casually swinging her leather shoulder bag, she crossed the road. As she entered the shop Ivy Dodson said, "Beryl Lisamore wasn't all that well liked." Noting the past tense, Letitia glanced apprehensively behind her and saw the first of the strange cars sweep in. Two men jumped out, grave and businesslike in dark suits.

"What's happened?" she asked, addressing the women grouped together in the window.

The tale poured eagerly from half a dozen mouths. Charlie Ellis had telephoned Denise to say he wouldn't be able to get back to fix her broken washing machine, so Denise had phoned Dolly Oswhistle at The Fox and Hounds to ask if Bert, who was a handyman outside of pub hours, could come over. She had already contacted Loughtons Electrical Repairs in Castle Manton who couldn't send a man until after the weekend. And why couldn't Charlie come home? Because Beryl Lisamore had been murdered.

"What's going to happen about the show, now?" Mrs Walker's voice, seldom cheerful, crept to the edge of doom. Never before, in its eighty-year history, apart from wartime, had the Halfpenny Dun Annual Summer Show been cancelled.

"How can it go on? Wanton disrespect for the dead, that would be," said fat little Mrs Smith, standing head high to the chocolate bars.

"She wasn't so well liked," opined the postmistress again, offering her customers a second chance to discuss the matter. "There was that funny business about the parrot. Accusing them boys. I never heard the bird myself, but I believe its vocabulary's disgusting."

"That doesn't mean anyone would want to murder her," Letitia snapped, nerves jumping because the police might, and probably would, need to know where everyone had been last night. She hadn't had a baby-sitter in, and everyone knew she never left Candy and Oliver alone in the house, in the daytime, much less at night. Yes, come to think of it, she had a good enough alibi. But Anthony! She stifled a gasp. Anthony hadn't.

Mrs Walsall, entering, tripped on the step because she was looking backwards at Badger Cottage as she came. Emma Nesbet, Marigold Ashenden's au pair, reached out an arm and steadied her. "Someone must have something against her," conjectured Emma, thinking aloud about the unsolved mystery of the bottles on Beryl's lawn. "Empties can easily be disposed of in the hedgerows. That was deliberate."

"She were secretive," Mrs Parker, the butcher's wife reminded them. "You never knew much about her."

"Nobody really believed the local children were to blame," added Ivy, referring to the parrot.

Zelda Beard, who lived in The Little Cottage in the high street, arrived in a great hurry and bought one second class stamp. She had heard the news at the greengrocers. She was sorry about Beryl, of course she was, but she couldn't help feeling peeved that fate had chosen this particular day. Her raspberry jam, made with her own berries that had never been better than this year, had a very good chance of a win. Unable to say that out loud, she was obliged to content herself with remarking what a shame it would be for the children if the show were postponed, for they did look forward to it, especially the-five-to-eight year olds who had worked hard on their plasticine animals and their posies of flowers.

Letitia bought six firstclass stamps and left to telephone Anthony.

The store filled up, but Ivy Dodson was kept only moderately busy, for nobody bought more than one item, the price of standing room. The answer to whether they should get on with their baking, or not, seemed nearer here than in their own homes. Cheese and chive scones, fairy cakes, bread pudding, all these, inevitably, were left to the last moment in order to be absolutely fresh. Everyone baked the day before.

* * *

Over at Badger Cottage the scene-of-crime team moved in. Fingerprint experts went to work on the surfaces, the police photographer took his pictures, Dr Fairway came post haste from Headquarters to examine the body and pronounced that the victim had been strangled. There were bruises, so one could assume she had put up a fight, and a number of random small cuts – holes rather than cuts – that looked as though she had been jabbed with something sharp.

PC Ellis told them about Ben Finlay and his damaged bicycle, hastening to add that Ben was a simple boy and wouldn't hurt a fly. Detective Chief Inspector Perce Paton, Chubby Paton as he was known, a heavily built man with sandy hair and a beer gut, he who had seen simple boys grow up into aggressive men, made some notes in his book.

While the doctor talked on the telephone, arranging for the removal of the body, the inspector lumbered upstairs. He examined the two bedrooms and the bathroom, then climbed to the attic rooms. Nothing disturbed. He clumped back downstairs and into the sunroom. Sergeant Donovan followed him, with PC Ellis bringing up the rear.

"Oh hell!"

Paton did a double take.

"The parrot, sir," said Constable Ellis, pointing. "Over there. In that cage. Got quite a lot to say, it has. Worse than that, too."

Paton crossed the room and stood looking down at Quixote. He was followed by Sergeant Donovan, a long, skinny youth with a mournful face, a comic in his back pocket and ears that stuck out. They were an odd couple, the heavily built inspector aged forty-five, his sandy coloured hair thick as a mat at back and sides, fluffy, thin and lank on top, Donovan with a riot of curls so nearly the same colour they might have been father and son. Paton had learnt a great deal about people during his years in the force. His love for his work came out of his interest in his fellow men. One could see from his shrewd, kindly eyes he was resigned to the human condition. It was a great pity he could not apply this tolerance in his own private life.

He and Barbara had married during her period of rebellion against her parents' establishment background. Less than five years later she came to her senses, as her family put it, and the following fifteen years of the marriage had been a kind of hell. Chubby had survived because of his absorption in his work. Barbara, who had not been encouraged to train for a career, it being assumed she would marry into the army, spent too much time alone. London was lonely, she said. He had to live in London because of his work. Babies with their good will and dependence had not come to heal the wounds and knot them together. They endured because their backgrounds had bred endurance in them, Chubby's from poverty, Barbara's from military discipline. Besides, neither of them happened to meet anyone they preferred.

Donovan, too, had problems. His stepfather, jealous of the close tie between mother and son, had thrown him out. "Get yourself a girl of your own," he said, but competition for the kind of girl Kelly Donovan admired was brisk, and one or two knock-backs had made him wary. He lived alone in a bed sitter in Wandsworth and wished he could go home again.

"Shit to you, too," said the parrot.

"Blimey!" ejaculated the inspector.

PC Ellis explained, "Miss Lisamore kept his cage outside in good weather. She said little boys came into her garden and taught him bad language."

Paton grinned. "Sounds like little boys to me." He could imagine himself enjoying such an opportunity thirty-five years ago. "These African Greys are amazing mimics." Putting the diversion behind him, he asked, "Who's her next of kin?"

Ellis hadn't any idea. "I dare say they'd know at the school."

"Find out, then. Detective Inspector Fowler is sending some men over from Headquarters. They can start on a house-to-house. Where's the village hall, Mr Ellis? I presume there is one?"

"In the high street, sir, opposite the old people's houses."

"Council houses?"

"You'd never know," said Charlie Ellis with shy pride. "There's a half circle of bungalows with the warden's flat at one end. You can't miss them, sir. There's a lawn in front, and flower beds. Very nice."

Chief Inspector Paton focused his eyes hazily on a spot about two inches from the constable's nose and rocked backwards and forwards on his heels whistling through his teeth while he summed up the local man. Sergeant Donovan, embarrassed, gave Charlie Ellis an encouraging grin. He knew Paton was having trouble at home. Life could be difficult for everyone when affairs were out of kilter at 5 Donkey Lane, the incongruously named little street in Fulham where his superior lived.

The standardised country constable, Chubby Paton decided intolerantly. Uncorruptible, unpromotable. "D'you know who has the key to the hall?" he asked. "We'll need it for an incident room."

"I can get it for you, but what shall I do first, sir? The hall, or the school?" Charlie was anxious, as always, to please.

Chubby Paton pulled his hands out of his pockets and his notebook from under his arm. Glancing down, he caught sight of a stain on the front of his otherwise impeccable shirt. Marmalade! That damn runny marmalade Barbara's mother had given them! "Just because somebody gives us something we don't have to eat it," he had grumbled, but Barbara, on a short fuse, had snapped back with a reminder that he refused to eat the bought stuff and she certainly hadn't the time, what with his parents coming to stay, to get down to some home-made. Barbara didn't get on with his parents. They thought her hoity-toity. She thought them common.

He went into the kitchen and found a tea towel, put one corner under the tap and rubbed the stickiness away.

"I'll go and have a word with this fellow, Finlay," he said, emerging with a wet patch on his front. Sergeant Donovan saw it and tactfully found the view of the garden interesting. "Though the man seen coming away from the scene of the crime in broad daylight is never the killer," Paton added. "Not unless he was blind drunk at the time." He looked up, pulling one ear lobe, frowning, then remembered the constable's query. "What did you say, Mr Ellis? Hall or school? Open up the hall." He walked over to the computer. The green light had disappeared. He glanced down at the plug. Someone had turned the power off. "Know anything about computers, Mr Ellis?"

The constable shook his head.

"Find someone who does. Number three, High Street Close, you said?"

"Ben lives with his parents. If he's not there, he'll have gone to catch up with the milkman. If you see a milk float, he might be on it. That's his job, delivering milk."

Side-stepping Gregson who was taking measurements, Paton left by the front door.

"Hall. School. Computer," muttered Charlie, looking round for his hat.

"You should see yourself!" screeched Annie Finlay at number three High Street Close, quite forgetting that only five minutes earlier, going to make Ben's bed and finding he had not slept in it, she had been distraught. "And smell yourself!" she added in disgust. "Ugh! You smell like a sewer. Don't tell me you haven't been drinking," she ranted on. "Now, you just tell me who put you up to it. That's what I'd like to know. Who put you up to it?"

"Nobody," said Ben, balancing his bony bottom on the

edge of a kitchen chair, his poor head that weighed a ton drifting down until it rested on his knees. "I been sick, Mum. Me 'ead's thumpin'. Don't go on at me. I can't bear it. Me head!"

"You are a disgusting sight." Annie had the neck of a plucked bird. In it her Adam's apple, big as a man's, shot up and down like a piston. "I don't know what the world's coming to, I really don't, when a boy your age can get himself into this state. Sit up – you can sit up, can't you? Just look at your clothes, will you. Who d'you think's goin' to wash yer clothes? Me?"

"I'll wash them." Ben raised his head, begging for mercy. "Don't go on at me, Mum. Mum, I think I'm goin' ter die."

"You're s'posed to be on your milk round. And I'm s'posed to be doing for Mrs Tate." Annie Finlay was unstoppable in her anger and relief. "D'you think she's going to pay me for standing around 'ere worrying about you? And d'you think George Reid's goin' to pay you for not turning up for the milk round this morning? We're not made of money, you know."

"Can't I go to bed?"

"Ben!" She shrieked as her son's thin body convulsed, his mouth opened, and what was left of yesterday's food and drink sprayed across the linoleum.

It didn't take much cleaning up. Annie was good in normal emergencies, and this was normal enough now, a child being sick. She was gentle as she put away the mop and the orange plastic bucket. "Come on," she said with love, and raising Ben, unresisting, she supported him into the bedroom where she proceeded to undress him.

Leaving his car outside Badger Cottage, Detective Chief Inspector Paton walked down the high street that had been deserted when he drove in, but which was now dotted with little groups of sightseers. Huddles, rather than groups.

A scene with which he was only too familiar. Huddles accumulated within an hour of the police arriving on a murder investigation. They fell silent as he approached.

Chubby Paton, brought up as a townie, knew little of country villages. In the inner cities unwashed hair, unshaven chins, shifty eyes and a propensity to run at sight of a police car meant what it said, but he had often heard his father, who had been a country man, say that sometimes things that went on in a picture-postcard country village with thatched roofs and big labrador dogs taking up the best seats in the pub, could make your hair stand on end. It might be a million miles, said his old Dad, from the bland outer shell of the hairy dog's tooth tweed to the shrivelled heart locked away beneath it. Well, thought his son, we shall see.

He passed the old-age pensioners' houses, acknowledging them to be very nice, as the constable had said, then the village hall, set well back on the left with a gravel forecourt and neat squares of lawn. Handy position for a headquarters, he acknowledged with satisfaction.

High Street Close was on the right-hand side, an unedifying group of double-storey brick buildings put up in the sixties with regrettable over-regard for economy. Chubby Paton, who had an eye for good architecture, regarded them with dismay and came to the measured decision that the housing committee of the time ought to have been taken out and shot, one by one. He glanced down at his shirt front and was gratified to see it had dried without leaving a stain, then went up the concrete path and in at the communal entrance marked 'Flats 1–3'. In the bleak passageway, leaning up against the staircase, there stood a man's ancient bicycle. He bent to look at it. The front mudguard was a mess. Some of the spokes were broken and tied in place with string. It was not beyond the bounds of possibility, he decided, that these had caused the lacerations on the victim's body.

He rang the bell.

Chapter 7

At The Red House in Pieman's Lane, Letitia picked up the telephone and tapped out Helen Tate's number.

"It's Letitia, isn't it?" Helen leaned against the bannisters by the telephone table, slim and sweet in the Liberty print dress she had been wearing for four years, hoping Geoff wouldn't notice. Her entire allowance had gone to Stephen this year, plus as much as she dared siphon off from the housekeeping.

"Listen," said Letitia, her voice jumping, "I'll tell you why Annie Finlay hasn't turned up for work this morning. Beryl Lisamore's been murdered."

"No!" Helen jerked upright, her pretty blue eyes bulging.

"The high street's crawling with police. Ben's involved."

"You're joking!"

"It's not my idea of a joke." Letitia, unstrung because she couldn't locate Anthony, was battling with tears.

"Ben wouldn't hurt a fly." Helen fearfully rejected Letitia's news. There must be some mistake. He had been educated, so far as that was possible, at the village school. When the Tates went on holiday, they left their key with his mother. She baby-sat for them. Even her brutish husband belonged, his potential ignored because it had not been realised.

"I tried to stop him in the high street but he ran like a rabbit. There's a crowd in the Post Office, gawping. Listen, Helen, Ivy Dobson's telling everyone she saw Ben come out of Badger Cottage. You'd better go and see his mother. You'd better get that husband of hers home before the police start asking questions. You'd better—"

Helen sharply protested, "I can't leave the baby, and I can't take her over there. Not if Ben – not . . ." Her voice trailed away.

"Helen, are you there? Are you there, Helen?" Scarcely knowing what she was doing, Letitia slammed down the receiver. Biting hard on her index finger she moved distractedly to the front door, returned to the study, then went back to the door. Once again she picked up the telephone and feverishly tapped out the number of Anthony's antique shop, then without waiting for the connection, dropped the receiver back on its stand. The girl had promised he would ring the very moment he came in. She must get herself in hand. What on earth had possessed her to make that witless call to Helen? She went in to the kitchen. Coffee? No. One of those herbal tranquillisers? No, better not. Keep alert. Dear God, let Anthony ring before Brian comes home.

In the hallway at Spring House, Helen dazedly reached behind the vase on the telephone table and brought out the little book in which she kept local telephone numbers. Jack Finlay was a farm hand. She rang the estate office and asked Jim Whitehead, Lord Oaks' manager, to send him home.

"Something wrong, Mrs Tate?"

"Er – he will explain. I'm sure nothing serious," she floundered, "but I'd be grateful – I mean, Mrs Finlay would like – I'm sure he won't be away long."

"Very well, Mrs Tate." Whitehead sounded puzzled. "I'll send him down."

Ben's mother scuttled through the back door of Spring House, dropped her plastic bag on the floor of the utility room, slid bony little feet into the slippers she wore indoors, tied her apron round her waist and burrowed into the hoover cupboard. She looked up guiltily as the kitchen door swung inwards, misread the expression on her employer's face and muttered apologetically,

"Ben's sick, Mrs Tate. I couldn't leave 'im. Not the way 'e was." She put her head down again and tussled with the cleaner that had a mind of its own when you were in a hurry. "Come out, you silly thing. Oh, you are a silly thing, and no mistake," Annie puffed.

"Mrs Finlay."

"Yes. I got it now. Don't you worry about me, Mrs Tate. I'll rush through fast as I can," Annie rattled on, not wanting to be questioned. Mrs Tate would know there were only two things that kept a boy out all night, drink, and girls. Down on the floor unwinding the cord from the shafts, smarting from her secret shame, Annie saw her employer's slim bare ankles directly in front of her, not moving. The habit of obedient dependence brought her upright.

"What has happened to Ben, Mrs Finlay?"

Annie's thin cheeks turned a fiery red. "'e woke up sick," she said, stubbornly improvising, then bent to lift the machine. "That's all. 'E just woke up sick. 'E'll be all right."

"I'll make you a coffee," said Helen, unnerved by the woman's intransigence.

"Thanks. I'd rather get on." Annie hustled the tools of her trade into the hall, taking her problem with her.

In the kitchen Helen considered with despair that she did not know how to tackle the matter. Her own bizarre secrets were testimony to her incompetence when faced with life's more freaky challenges. Not only did she want to send Mrs Finlay home, she wanted her out of the house. She was being ridiculous, she knew. Why should Ben's mother . . . even if Ben had . . . But Letitia had been near to hysteria on the phone. Why? Why had she demanded I get Jack home? Why didn't she do it herself? Was she warning me? Poppy, the baby, was asleep upstairs in her cot. What would she do if Annie refused to go home . . .

Helen put Nescafé into two cups, and waited, tap, tap, tapping her foot on the tiles. Beyond the kitchen door the old Hoover crawled inefficiently around the ancient grandfather clock, inherited from Geoff's family, beneath the gold-framed portraits of Poppy and Simon and Tom, filling the downstairs rooms with its rage. The kettle came to the boil. Helen filled the cups and tossed some biscuits on to a plate. One of them skidded to the floor. She left it there and went to stand in the doorway, waiting to attract Annie's attention. "Coffee's ready," she mouthed when the little figure swung round. Reluctantly, Annie put her foot on the button and the machine groaned into silence. She followed Helen's erect figure into the kitchen and looking like a cornered fox, settled on the edge of her chair. Helen seated herself on the edge of another chair, and offered the digestive biscuits.

"Mrs Grey rang to say there had been some trouble in the village."

Annie swallowed and the Adam's apple jerked.

Helen waited. Annie stared at her cup.

"I've telephoned the estate office and asked for your husband to be sent home. I think you had better go home, too."

"What's wrong, then?" Annie looked up, her eyes glassy with fright. "Why should Jack come 'ome?" she asked, knowing already it was not Ben's health that was at stake, nor even his reputation. "'e's not dying, Mrs Tate." Ben must have done something, and Mrs Tate knew about it.

"There are police in the village."

Another long silence. Then, "I don't know what you're saying, Mrs Tate," Annie muttered at last. "My Ben never done nothing wrong."

"No, I'm sure. But apparently—" Unable to bring herself to break the terrible news, Helen said, "If the police want to interview him, I'm sure you would like to be there. And your husband ought to be there, too."

"Why should the police interview 'im?"

Helen took a biscuit she did not want and stared at it intently. She tried, and failed, to say Beryl Lisamore had been murdered. "I expect they're going to interview everyone," she said, adding consolingly before recognising the implications of what she was saying, "I dare say they'll want to interview me."

"Why?" Annie stared at her employer, wondering at her sudden and obvious discomfiture. "What 'appened, Mrs Tate? There's something 'appened, isn't there? My Ben's been out all night," she admitted. "What's 'e done, Mrs Tate?"

A child's long-drawn-out wail came floating down from the floor above. Helen jumped up. "I must see to Poppy. You be on your way. Don't worry about the Hoover," she called as she fled upstairs. She went to the nursery and picked up the child. "My darling, you're soaked." She changed the nappy, then held her close against her heart, needing the comfort.

Downstairs, frustrated and angered by her expulsion, Annie dragged through to the utility room, removed her apron, put on her shoes, picked up her plastic bag, and left.

Helen, having put the baby back in her cot and set the mobile dancing, went down to the hall. The telephone book was on the table. She turned the pages. Pinmartin 370.

"Hello. Is that the Prince Albert hospital visitors' canteen?"

"Yes."

"It's Helen Tate here." She knew all the voluntary helpers, and they knew her.

"Helen. What can I do for you? It's Celia."

"Would you be a sweetie, Celia, and look at the roster? I want to know who was on duty last night."

"Can you speak a little louder? I can scarcely hear."

Helen dragged her voice up from where it had slipped, and repeated the question.

"Half a mo." A pause, then, "Letitia Grey and Molly Fox were on duty. Is that all? Are you there, Helen? Helen! Are you all right?"

"I'm fine. Thanks. Thanks a lot."

"You don't sound a bit all right. Are you sure there's nothing wrong?"

"A bit of throat trouble, that's all. Sorry about the voice."

"Have a gargle, dear. Catch it before it takes hold," her friend suggested kindly.

Helen replaced the receiver and went into the drawing room. She crossed to the glass doors and stood staring out over the long garden with its tennis court flanked by slim cuppresses, hugging her bare arms, tasting fear. Could she trust Letitia to supply her with an alibi without asking questions? Letitia was a darling, but she could be mischievous. She decided to try Maureen Fox who was not a woman she would choose to ask to lie, but who was more suitable by virtue of the fact that she lived eight or ten miles from the turmoil of Halfpenny Dun. Helen found her number. Castle Manton 512.

"Looking for an alibi?" repeated Maureen, her voice thin and potentially critical.

"I just want you to say, if anyone asks, that I was on duty at the canteen last night."

There was a long pause, then, "I don't think so. I'd rather not, if you don't mind."

Helen tried to say, "Don't worry," and failed.

"All right?" Mrs Fox asked in a fiercely cheerful voice.

"Yes. Yes. Of course." Helen replaced the receiver. Better ring Letitia now, before her nerve went completely.

"Hello." Letitia sounded at once frantic, breathless and relieved. "Is that—"

"It's Helen."

"Oh God!"

"What's the matter?"

"Nothing. Absolutely nothing. What do you want?" Letitia's voice snapped like an elastic band.

"Last night. You were at the canteen last night—"

"I wasn't. Actually, I wasn't. I told them I couldn't. They found someone to step in. Why do you want to know where I was last night? What the hell's it got to do with you?" flared Letitia.

Bewilderedly, Helen replaced the receiver. The child had begun to scream again.

There was a middle-aged stranger standing at the door of number three. As Annie came up the steps and into the lobby he took his finger off the bell and came to meet her. "Mrs Finlay?" He held out a card bearing a photograph of himself. "I'm Chief Inspector Paton. May I have a word with you?"

She did not invite him inside, she was too terrified to speak. She unlocked the door and went ahead, expecting him to follow, assuming the police had a right to go anywhere they wished.

Chapter 8

Chubby Paton stood in the middle of the small living-dining room with its stiff, mock-leather sofa, hardwood chairs and chipboard table thinly disguised as oak.

It was not a room for the artistically sensitive, but Annie was proud of it. The extra money coming in from Ben's milk round had paid for the new carpet which they had bought in Castle Manton when the recession hit the high-street shops and prices tumbled. Jack had said, quoting his mother, it was an ill wind that blew nobody any good. Annie regretted that the snaking nasturtium vines and orange streaks in the carpet did not match the cochineal red of the curtains, but beggers can't be choosers, said Jack, quoting from the same source.

"Where can I find your son Ben, Mrs Finlay?" Noting the terror in the woman's eyes, Paton spoke gently. One of the less attractive angles of his work was that his mere presence too often put the fear of God into innocent people.

"What's 'e done?"

"Nothing, that we know of. He was seen wheeling his bike out of Badger Cottage. That's why I want to talk to him." Paton wrinkled his nose, wondering at the faint but insistent smell of vomit in the room.

Annie's little eyes blinked sharply several times. If she had been a cat, Paton thought, her fur would be standing on end. "'e wouldn't take 'is bike inside Miss Lisamore's house. What would 'e do that for? Inside?" asked Annie shrilly.

"That's what I was told."

"It's broke," she said. She tried to visualise Miss Lisamore mending Ben's bike, and failed, but why else would it be in her house?

"I'd like to speak to him if he's here. Would you mind calling him?"

"'e's in bed. 'e's sick."

"I'm sorry. But I must see him." The inspector was patient.

It was a long job, waking Ben. They eventually transferred him to the living room where he sat whey-faced and red-eyed, with a cup of black coffee in one trembling hand. Disadvantaged though he was by the brief and heavy sleep, he was able to give a halting account of the mindless self-indulgence of the previous evening. Paton sat on a hard chair, hands clasped between splayed knees, forearms resting on his thighs, watching the boy's face. Annie, diminished by the emphatic roses, stood by the window, tallow-faced and blank.

Suddenly she came to life. "Why were you drinking in Miss Lisamore's garden? 'oo was with you? You can't buy liquor. You're not eighteen. It's that Ollie Mitchell, isn't it? Did 'e buy the stuff? 'ee's eighteen. 'ee could."

Ben nodded miserably.

"'oo else?"

"I told you," said Ben wanly, "it was only me, last night."

"Why?"

"She took me bike," muttered Ben.

"She's got a bike of 'er own. Why would she want a man's bike?"

Ben felt there was an answer to that. He tried hard to find it.

"Your dad's gunner wallop you, and no mistake. Drinking!" Annie diversified her threats, "Just wait till 'ee gets 'is 'ands on that Ollie Mitchell."

"She broke me bike." Ben looked as though he were going to cry.

"So what did you do to her?" asked Chubby Paton encouragingly, deeming this was the moment to step in.

"Nuffin'. I didn't see 'er. Miss Rutherford from the school was there. She found me broken bike in the 'all."

Paton spoke reasonably, "Now, why would Miss Lisamore break your bike?"

Ben was silent, wondering. "Dunno," he managed at last.

"Where was she?"

"Dunno. Miss Rutherford was lookin' for 'er. She weren't there. Couldn't 'ave been, or Miss Rutherf—" He broke off as the door opened. They all looked up.

A brutish-looking labourer came into the room. He stood with dusty, booted feet apart, thick, straw-coloured hair standing up where he had pushed at it. Clean, it would have fallen back into place, but it was not clean. Annie dutifully washed her husband's clothes, but she dared not mention other needs. There was no shortage of water in council flat number three, but Jack Finlay was a man of habits as ingrained as the dust and dirt he acquired in the course of his job. He had not been brought up to wash. He looked from Annie to Ben and his little blue eyes came to rest on the inspector, but when he spoke it was to his wife.

"Mr Whitehead brought me down in the car," he said. "What's this about Miss Lisamore being murdered?"

Chubby Paton watched their faces and could feel only pity for the mother, shrinking against the wall, one hand to her gaping mouth. The incomprehension on the boy's face was not assumed, but how much would he remember after drinking an uncertain quantity of gin, whisky and vodka? He turned back to the father. "I'm Chief Inspector Paton," he said. "I'm in charge of the investigation."

The man looked sullen. "We're decent people 'ere," he muttered. "Ask anyone. Ask anyone in the village. We don't go round murderin' people, if that's what you're on about."

"It's my job," said Paton mildly. "Ben was at the scene. I have to question him." He turned to the boy. "So you were under the laurel bushes, Ben, from about seven o'clock until you woke up – around what time?"

"Nine." Ben was quite definite about that, for he remembered looking at his new digital watch, bought with his milk-round money at a stall in Castle Manton market only a few weeks ago.

"While you were under the laurel tree, did you see or hear anyone come into the garden?"

Ben shook his head. "I must've gone to sleep."

"Think hard, Ben. You must have seen someone go in or out."

Ben was frowning, rubbing his forehead. "Goldie Montrose come out," he remembered. "But that was before. When I was takin' the cream in."

"The film star?" The inspector, suspecting hallucinations, frowned.

Annie explained, "She's 'ere in the village. She's rented Wayside Cottage. Lord Oaks got some cottages 'e rents out."

"Oh." Paton resumed his encouraging manner. "I'd like you to think about that bike, Ben. I doubt very much if Miss Lisamore would break it. If it was intact when she took it up the garden path, I mean, if it wasn't broken then, and you didn't hear any banging, how do you think it got broken?"

"Dunno."

"I think there was some violence in the house," said Paton, watching Ben's eyes.

"You tellin' the truth, Ben?" His father scowled at him. "I'll wallop you if you're lyin'."

"Yeah. Course I am." Volatile resentment rose beneath a thin skin of inertia. "D'you think I had a fight with her, or sumpin'?"

Paton could feel tension building up in the room and silently cursed the interfering ass who had brought the father home. He addressed Finlay, "There's really no need for you to stay. I expect you'll want to get back to work."

"Yeah. I'll talk to the boy first."

Paton rose, feeling resigned. "I'll show myself out," he said. Poor kid. He knew what happened when simple, ignorant people were scared, and had someone to blame.

They allowed him to go. There were no goodbyes. He heard the wail of pain and protest as he descended the steps into the close. He was sorry his job too often stirred up the baser elements in the human psyche. He thought about his cat bringing live voles into the house. The inevitability of the vole's misfortune, one's knowledge of cats, somehow precluded interference.

"You no need to clout 'im like that," protested Annie, holding Ben's poor head protectively against her bony rib cage, feeling his tears trickling through her fingers.

"So what've you done?" bullied Jack. "If you've brought disgrace on this 'ouse . . ." Breathing heavily, he pondered on a choice of punishment.

"I 'aven't done nuffin'," sobbed Ben. "I drank what was in the bottles, that's all. And some of it was mine, anyway."

"So that's what you're spending your money on," ranted his father, "and us not knowing where to find the poll tax." The poll tax was something Jack Finlay understood they should not be paying, though exactly why he did not know. "You can give all your wages to your mother in future. If you can't keep yourself out of trouble, we'll keep you out. Now—" He broke off, for to say the word "murder" brought unacceptable matters too close. "What about Miss Lisamore?"

"I ain't done nuffin' to 'er," roared Ben through his tears.

"Make me a cup o' tea, Annie, and be quick about it." As she moved away Jack vented his fear and anger by cuffing Ben once again across the ear. "She broke your bike. You said that. You said she broke your bike." He cuffed the boy again.

"That was after," sobbed Ben, retreating to a chair.

"What d'you mean, after?"

"I saw it was broken after she wasn't there." Ben was incoherent with fear, pain and grief. "Miss Rutherford told me it was in the 'all. I went in and it was broke. I didn't see 'er. I wouldn't murder 'er. I wouldn't do nuffin' to 'er. Why would I?" sobbed the boy.

"Because she broke your bike." It wasn't that Jack thought his son was a killer, but he had to know for certain. He'd belt the truth out of him if he had to stay here all day. Jack was born to be boss, but lack of education meant his life had to be spent taking orders, Yes sir and No sir-ing. There was more energy and power in him than could be used up ploughing, digging, and carting bricks. It was something Annie managed to keep from the village, this serious threat to the family.

Mrs Tate always said not to take water from the hot tap, on account of the copper pipes. Annie thought as she swiftly ran a precise mugful into the electric kettle and switched it on that one lapse was unlikely to cause serious damage to her unloving mate. The kettle boiled in double-quick time. She poured the water into the mug and trotted back, anxiously swilling the tea bag around by its string.

Jack slurped the tea down. He never thanked Annie. Gratitude smacked of weakness, and anyway, wasn't it a man's right to be waited on?

Annie bent over Ben, wiping the tears from his face. "'ere, take my hanky and blow yer nose." She recognised this was something they had to go through.

"Why didn't you say you saw some men go in?" Jack slammed the mug down on the table and began again. "You could've said that. They're gunner blame you, whether you done it or not. You could've easy said you saw some men, and 'eard her scream."

Ben accepted the rebuke in silence.

"Why didn't you, then?" Frustrated by the boy's lack of reaction, Jack cuffed him again. It was the only way he knew. Thus had his own father interrogated him.

"I didn't think."

"You bloody ought to 'ave thought." Jack went to the window and scowled across the close. The Harris' lace curtains twitched. There was a shadowy face at the Medway's bedroom window. Old Gus Bristow, whose daughter lived at number sixteen, was banging eagerly on the door of number fourteen. Jack's blood boiled. Eve Cross came in a flurry from her flat and hurried out of the Close, casting a surreptitious glance in the direction of number three. Jack felt he was drowning in a rising tide of shame. He swung round, "It's all over the village," he shouted. "They all seen that inspector come 'ere. You stupid little sod." He cuffed his son twice in quick succession and felt marginal relief. Ben, roaring, flung himself upright and ran to his bedroom, slamming the door behind him.

Annie made a weak gesture of protest in his defence. "Jack. Hadn't you better go back to work?"

"It'll be all round the estate by now," he said bitterly, ignoring her plea.

"They'll find the culprit," said Annie, comforting him. "Go back to work now, Jack.

He moved towards the door, then paused. "You keep an eye on him," he said, quietly threatening.

"'e wouldn't 'urt a fly, Jack. You know that. You're just upset. Go back to work. Go on."

He went. Annie quietly opened the door of her son's room. He was lying on top of the bed, spreadeagled, perhaps even asleep. Though regretting the violence, she could not but be glad her husband had been brought home. She couldn't conceive of coping alone. She didn't mind being knocked about herself. Violence was a part of her *raison d'être* in an otherwise uneventful life. She saw it as part of Jack's loving.

But hitting Ben was different. She closed the door quietly and went to make herself a cup of tea. Seated in the middle of the sofa, waiting for the tea to draw, she stared blankly at the opposite wall, suffering.

Chapter 9

Lisa couldn't stop crying. She had cried herself to sleep the night before, wakened with swollen eyes, momentarily wondered where she was, then remembering, had broken down again. Her feeling of abandonment was primeval. She thought it must have been like this when she was handed over to her adoptive parents, a fragment of humanity – she saw herself, romantically, as that.

"I do not want this – thing? Creature?"

It had not been explained to her, why should it have been, for the Kings thought of her as their very own, that in the same moment of being abandoned by A, across the corridor in the hospital she had received an emotional welcome in the arms of B. Blind and unknowing, she felt she had been part of a charitable and shameful bargain – Beryl Lisamore's shame, the family King's charity.

She made coffee in the tiny, efficiently modernised kitchen, took it into the oak-beamed living room and, seated among her crushed dreams, wept while it grew cold. She thought about the photograph she had seen on the table in the front room of Badger Cottage, wondering emotionally whether Beryl had now destroyed it. She had already decided her father must be famous. At least he had had a moment of fame, or his picture would not have been in a newspaper. If only she could get hold of that photo, she thought she might be able to trace him. With luck, part of an article or story on the back of the picture would enable her to pinpoint the date of issue. She felt it must be recent. Newspaper cuttings did not remain new looking for long.

She decided to return to Badger Cottage. The door would be barred, now. She wished she hadn't told Beryl how she had gained entrance. With luck, maybe she would find a vulnerable window. She went back upstairs, washed her face at the pink basin – everything in Wayside Cottage was pretty, 'twee' she would have called it in a happier mood, patted her swollen eyes with a wet flannel, and pulled on a pair of jeans and T-shirt. She felt certain she would be perfectly safe, even through lunchtime, for Beryl would be involved with serving, or overseeing, school dinners. She believed that was what state schoolteachers did. She had attended an exclusive boarding school, herself. Anyway, why should she worry about being caught? She looked at herself defiantly in the mirror as she ran a brush through her long hair. A girl had a right to enter her mother's house; a right, also, to know who her father was. As she walked up the leaf-shaded lane she decided fiercely that she would break a window if she had to.

As she approached Cobblers the door opened and Romy Childs came down the path in a deceit of Romany garb, swirling black skirt and red blouse. Her thick hair streamed down her back, too long and too dark for a woman of forty-two.

"Good morning, Goldie Montrose," she said, resting her elbows on the wooden bars of the gate. "You're troubled, I know. I feel it, here." She touched her fingers delicately to a shapely left breast. "I felt it last night, and again this morning."

Lisa gave her a nervous smile.

"The crystal," volunteered Romy indicating the large tear drop that hung on a chain round her neck, "tells me you need help."

Lisa superstitiously eyed the faceted jewel glittering in the sunshine. "I'm really in rather a hurry," she said.

"Come and have some coffee with me later."

"Thank you." She edged away. Romy had already called on her, evincing an unwelcome curiosity in her presence here. She was a little afraid, not of the white witch, but of herself in the white witch's hands. She had no intention of further antagonising this new mother by confiding in the neighbours.

At the back entrance to Badger Cottage some sixth sense caused Lisa to turn. The white witch was still there, watching her. She continued on round the corner.

"There's that actress, Goldie Montrose!" The crowd in the Post Office seethed forward. Zelda Beard, greedily snatching the opportunity of a close-up look, slipped out of the door and crossed the road, stepping on to the pavement just in front of Lisa. Lisa, disconcerted, glanced to her left, became aware of a jumble of faces peering at her from the shop window opposite, turned her head and saw three men standing around the front door of Badger Cottage. Then she saw that the car parked in the road directly in front of her was a marked police vehicle. She came to a stunned halt, remembering that threatened to report her to the police.

Sergeant Donovan glanced up. Goldie Montrose! Irresistibly drawn by the prospect of one moment of glory in his local ("Guess who I was talking to today!"), he rushed down the path and eyes popping, face grinning foolishly, addressed her across the low wall. "Good morning – er—" After all, exposure to the peerless proved too much for him, and he could not go on.

I—" She burst out in a shrill, defensive voice, "I'm her daughter. Didn't she tell you that? I'm her daughter."

The chief inspector was at that moment leaving for the village hall to oversee the setting up of Headquarters. He came round the side of the cottage, the hall having been sealed off by the Scene-of-Crime team, in time to hear Lisa's words. "Come inside," he said, his sandy brows half way to his hair line, and ushered her across the lawn at the side of the cottage. Kelly Donovan, flushed with a mixture of excitement and embarrassment, followed. "I'm Detective Chief Inspector Paton," he said as they went. He led her into the sunroom. "Do sit down Miss – er—"

Lisa stood looking bewilderedly round the room, searching for Beryl, seeing the computer, the parrot in its cage, the pot plants on the window sill, the untidy sofa.

"Do sit – er—" For the life of him, Inspector Paton could not say "Goldie Montrose".

Donovan supplied it.

Lisa came to life. "I didn't mean any harm," she burst out defensively. "I can't believe this. I simply can't believe it. I told you, I'm her daughter." She looked from Paton to Donovan, then back to Paton, lips trembling.

"Do sit down." The inspector repeated his invitation. The sergeant hurried over to pick up the newspapers that lay on the sofa in order to create a space for her.

Still wearing the stunned expression, Lisa obeyed.

"When did you last see Miss – your mother, Miss Montrose?"

"I'm Lisa King," she said.

"When—"

"What are you talking about? You must know I saw her last night. She must have told you that."

Paton said gently, "Did you know she's dead?"

Lisa thought she was going to faint. "Dead?" she managed. They both watched her, waiting. "No!" she cried hysterically. "No. Last night she was alive."

Holding on to the gentleness, Chubby Paton told her what had happened. She listened, her blue eyes enormous, her slim fingers twisting and untwisting.

"I only met her last night." Her voice trembled and there were tears in her eyes. "I came to tell her I had discovered she was my mother. I had found out her name. I traced her here. I took Wayside Cottage down the road. I wanted to get to know her. I came last night . . ."

Chubby Paton considered her outburst with astonishment. "I'm afraid we will have to ask you some questions."

Lisa said, whimpering, "I couldn't. I mean, I wouldn't. I mean, you don't think . . .?"

"What time were you here?"

Sergeant Donovan pulled his notebook out of his back pocket and the comic slid to the floor. He hurriedly picked it up and put it back, hoping the inspector hadn't noticed.

"I don't know. It wasn't dark," she said, her voice trembling. "Maybe about seven."

"Kill you," said the parrot.

All three reacted involuntarily. The inspector said, "Hell's teeth!"

Donovan jerked to attention.

"The parrot was a witness," said Paton when he could get his breath.

Lisa was too frightened to say it could be her own stupid threat that the bird was repeating. She thought they would arrest her, quick as a flash. "Maybe Beryl disturbed a burglar," she offered in a frantic effort to put them off her scent. "Maybe he said he would kill her if she didn't hand over some money. She was wearing a necklace that looked valuable."

"When intruders are disturbed they don't tend to spell out what they're going to do." Paton's eyes strayed to the bird, then back to her.

The guilt and confusion proved too much, and Lisa wept. Chubby Paton went to the window and the lanky Donovan sloped tactfully after him. They stood together, looking out, waiting for her to calm down. The sun had come round and was beating down on the lawn that was brown from the long, hot summer, though the enclosing bushes and shrubs with their deep, established roots had remained green. Paton opened two of the windows, letting in the scent of leaves. A solitary thrush, hidden among the foliage, began its song.

"I'm sorry." Lisa spoke to their backs and they turned. Kelly Donovan thought he had never seen anyone so beautiful as Goldie Montrose with the shine of tears on her cheeks and that blonde hair curtaining her delicate face. "I'm sorry, I seem to have gone to pieces." She squeezed a soaked tissue into a little ball between the palms of her hands, and sniffed.

The parrot said, "You little bugger, you." Lowering his gorgeous head, lifting his feet slowly and deliberately, he moved along his perch.

Paton glanced at his sergeant, mouth twitching. Donovan looked interrogatively back. Paton nodded. Kelly opened his notebook and obediently wrote down "Kill you". And "You little bugger, you."

"I think you had better tell me the whole story," Paton said to Lisa, backing into the hard chair by the table. "Take your time."

Extending her hands palms upwards to expose the little ball of wet tissue, Lisa said in a broken voice, as though this was the ultimate tragedy, "I haven't got another tissue."

The sergeant said, helpfully, "There's a paper roll in the kitchen."

"All right. Get her a piece," his superior snapped. "Look sharp. It won't bring itself." If there was one thing he could not stand, it was sniffing. He addressed the girl, "There were two mugs in the sitting room."

"I didn't stop for coffee. She went to make some, but I left. Ran away," said Lisa. "She probably drank both of them herself."

Paton considered the possibility. They would have been fingerprinted, anyway. "Why did you run?" he asked.

The sergeant returned with a paper towel and handed it to Lisa. "Thank you. I was upset. She said I'd made a mistake. She said she wasn't my mother. She wasn't going to admit—" Lisa swallowed and dabbed at her eyes with the absorbent kitchen paper. "She wouldn't admit anything."

"Do you know who your father is?"

She told him about the newspaper cutting in the leather frame. "It's on the table in the sitting room. I'll get it," she said, jerking forward on her seat.

"It's not there now."

"Who took it? You? The police?" She sat poised on the edge of the sofa, her face raised and twisted with anguish. "I need it. I want it. It's mine, now."

"We didn't take it. It wasn't there. If we find it, we'll let you know. The place will be thoroughly searched." It had been searched by the scene-of-crime team. He wondered what they had done with the photo.

She sank against the sofa back, looking crushed. Paton thought how young and vulnerable she looked and regretted his formal manner. "Did you see anyone on your way back to your cottage?" He was making a conscious effort to be more gentle with her.

"No. But some boy was prowling around the garden. Much later, that was. He came to the window. I was frightened. I told him to go away."

"Have you any idea who he was?"

"He said his name was Sammy."

Paton looked across at Donovan. "Ask Ellis." The sergeant left the room. "Do your parents – your adoptive parents – know you're here?"

She wiped the corner of one eye, hesitated, then as though finding the answer difficult, wiped the other. "They know I'm in Halfpenny Dun," she said at last.

"Do they know the rest? That Miss Lisamore was your mother?"

She was all at once terribly young and defensive, like many a teenager he had known in a state of defiance compounded of ignorance, guilt, and sheer bloody mindedness. "They didn't want me to find my mother. So I didn't tell them."

"Were they against your looking?"

Fear showed in her eyes. "They're not murderers," she

said, "if that's what you're thinking. They wouldn't kill her. That would be ridiculous. I'm an adult. I don't belong to them any more. I don't belong to anyone. Let me look for the picture of my father. Please," she begged, flinging out both arms, palms turned upwards, big blue eyes beseeching.

"Shit," said the parrot.

The inspector, embarrassed by the unexpected role-playing, welcomed the diversion. Donovan and Ellis returned.

"Sammy," said the chief inspector looking directly at Ellis. "Who's Sammy, Mr Ellis?"

"Sammy Smeed, sir. He's just a boy. Not very bright. Wanders round the village with his radio blaring."

"At night?"

"Yes. Day and night. They can't seem to keep him at school and his mother can't keep him in at night, but he's harmless. Never done anyone any harm."

"Where does he live?"

"Foundry Cottage, down the high street."

"Thanks, Mr Ellis." He turned to Donovan. "Get that, Sergeant?"

Donovan nodded and Charlie Ellis went back to his post at the front door. Kelly wrote something in his notebook.

Paton turned to Lisa, "Could you give me your parents' address and telephone number?"

Her mouth buttoned up.

"In a case of murder it's necessary to interview everyone concerned."

"They're not concerned."

"Everyone connected in any way with Miss Lisamore is concerned," Paton told her gravely.

"No, I won't. They're not connected with her in any way. They never met her. Never." Lisa was frightened, defensive, indignant.

Paton noted the emergence of some deep-seated crumb of loyalty. He adopted an avuncular air, "We have to cover everything, Miss King. We can get their address, but it would save a lot of trouble if you gave it."

She was silent for a moment, then said sulkily, her voice barely audible, "Fifty-four Green Lane, Chobworth, Surrey, if you must know, but I wish you wouldn't. It's nothing to do with them. Nothing."

"Their names?"

"Mollie and George King."

Paton turned his head. "Got that, Sergeant?" He repeated distinctly, irritated by his sergeant's besotted expression, "Got that?" Returning his attention to Lisa, he asked, "Are you going to be in the village over the weekend?"

"Why would I leave? It's my mother who has been murdered." The tears spilled over and again rolled down her cheeks. She did not bother, this time, to wipe them away.

Paton recognised her need for sympathy. "Why don't you get your parents down?" he suggested kindly. "You shouldn't be on your own."

"Let me search for my father's photo. Please. Please, Mr Paton."

"I'm sorry, my dear. If it's here, it will be found. We'll let you know."

"What about a little drop of gin?" asked Quixote, though without hope.

Chapter 10

PC Ellis returned flushed with heat for the day was growing warmer. He stood in the doorway looking across at Paton who sat astride the sofa arm, "I saw the headmistress. She says Miss Lisamore has a brother in Oxfordshire. They don't know his address, though. She didn't visit him, or have him down. They weren't on good terms, it seems."

"How do they know – the school?" Paton always wanted the facts behind the facts. Ellis hadn't learned enough. He thought crustily that he should have sent Donovan.

"She's been teaching there for a few years. They're bound to know a bit about her." The constable looked hurt.

Paton wondered. "Not necessarily. Some people are secretive."

Up at the village school on the green that was what the headmistress was saying, "Beryl, when one comes to think of it, was a secretive girl. She never talked about herself – I mean, in any way that didn't concern the village. Angela, dear, you really must pull yourself together."

The school secretary wiped her eyes. Miss Hagan was glad to note that the fast bicycle ride had put paid to Angela's weedy fringe. She thought a bare forehead made a woman look intelligent. Her own broad brow was meant as a shining example, though no one copied.

"I'm in shock, Miss Hagan."

"Oh, come. That is an Americanism you no doubt picked up on your visit to Disney World." The head never allowed Angela to forget what she thought of

78

that folly. She had nothing against Americans, although a good deal against the over-abundant and easy pleasures of Disney. As for her staff saving up to fly to Florida to visit it when the world was full of natural wonders, words failed her. On the demerits of Disney opening in France she would only say the French could always be counted on to let one down.

"If you were in shock you'd be hospitalised and sedated," she pointed out, ever vigilant to maintain the purity of the English language, at least within the bounds of the Halfpenny Dun village school. Ignore the growth factor. Keep cockney out. "Within a certain radius of London all schools are menaced by cockney," she would say. "One must fight it." She was not one of the "They'll grow out of it" brigade. Miss Hagan was a nipper of buds.

"I'll take this coffee to my office," she said. In the passage she hesitated, then stalked back. "I'd rather you didn't discuss the matter. Try to keep things normal. Angela, grit your teeth and get on. If you can't, you had better go home." The head deplored the passing of the stiff upper lip.

"Yes, Miss Hagan," Angela replied, swiftly considering the advantages of going home to work on her dried flower arrangement for the Horticultural Show. That, she felt, would be therapeutic.

Leslie Hardiman, who was suspected of being gay – male homosexuals knew better than to emerge from the closet in Halfpenny Dun – said bitchily, "Beryl had a canter with Anthony Rowsell. Did you know? That's who gave her the necklace."

It was Miss Hagan's aim also, and mainly successful, to foster good old-fashioned decency in her staff. Corpses were not fair game. "True or false, I'd shut up about it, if I were you," said the infant mistress, glancing apprehensively through the open doorway in the direction the Head had taken. "He's been happily married for years, as you well know."

Leslie pursed his lips. "It was years ago. BS."

"What d'you mean, BS?"

"Before Susan."

"Forget it, Leslie."

"In the circumstances that there's a murder to solve, nothing ought to be forgotten," Leslie retorted primly. "Keep your wits about you, that's what I say." He slid his narrow bottom off the table and with a barely perceptible twitch of the hips, went back to his classroom.

Down at Badger Cottage Detective Chief Inspector Paton was saying, "It's not beyond the powers of Policewoman Sellars to run a man called Lisamore to ground, wherever he lives, Oxfordshire or Timbucktoo. Get on to her, Mr Ellis."

The Post Office Stores had emptied. Even with a murder in their sights, the voyeurs needed lunch. As the inspector crossed the road he noticed the floodlights set in the upper façade where the living accommodation lay. Ivy Dodson, a wiry little woman of forty-three, with thick brown hair turning grey, was closing down the counter grill. "We open again at two," she said firmly. "I'm sorry, but I have to make it a rule not to allow customers in, in the lunch hour."

She added a brisk apology of sorts, "There's always someone peering through the glass door dead on two o'clock and certain persons who shall be nameless can turn nasty if you're a minute or two late opening up." She came out of the barred-off post office area and purposefully locked its separate door.

"Detective Chief Inspector Paton," he said, pausing by the fruit display that was filling the store with the ripe scent of conference pears and blushing cox's orange pippins. "Could I have a word with you, please?" He didn't bother to flash his card. She knew what was going on over the road.

She cast a warning look at her husband, a short, plump man with earnest eyes who made a sudden decision to search assiduously under the counter. "I'd rather not, if you don't mind, Inspector. I've got to keep on the right side of my customers," she said, fussing with some left over newspapers lying on a shelf in the window, pushing them out of line, then straightening them. "There's people around, if you don't mind my saying so, who could answer questions without doing themselves harm. I don't want to be unco-operative," said Ivy, "but."

Paton recognised that was the end of the sentence. He said mildly, "You may not know it's an offence to withhold information from the police. You're in a crucial position, opposite Miss Lisamore's cottage. I need to know if you saw anyone in the vicinity last night." He added, "You've got some powerful floodlights out there."

Ivy's mouth buttoned up.

"You'd better tell 'im," said Fred emerging from under the counter to nervously address his wife.

The inspector opened his mouth to ask Fred what she had better tell, but Ivy flared, "We'd be out of business in no time if I nosey parkered on everyone I saw around at night."

Paton, recognising that Fred was not to have a say, returned his attention to the postmistress. "I thought you might have seen Ben Finlay, for a start." Fred, adopting a humble stance, looked down at his size tens.

"Course I seen him this morning. Charlie Ellis seen him, too. I didn't see him last night."

"Maybe you saw the Smeed boy last night?"

"Sammy walks round the village day and night. Anyone'll tell you that. He wouldn't hurt anyone. Gentle as a lamb, he is."

"Anybody else?" Her mouth shut like a trap. Fred nervously raised his head, then returned to uncertain contemplation of his feet.

"Just because someone was in the area," Paton pointed out patiently, "it doesn't mean he was the murderer. But he may have seen something suspicious."

Fred raised his head again.

"Nobody," said Ivy.

Paton saw the beseeching expression in Fred's eyes and took it as a lead. "I think you had better tell me who you saw, Mrs Dodson," he said, using his officer-in-charge voice.

"It can't do any harm, not to a man like him," Fred ventured.

"A man like . . .?" The inspector left the sentence open ended, waiting.

Fred bravely addressed the inspector without taking his eyes from his wife's face, "Mr Rowsell's a member of the Council. Highly respected. He wouldn't be doing any harm."

"You saw this man Rowsell come out of the cottage?"

"Out of the lane," Ivy corrected him fiercely. "Out of the lane."

"What time, Mrs Dodson?" Paton recognised her husband had spoken all he dared.

"We were going to bed. Ten-thirty, I expect. Maybe eleven. And if you think Mr Rowsell would murder that poor woman," Ivy's chest puffed up with indignantion, "you got another think coming. He's got a lovely little wife and children. Lovely family. Lovely."

"I'm sure we shall be able to eliminate him. Does he work locally? Rowsell?"

"He's in antiques," volunteered Ivy, looking accusingly at her husband. "In Castle Manton. Very respectable business. Very respectable family."

"Thank you for your help." Paton heard no more than a quiet click as he shut the glass door behind him, but turning he caught a glimpse of Ivy's malevolent expression as she turned to her husband and regretted he had had to spoil their lunch.

Down at The Fox and Hounds the landlord said as he

pulled a pint of bitter, "Young Smeed wanders round the village most nights. A bit light-on in the upper story, but harmless. The menu's over there on the blackboard. I can recommend the cottage pie. It's my wife's speciality." Dolly, a startling redhead, full-bosomed and chatty, said cheerily, "We've got lasagne as well. And pork pies. And salad. Have a look, anyway. Take your pick."

With no warm cooking smells to guide him, Paton, feeling slightly guilty, chose the lasagne though when he saw the effort put into separating his portion from the main body in the dish he wondered if he had been wise. Dolly warmed it in the microwave. "Salad?" He nodded. With the care she might have bestowed on quails' eggs, she forked some pieces of wilted lettuce and sad-looking beetroot on to the plate and handed it over the counter, smiling from the heart, as though conferring a beautiful and well-deserved prize. "That'll be two-fifteen, thank-you-very-much, sir."

There were only two others in the room, a serene-looking silver-haired pair wearing His and Hers leisure gear in lemon-coloured fine wool. They glanced up, caught his eye, and smiled. Paton smiled back, thinking that Goldie Montrose, at seventy, might well look like that woman if life decided to treat her well. He watched them covertly as they chatted and smiled and concerned themselves with each other's needs. "Pepper?"

"Thank you, darling. Do you want a roll?"

He practised saying it in his mind. "Pepper, darling?" and knew he and Barbara hadn't tried hard enough.

Sergeant Donovan barged through the door and came to join him. "I've got a chap coming out from a computer company in Castle Manton," he said. "Pity it wasn't a recorder. It's voices we need, isn't it?" He looked longingly at the chief inspector's ale.

"Go and get yourself one," Paton growled, put out of sorts by a combination of his recognised guilt and his unfortunate choice of food. "Keep off the lasagne. It's grade one lousy. Three weeks old. I should have taken her advice. There could be letters on the machine. That's the thing about computers, they keep copies. Try the cottage pie. She recommended that."

"Oh, by the way, your wife rang," said Donovan diffidently. "Wants you to ring her back."

Paton was annoyed with him for being so blatantly tactful. He pushed the half-eaten lasagne aside, picked up a piece of beetroot in his fingers and ate it thoughtfully, then finished his ale while the sergeant went to the bar.

"There's a phone over there by the door," said Donovan, returning and dropping, loose boned, into the seat opposite. He gestured with one hand while spooning a forkful of potato into his mouth with the other.

Paton deliberately stayed where he was, staring at Donovan until he squirmed. Barbara's emergence into his day always brought out the worst in him. The warm meaty smell of the cottage pie made his nostrils quiver and added regret to his mood. "Ever thought about getting married, Sergeant?"

"No." Catch him telling his superior about his failures!

"Why not?"

"Never met one I wanted to marry, I s'pose. Seen them. Never met them."

"Beauties can go off, you know. They can go off to hell. Look at that one behind the bar. I'll bet she was a kitten once." He sidled along the wooden seat, holding his stomach in.

"It'd be nice for a while, though." Donovan forked another lump of cottage pie into his mouth. "Imagine walking into a restaurant with Goldie Montrose on your arm." The imagery lit his mournful face, straightened his long back and brightened his cheeks.

Paton grinned. "That's having ideas above your station, all right." He thought, if he had had the choosing of a wife, which he had not for Barbara it was, in her frenzy to get away from her family, who had swept him off his feet, he could have been said to have had ideas above his station. He thought he had done well, but his rise to chief inspector was not success in his in laws' eyes. They never made any effort to recover from the disappointment of their only daughter failing to marry a banker or stockbroker, or a young officer with the right connections who could have been a brigadier by now.

He often wondered if things would have been different had they had been blessed with children, a couple of stalwart sons who wanted to join the police, but he knew in his heart that it would not have happened that way. They would have been given the right introductions and joined the army, or gone into the city with one of Barbara's toffee-nosed cousins and married toffy-nosed girls who would treat him the way Barbara treated his parents, with occasional tolerance but mainly indifference.

Fiddling in his pockets for change, he found himself hoping that mixed-up little monkey Goldie Montrose didn't find her natural father and break her parents' hearts. But she would, he thought. Short of a bloody miracle, she would, for that was the way of life.

He lifted the receiver and dialled.

"Chubby, thank goodness you've rung." Barbara's voice sang happily. Someone was listening, Paton thought sourly. "Mother's had a fall and maybe cracked a rib and they're having drinkies tonight. She's determined to go on with it so I'm dashing to take the helm. My battery's flat as a pancake so Wendy Pitt is running me over. She's here now. Can you join us for supper and bring me home?"

He said, "I told you I'm on a murder case. I can't guarantee—"

Dropping out of the role of happy, confident wife, she broke in impatiently, "Of course you can. You can if you want to. You can't work round the clock. I mean, you don't have to. You're in charge—"

"It's because I am in charge that I can't drop everything,

you know that, Barbara. Get Wendy to take you down to the garage and ask for the loan of a battery—"

"Don't be silly," Barbara snapped. "You know perfectly well I can't change a bat—"

"If you'd let me finish, I was going to say young Joe will change it for you. It's a two minute job."

She was bleakly silent. Then she said, "And it's a halfhour job for you to run over to Mother's when you finish. I wouldn't ask you if you weren't in the area."

The line went dead. Paton left the booth wishing every conversation, even when it started well, didn't have to end badly. Donovan had gone. He nodded to Bert Oswhistle, polishing glasses at the bar, and went out into the street.

Chapter 11

The front door bell of Badger Cottage rang.
"I'll go." The hall having been sealed off by the scene-of-crime team, Constable Ellis went round through the garden to the high street entrance and returned escorting a young man, whip-thin and bouncy as a sparrow. He wore a dark suit and sported a thirties haircut, short back and sides. "Mr Belcher," he said, leaping forward and holding out his hand. "I've been sent by Touch-Lite Computers."
"Detective Chief Inspector Paton."
"So what's the prob?"
"Can you start up that thing?" Paton nodded towards the computer.
Belcher crossed to the table, fingered the empty slots below the screen, and turned to ask, "Where's the master disk, then?"
"There's a box of them in the drawer on the right."
"A *box* of master disks!"
"I don't know what they are." Paton spoke brusquely, indicating the drawer, "Have a look for yourself."
Belcher flipped open the drawer, lifted out a box and slid half a dozen disks into his palm. "I can't boot it up with these," he said, sounding hurt.
"Boot it up!" Paton thought of football hooligans, bovver boots, and ton-up motor bikes.
"Don't you know anything about computers?"
"Listen, young feller," said Paton heavily, "I'm a cop. If I'd been a computer expert I wouldn't have sent for you."

The bones beneath the shoulder pads twitched. Paton hazarded an eccentric guess that the little squirt was plugged in to a battery. Or had he got St Vitus's dance?

"I can probably get a master disk, but I need to know what software was used."

"Software?"

"Is there a manual anywhere?" asked the expert, exasperated.

Donovan came forward and rummaged through the drawers. Belcher pounced on a three-inch square, black with a silver tag. "There it is. That's the master disk. I can boot it up with this, but I need the prog disk as well."

"What?"

"Programme," said Belcher, wearily resigned to their ignorance. "I need the programme disk to get at the files. Those disks there," he pointed to the box, "will have text on them, but I can't get at it without the prog disk. And that's what's not here."

Paton rummaged through the drawers and brought out a black book. "What's this?"

"Wordsort." He pointed, with infuriating condescension, to the big white capitals on the front.

"All right," grumbled Paton. "I can read."

"I mean, that's the software. Wordsort. Understand?" The muscle jerking went into recession while he waited for an answer.

"No," said Paton. God! What a horrible haircut!

Belcher sighed. "I'll have to go back to the shop to get the necessary."

"Necessary what?"

"Wordsort prog disk. I told you that's what's missing. We won't get anywhere without the prog. It goes in there." He pointed to a slot below the screen, "And one of these," he indicated the box containing the disks, "goes in the other slot." His skinny fingers slid into a pocket, found his car keys, set them tinkling and rattling.

"Right," said Paton. "Go ahead. Get the prog – whatever. We'll be waiting for you." He had no intention of coming to terms with this new breed of illiterate who took to computers like a duck to water. Heads full of bricks. Nothing to unlearn. Kids thought them a doddle. That said something.

In the kitchen Sergeant Donovan, having exhaustively and without success searched the cottage for the picture of Goldie Montrose's father, had now emptied the contents of the waste bin on to newspaper, and using the tip of a knife, was delicately engaged in prodding through its malodourous contents. Paton gazed upon it with distaste; apple peelings, something white that looked like rice pudding, a river of thick gravy, and a lump of rather smelly fish.

"Funny that disk disappearing," he remarked, thinking out loud.

"Suspicious," agreed the sergeant.

"Not suspicious. Funny. Odd. Why would anyone take the disk that works the machine? It can't have anything incriminating on it."

Sergeant Donovan, having long ago learned to recognise rhetorical questions as part of his superior's thinking processes, kept his mouth shut. Besides, he didn't have an answer.

Paton pulled his hands out of his pockets. "Hey, what's that? Looks like a bit of a leather frame. Haul it out, Sergeant."

Donovan lifted the object between finger and thumb. It was indeed a framed photograph. A crumple of kitchen paper had mercifully protected most of the leather from the swill. He wiped the glass and frame with a kitchen cloth before handing it over.

Paton stared, narrow-eyed. "I know that face."

The sergeant, down on his knees again wrapping up the debris in newspaper, asked, "Who is he, sir?"

"That chap Street, headmaster of – what's the name of

it? Brockley Martin Abbey. That's right, Brockley Martin Abbey. A boys' public school in Wiltshire. He's been suspended while they wait for the verdict in a paternity case. So he's the girl's father! Well, I'm blessed," marvelled the Inspector. "He's still getting it up, then."

Donovan ruminated, as he carefully lifted the envelope of wobbly kitchen refuse, that he'd have been chastised for daring to say that. "In English law a man's innocent until proved guilty," he silently mouthed as he went outside, thinking of himself as a comical chap. Having bundled the rubbish into the waste bin which he had earlier found hidden behind a piece of trellis near the back door, he returned to the garden room to find the inspector thoughtfully placing the photo on the table.

"Are we going to give it to her, sir?" Donovan tried to imagine his own father, or his stepfather, involved in a paternity case, and failed. "She could do with not finding out, couldn't she?" he asked, feeling sorry for the lovely Goldie Montrose. "I mean, she's just lost her mother."

"Yeah. I don't need reminding. This clown's pretty loseable, too. But we're going to have to pull him in. Look at it this way. The victim's seen Street's photo in the paper. She knows he's in trouble. They're obviously not on good terms or she wouldn't have to resort to a newspaper photo, she'd have a proper one. What's to say she hasn't seen him since their affair?"

"She's – was – only about fifteen or sixteen then," Donovan pointed out. "Seduction, wasn't it."

Paton said, "Yeah," without looking up. He walked back to the computer and stood looking at the box of disks, holding the frame in one hand. "I can't help feeling it's all here. When Jumping George gets back we may have the answer. Maybe she wrote to him crowing: 'My moment has arrived. I'm going to get my own back.' That sort of thing. She goes on to say she's going to offer evidence in court that he was seducing schoolgirls more than twenty years ago. He decides to do her in. He comes to visit, sees the computer and realises he has to take the disk with the copy on it."

"So he goes over to the computer, slips out the disks, and pockets them," suggested Donovan eagerly.

"We're assuming he knows how to work this particular machine."

"Maybe he forces her to give it to him. 'Gimme the letter or I'll kill you,'" suggested Donovan, his little grey eyes lighting up, "and she's clever and gives him the program disk, leaving the one with the letter on it in the machine."

"Yeah. But it's not there," Paton pointed out."

"Maybe it's in the box.

"Let's hope so.

"Kill you," croaked Quixote in the background.

They both turned to look at him. "Doesn't half give you a turn, does it?" Paton put the frame down on the work table and went over to the cage. "Who's going to feed this chap? What does he eat? Somebody ought to know."

Quixote put his beautiful head on one side and remarked conversationally, "I belong to Beryl." He edged along his perch, came back again, then added, "Shit."

The sergeant waited to see if Paton would ask him to write that down, but he seemed not to have heard. "Nuts or seeds or suchlike," he suggested.

The inspector looked at him blankly.

"The parrot, I mean. You asked what he'd eat, sir."

"Oh. I was thinking. That girl wants the photo."

Donovan said, "Why don't we throw it away?"

Paton pushed his hands down into his pockets and staring at the toes of his shoes walked the length of the room. "Take a chap's fast car away and sure as eggs is eggs, he'll fall off a bus."

The sergeant tried to look intelligent, as though he understood.

The parrot said, "Ho, ho, ho and a bottle of rum," then lapsed into silence.

"So, what about it?" Donovan picked up the photo.

"People's problems are their private property. You don't steal private property."

Donovan stared. "You mean 'photos'?"

"I mean problems."

Donovan scratched his head.

"If you remove problems, you stunt their owner's growth. Know that?"

"Er—" He wondered if the inspector's telephone call to his wife had brought on this wierd mood.

"You know it now." Deep in his crisis of conscience, Paton stared at the picture in the sergeant's hand. "She's going to know anyway, if he turns out to be the villain. Tell Ellis to run it down to Wayside Cottage."

"And God help her, poor little trout," he muttered as he went off to the incident room, but the sergeant did not hear.

Chapter 12

"Letitia?"

"Anthony! At last! Thank God! Have you heard the awful news about Beryl Lisamore?"

Anthony stiffened.

"Anthony, are you there?"

"Yes," he said indistinctly.

"Beryl's been murdered. She was found dead in her cottage this morning. Anthony, are you still there? Anthony!" She waited in a fever of expectancy.

The answer was slow in coming. "Y-es."

Letitia said feverishly, "You've got to think up an alibi that doesn't include me."

"Why—" He cleared his throat and began again. She thought his voice trembled. "Why should I need an alibi?"

"The police will want to know where everyone in the village was last night. Don't you see! What a mess!" She was thinking that Brian was coming home today."

Anthony said, thinking of Sam Smeed and the car lights on his face as the unidentified vehicle crawled past, "I could say I had gone for a stroll and dropped in with – say, the notices for the choral society—"

"They're not printed yet. Why don't you say you went to join Susan for the night?"

"Susan would have to back that up," he said cautiously.

"Wouldn't she? She's a loyal wife, isn't she?" When he did not answer her panic escalated, "Promise me you won't involve me. Candy and Oliver are my alibi. Everyone knows I wouldn't leave them alone at night. But if Brian finds out about us – he would kill me. And you, too, probably. Anthony, are you there?"

He was a whole lot less worried about Brian than he was about Sam Smeed, who was dim as a donkey and could not be relied upon to keep his silly mouth shut. And again, what about that cruising car? The implications of adultery were as nothing beside the fact that some local car driver had seen him leaving the victim's house. He had to be local for why should a stranger be cruising along Old Wood Lane at half past ten at night?

"Plenty of people won't have alibis," he said, aware of sounding out of kilter, suddenly too brisk. "I think you're worrying unduly. I don't see why we should be questioned – either of us – but if we are, I shall simply say I was at home."

"It's not going to be enough," Letitia wailed. "People could have called around, or telephoned. If you don't answer the phone, you're not at home. Think, Anthony, think."

"Yes," he said bleakly. "I'll think. I've got to go now." He thought her problems petty in relation to his. He'd square things with Brian, if it came to that. He replaced the receiver and sat with elbows on the table, fingers steepled beneath his chin, staring at the carriage clock that was waiting to be repaired, thinking of Susan and the Buckinghamshire estate she was imminently due to inherit, pondering bitterly on the always uncertain hand of fate.

He thought of his father-in-law, lingering on in that beautiful brass bedstead (worth thousands on a good market). Ever since old Teddy Lambert became ill Anthony had been making plans. He had decided to put a manager into the shop, for there would be no buyers coming forward until there was a shift in the economy, and take himself off to Cirencester for a course in farm management. He easily envisaged himself in the role of country squire, or its 1990s equivalent. A man of property hadn't the standing of his ancestors (Susan's ancestors), but the structure of English society still required a man of substance to take his place in a country community. Anthony fancied himself as a man of substance.

Through the glass panel he could see into his showroom where the girl was polishing an eighteenth-century table, brass inlaid. People had stopped buying that kind of thing a couple of years ago. Luxury trades were always the first to be hit by a recession. Anthony didn't need telling it was possible to exist without intricately carved William and Mary sideboards, nests of Jacobean tables, snuff boxes and icons. He had managed to keep the depth of his troubles from his wife, but if her father didn't die soon he was going to be hard pressed to meet the mortgage payments on the house.

Yes, Anthony decided, he would say that he was at home all evening. If he stuck to his guns, who could prove otherwise? If someone said they had telephoned – who on earth was going to say that? Surely the police weren't going to ask everyone who they had telephoned last night? Anyway, he could always say he had gone for a long walk. Then read a book in the bath. He couldn't hear the telephone from the bathroom. Stop worrying about the telephone. Nobody was going to bring that up.

If pushed into a corner, he would admit that he had visited Letitia. There was no reason why Susan should know. He sucked in his breath. Unless Letitia, crossing swords with Brian, turned spiteful. But why should she? They were old friends, before they were lovers. For heavens' sake, this was 1992. What was so dire about helping yourself to a bit of tail? Everybody did it. If one was to believe what one read in the papers, one child in three these days was the result of extra-marital sex. That was the least of his problems.

Oh hell! Damn and blast it! He leant over the desk,

elbows on the leather, and covered his face with his hands.

In the high street of Halfpenny Dun Elsie Smeed was shouting, "'Ere, Sammy. Come back 'ere. I want ter wash them jeans."

Sam, who hated being parted from his clothes, put his head down and ran but he was knock-kneed and slow compared to his mother, a lively thirty-three. She caught him easily, took him by the ear, and led him triumphantly back to Foundry Cottage, conscious of the amused grins of two policemen standing by their cars. Showing off. "Now you gimme those jeans or I'll take them," she threatened as they went inside. Sam regretfully shed the offensive garment. "My, how they smell! Where you been, I'd like to know, to get to smell like this?" she asked, though knowing it was his habit to paddle in the muddy stream that fed the allotments, then rub his feet dry with his hands, and wipe his hands on his clothes. Sam couldn't keep a handkerchief for five minutes. "T-shirt," demanded his mother.

"Aw, Mum." He pinned it to his chest with both arms. Elsie took it by the hem and wrenched it over the back of his head. "Now go and get into some clean things. Goodness knows, there's always clean clothes in your room. Don't I wear my fingers to the bone washing and ironing for you?"

Sammy, all white skin and jutting bones, disconsolately climbed the narrow stairs in his briefs. Elsie went through to the kitchen, turned on the taps over the sink and proceeded to empty Sam's pockets. A tangle of string, a half-chewed peppermint, two small nails and a matchbox full of dead beatles. "Ugh!" She flipped the other one inside out. Unidentifiable junk rattled on to the bench. "Come and get your rubbish, Sammy," she called over her shoulder as she tipped a handful of soap powder into the water and turned off the taps. "I don't want it cluttering up my kitchen." When he did not appear she shouted, "Come and get your rubbish, I said." She waited another moment then tossed it all out of the window.

The Meads had never made a garden. Tourists wandering down the high street admiring the old houses in their variety of periods and shapes were charmed by the diamond-paned windows of Foundry Cottage that caught the light from slightly different angles, the hanging tiles glowing in the sun and the magnificent mauve wysteria rampaging across the façade. They could not see the small area behind that was cluttered with bars of rusted iron, an old grating, broken fire-backs and other detritus of a working forge that had gone out of business years ago when the smithy died and the Smeeds moved in.

Nobody had bothered to clear away the mess. Dick in his time had grown vegetables in an allotment. Rather the allotment with its good loamy soil and the company of neighbours, anyway, than this rough little patch of clay.

The door-knocker banged. Elsie pushed the clothes down into the suds, wiped her hands on her apron and went to answer it.

"I'm Detective Chief Inspector Paton." Chubby Paton held out his identification card. "And this is Sergeant Donovan. We would like to see your son Sam, if he's at home."

Elsie's little brown eyes skittered briefly over the card without reading it. "Miss Lisamore! She got murdered, I know. I 'eard it in the village." Her terrified eyes lifted to Paton's face, then swivelled to the waiting Donovan. "But it's nothing to do with my Sammy. He wouldn't do a thing like that. Never."

"May we come in?"

She backed like a cornered mouse and they entered a tiny living room made dark even on this sunny day by a combination of the small paned windows and a heavily beamed low ceiling. There was a narrow wooden staircase leading to the floor above, the treads set between two rough hewn oak stays. Elsie went to the bottom stair, grasped the bannister, and called, "Sammy."

"I'm getting dressed, aren't I? You told me to get dressed." The whine dwindled down the stairs.

"He's an obedient boy," said Elsie, nervously twisting her fingers in her apron bindings. "Does as 'e's told. Never 'urt anyone." She pounced on one dirty trainer lying on its side as though thrown from the front door, and keeping her face averted from the men, searched assiduously for the other. The room was shabby and sparsely furnished. A vast inglenook fireplace stacked with logs dominated the side wall. Paton wandered across to take a close look at the ancient fireback decorated with plunging war-horses ridden by armoured soldiers. He hazarded a guess it had come with the cottage, and that the woman was unaware of its value.

"You've got a nice lot of logs there, Mrs Smeed."

She found the shoe under an old rocking-chair and came upright. "A tree come down in the churchyard, hurricane night. Lord Oaks sent Jack Finlay with his electric saw to cut it up and Vicar said we could 'elp ourselves and put something in the plate. What we can afford, like." What they felt it was worth, was actually what he said. The wood was worth a lot to the Smeeds, but Elsie put nothing in because he'd shot her husband, hadn't he? Well, someone had. If not him, then one of his friends. Accident or no accident, Dick ended up dead and she reckoned the estate owed her the wood.

Donovan was gazing at a large glossy print of the queen fixed with sellotape to the back wall. Paton said kindly, "Nice, that."

Elsie looked pleased. "They was givin' them away with a packet of cornflakes. You 'ad to buy the large one. You 'ad to fill in a paper saying what you liked about these cornflakes. Sammy done it," she said in a proud, defensive voice. He wrote, 'I like it because my Mum gives it to me.'"

"Clever," said Donovan. "Would you mind calling your son again, Mrs Smeed?"

She returned to the foot of the stairs. "Sammy, there's some men to see you, an' they're in a 'urry."

A pair of jean-clad legs appeared, then the skinny hips, and finally the pale face framed in its mousey coloured hair spikes. Sammy stopped at the bottom of the stairs, his right hand grasping the rough bannister, his body swinging back and forth in embarrassed uncertainty, his left hand shielding the wart on his face.

Paton went to stand before him. Sammy stopped swinging and stared at the inspector's shoes. "Hello, Sam. I want you to tell me where you were last night."

"'e's a p'liceman, Sam."

"I wus walking round the village. Nuffin' wrong with that."

"Of course not," agreed the inspector. "And who did you see?"

"Go on, Sammy boy. Tell 'im," urged his mother anxiously.

"Goldie Montrose. I didn't see Mr Rowsell or—" His voice dropped to a mutter.

"Who? Bobby and who?"

Sammy giggled.

"Are they the people you usually see?" Sam looked suspicious, then confused, and Paton thought, I'm wasting my time. There's a screw loose here.

"Goldie Montrose asked me in," said Sam, fantasising.

"Oh?" Paton's voice sharpened. "What did you talk to her about?"

"She was crying. Watching the telly and crying. I told her," continued Sam, looking over the inspector's shoulder at the far wall, following his bolting imagination with halting words, "that it weren't true. The film weren't true. Nuffin' to cry about, I said." That, anyway, was what he would have told her, had he been invited in.

"You telling the truth, Sam?" asked Elsie, her thin mouth pursed in doubt.

"You never believe anything I say," whined Sam, swinging his left leg now, kicking his heel on the bottom stair.

"Mr Rowsell. You said you didn't see him." Rowsell, whom the postmistress had seen coming out of Old Wood Lane.

"Why? Why did you say you didn't see him?" asked Paton taking a shot in the dark.

"That's what he said."

"To say you hadn't seen him in Old Wood Lane?"

Sammy looked slyly at his mother, remembering Mr Rowsell's secret that he had promised to keep to himself.

Paton rephrased his question, "Did you see Mr Rowsell come out of the gate of Badger Cottage?"

Sammy considered. "Yes," he said. "Yes, I seen him come out," then added loyally, remembering his promise not to tell about the rubbish, "but I dunno what he was doin' there."

Paton turned towards the door. "Thank you, Sam. If you remember seeing anyone else, let me know. I'll be down at Badger Cottage, or the village hall."

"You go back and wait for Jumping George," he said to Donovan as they walked up the high street. "I'm going to the incident room."

"Are you going to get someone to look up that Paul Street, sir?"

Hmn. Let's wait and see what we find on the computer disks."

Chapter 13

Mr Belcher from Touch-Lite was back, jigging around in front of the computer while Sgt Donovan read the text on the screen. "Can't stay all day," he was saying impatiently as Paton walked in. "I can leave that disk with you, though."

"Listen, mate," said Donovan, "it's no use to me if I can't work the flipping machine. You're going to have to stay until the inspector has read this guff." He glanced up and saw Paton in the doorway. "We got one letter of interest, sir."

"Street?" The inspector was alert.

"'Fraid not. It's about that chap Rowsell. She's got it in for him all right. Had," Donovan amended wryly. "She had it in for Rowsell." He jumped up and offered his seat. "You have to sit down so the light's right on the screen."

"Liquid crystal," said Belcher knowledgeably.

Quixote said, "How about a nice cuppa tea?" Nobody took any notice. He hadn't said anything useful all day.

Paton read the letter Beryl had written to the Council asking for double yellow lines to be painted on the road outside the cottage. "I have asked Mr Rowsell repeatedly to put the matter before the Council and though he assures me he has done this, it is clear to me that he is lying. I know that various matters of importance to him have been implemented and I am concerned that a man who is motivated purely by self-interest should represent the village."

"The date," said Paton pointing, "is yesterday. The day of the murder. She may not even have sent it."

"She could have told him about it and said she was going to send it," suggested Donovan.

Then she gives him a cup of coffee and he strangles her, Paton finished in his mind. No, it would not do.

"I can't stay," said Belcher jigging and jumping with impatience. "I'm supposed to be in the showroom. We're short-staffed as it is."

"You can't go," said Donovan, his confidence restored by the chief inspector's arrival. "We've got to read the rest of the disks."

"All the instructions are in the book." Belcher lifted the manual out of the drawer and tapped it with his finger.

"Give it to me." Paton stood up, took the book from him and flipped through, then tossed it dismissively on to the desk. "Five hundred pages of gobbledy-gook," he said. "I think you over-estimate our ability, young fellow."

Belcher scowled.

"Oh bum," said Quixote, sounding bored.

The young men grinned and the tension between them eased. "Come on," said the sergeant in his most persuasive manner, reclaiming his seat in front of the machine, "it won't take long to read these disks. How's that for jargon – read the disks?"

"Big deal." Belcher refused to be drawn.

Donovan took a disk out of the box and handed it to the reluctant expert. Paton stood watching and waiting. "Go on. Shove it in." Belcher performed some miracle and print appeared on the screen. Donovan peered at it closely.

"School stuff," he reported. "Timetables. Okay, get rid of that and let's try another. There's only five files on this disk. Files? Get that?" Donovan was cocky and eager, enjoying the novelty of the machine.

Paton wandered over to the parrot and stood hands in pockets looking down at him. He heard Donovan say,

"Letter to the electricity disputing a bill. Come on, next file." Paton turned and went out on to the lawn. Donovan's voice followed him: "More timetables." He wandered a little way down the path and back, enjoying the sunshine. When he returned Belcher was protesting, "I can't stay to go through the lot."

"You'll have to." The sergeant looked up at Paton. "We can't work it without him, sir."

Belcher looked angry, then recognising from Paton's expression that he hadn't any choice but to stay, capitulated. "I'll tell you what. I'll write down exactly what you should do. Idiot guide. Unnerstand?"

Donovan scowled. "Wadderyermean, idiot?"

"It's just a name," said Belcher obscurely. "Here's a pen. Get some paper. There's bound to be paper in one of them drawers." The sergeant, though still offended, shuffled around and produced a sheet of quarto. Belcher stabbed at a key. They both waited. The machine buzzed, the text disappeared and a list came up on the screen. He removed both disks and switched off the power. The screen went blank. "Now look. Watch close. Do exactly what I tell you. Switch on." Donovan obeyed. "Put the master disk in the left hand slot." He added impatiently, "Do it, Sergeant. I told you, I'm in a hurry."

Donovan nervously inserted the disk in its slot. They waited while text flew across the screen. When the buzzing stopped Belcher said, "Now take that one out – write it down, Sergeant. Write, 'Take out master disk.' Go on. Write down everything I tell you to do. Everything. I'm giving you an Idiot Guide. How to work the thing, step-by-step, but you'd better not make a mistake because if you do you'll never get out of it. Okay?"

"Okay." Donovan was mollified, even interested.

"Now, got that? Put the program disk in its place. Go on, shove it in. Write that down. Now, put this in the righthand slot. Write down what you've just done."

Paton wandered back to the door and stood looking

out. It could have been a beautiful garden, he thought. He could imagine flowers flowing out of stone urns, little beds of annuals bordering the paths. But Miss Lisamore had not been into flowers, only curtaining bushes behind which she hid herself and under which young men, intent upon mischief and solitude, drank whisky, gin and vodka from half bottles which were all they could afford. An easy place to creep into to commit a murder. An easy place to get out of without being spotted, except that there were floodlights in the Post Office opposite.

Rowsell. He of the lovely family.

He decided that as soon as the Idiot Guide was done they would go and look him up. It seemed more important, at that moment, than wading through the computer disks.

It was five miles from Halfpenny Dun to Castle Manton. The road ran along the side of the very same stream that crossed the arable fields of Home Farm, made its way down Old Wood Lane, then shying off the high street, rattled over a stony bed between the allotments and the council houses in the high street. The park on his right, that surrounded Crumford Place, had been planted with oaks and chestnuts by his lordship's ancestors in the late 1700s. Those that had survived the hurricane were magnificent giants, but among them there were grotesque, broken-limbed skeletons. Lord Oaks had already spent a small fortune cleaning up the worst of the mess. Now, strapped for cash, he was concentrating only on the obligatory programme of restoring the public footpaths that ran through his land.

The park with its dry summer grass ended here and the road wound down a wooded slope, then out into open farmland that gave way to a series of apple orchards red with the glut of fruit so great this year that farmers could not afford to pay for their picking.

"Kill you. Give me your money, or I'll kill you." Paton considered the possibility of drug-crazed youngsters breaking in to Badger Cottage in search of money. Were there any drug-crazed youngsters in the area? It was hard to imagine. She hadn't been raped. Nothing sexual, the doctor said.

Sergeant Donovan, aware that the inspector didn't want to be disturbed, relaxed in his seat, dreaming of the computer. He wouldn't mind getting one for himself. You could have a lot of fun with one of those. He must find out how much they cost.

Following PC Ellis' advice, they drove round the one-way system and found themselves in a quiet square. "Two tall yews, Ellis said. There they are." Donovan pointed. Beyond lay a magnificent clock face planted out in golden marigolds, all in full bloom, the hands and hours marked in with a string of small blue flowers. "This council's got a soul beyond drainage and roadworks," Paton said, sniffing appreciatively at the scents in the air.

"Sure has."

"You like flowers, Sergeant?"

"Sure do. I got a pink thing in a pot on my window sill. Someone gave it to me." His mother gave it to him but he didn't want to say so. He was touchy about his mother, now.

"What is it?"

"I forget. It's got a name. It was on the ticket."

Paton grinned and Donovan tried not to look embarrassed.

As the car slid into one of the few spaces that had escaped the double yellow lines they saw the shop they were seeking standing back where the pavement had been raised and widened. Anthony Rowsell Antiques was written in gold lettering on a black background. There were window boxes full of pink geraniums and multi-coloured astors. They left the car and climbed half a dozen steps decorated on either side by small barrels of salvias.

"Very nice," said Paton. "Very upmarket. This cove is prosperous. Doing well."

Anthony saw them coming, recognisable policemen, each with a purposeful stride. He jerked at his cuffs, though knowing they would not hide the marks on his hands. Thinking loss, thinking of Susan and the two children, the Buckinghamshire estate, he suffered, bitterly regretting the stupid indulgences that had started a trail of events leading to this mess.

Paton shoved open the heavy glass door and came face to face with a man he immediately labelled the Eton and Oxford type. "Mr Rowsell?" Astute blue eyes, clean, floppy fair hair cut precisely short enough and precisely long enough for consummate effect. He stood loosely, one leg bent at the knee, neither welcoming nor indifferent. A courteous man. Chubby Paton was not at his best with Anthony Rowsell's type, amiable fellows whose very bearing brought lesser mortals running. Their serenity seemed to reach out and pull his inferiority into focus; his thinning hair, his beer gut; his humble origins.

Anthony nodded in acknowledgment of Paton's introduction, took the card and slowly read the print, giving himself a little more time. He glanced thoughtfully at Donovan, then back at the card. Paton allowed him his little prevarication. There was plenty to look at. On his right a glass showcase displayed antique jewellery, the very case, had they but known, from which Beryl Lisamore's necklace had come. There were highly polished tables inlaid with brass, a bowfronted chest, its surfaces gleaming from centuries of polish. Paton's grandfather, who had been a butler in a grand house, proudly boasted a flattened cushion on his right thumb. It was his badge of identification, he claimed, as a man who knew how to polish silver. He never used a cloth.

A girl was standing at the back of the showroom pretending to be absorbed in buffing up a hunting horn. She had watched the men come in, seen the production of the identification card. She knew they were policemen by the way it was done. Straightforward. Look! This is who I am. Salesmen and buyers had quite a different style. Cor! Glamourpants in trouble? She had worked in antiques long enough to know that sometimes the lines drawn between arbitrating skill and sheer theft were very thin indeed.

"Maybe you've heard," said the inspector watching Anthony's face, "that a woman in Halfpenny Dun was murdered last night."

Anthony wrestled with the choice offered and settled for innocence. "Good God! Who?"

"Miss Lisamore. I'll come straight to the point, Mr Rowsell. You were seen coming out of Old Wood Lane around ten-thirty last night."

Anthony glanced up, saw the girl standing pop-eyed, the hand holding the cloth arrested in mid-air, and realised she may have heard. "Let's talk in my office," he said. "Come this way." He ushered the two men ahead and shut the door behind them. "Do sit down. Over there. That chair's comfortable, Mr Paton. One of my William and Marys. Sergeant, do you mind that stool? Or, I could get you—" he looked vaguely round the office waiting for Donovan to say the stool would be all right.

"This is fine." Donovan, cheerfully unaware that he was being patronised, edged his boney bottom on to the high seat, treating it as a vantage point from which to get a good eyefull of the girl in the showroom.

"Yes, that's true," said Anthony, "I was walking in the village last night. But, good lord—" He settled on the edge of his desk, smiling with a well-blended mixture of charm and sophistication at the ridiculous idea of anyone suspecting him, "My wife's father is ill and she's been away all week with the children. I do go out walking in the evenings when there's nothing on the box I want to see." He rested one hand on the desk, shifted his weight a little, a man at ease with himself, a happily married man. "It's a bit lonely at home without the family," he said, warmly drawing the inspector in, pointing up a situation that he might be expected to understand.

Paton said, "There's a somewhat vitriolic letter on Miss Lisamore's computer referring to your lack of co-operation over a matter of double yellow lines." Donovan took his eyes off the girl and opened his notebook.

Anthony's laugh was tempered with just the right amount of outrage. "One doesn't murder over double yellow lines, Inspector."

Feeling small, overweight and regrettably scratchy, resenting his position on the chair looking up at Rowsell on the desk, Paton said, "I'd like you to tell me why you were in the vicinity of Badger Cottage last night."

Anthony shrugged. "It's inevitable, on a walk round the village, that one will at some point be in the vicinity of practically everything."

"So you must have seen people. Can you give me their names?" Donovan readjusted the notebook on his knee and stared at the point of his pen.

There was no hesitation. "I don't know that I did. I don't remember seeing anyone, actually."

"Ben Finlay?"

"The milkman? No. Why would I see him? I imagine he's tucked up pretty early. He must start work on the milk round about 4 am."

"Sammy Smeed?" Paton wondered if he detected just the faintest hesitation.

"Confidentially," said Anthony, bending forward in a confidential manner, "that boy's not all there. He wanders round the village at all hours of the night in summer. I've no doubt he was on the wander last night." He pondered, frowning, giving the impression of cudgling his brains. "Whether he would actually commit a murder . . . mmn. It's felt in the village that he's harmless." Anthony finished on a provocatively uncertain note.

"Did you see him, that's what I asked."

"No. I don't think so."

"Miss Lisamore?"

"No."

"Perhaps you could tell me exactly where you walked?"

Anthony lifted one arm and was casually rubbing the side of his head when he remembered the marks on his hands. Sick with fright, yet still managing to retain his urbane manner, he slipped them into his pockets. "Let me see." What he could see was the inspector's eyes on the protruding shape of his knuckles through the fine cloth of his trousers. He panicked. Everything went topsy-turvy in his mind. He decided to put them off the scent by saying he went in the opposite direction. "I went up the high street towards the church."

"You would have to pass the pub. There must have been people outside who knew you, or whom you knew."

"I don't think so." Now he'd botched it. Why the dickens hadn't he stuck to the truth? Anthony felt sweat trickling down from his armpits. "Maybe there were. I'm blowed if I can remember," he said, carefully orchestrating a small laugh at his implied ineptitude. "Then I went along the path between the high street and Pieman's Lane. Pieman's Lane," he explained, "runs more-or-less parallel with the high street, though in a curved line, and comes out at Old Wood Lane."

Hell's teeth! He had forgotten about the skips and the piles of soil and clay that had rendered the lane impassable just beyond The Red House. Too late, now. Keep going. Keep calm. For God's sake, keep calm. "I turned left there," he said, "and went up the lane. Quite a long way," he added, quickly distancing himself from Badger Cottage. "It was a pleasant night for a walk. Moonlight. Very mild. Then, I came back into the high street."

"About what time?"

"I haven't the foggiest. I wasn't timing myself. There was no reason to hurry home."

"You must have noticed the time when you arrived home, though."

"I'm not a great one for clock watching," said Anthony.

"Do you know what time you went to bed?" There was an edge to Paton's voice.

Anthony shrugged. "I had a bath. Actually, I spent quite a long time in the bath." His well-cut mouth curved in a naughty-boy smile. "I keep some paperbacks in the bathroom. There's nothing like a soak and a read when you're bored, don't you think?"

"Could I see your hands?"

"What?"

"Could you take your hands out of your pockets, please."

Anthony did so. He rested them on his knees, looking down at them, keeping the faint smile going. "You're wondering about the marks. I was cutting some wire. Mending a hole in the fence." He frowned convincingly, letting the inspector know he was displeased with himself for his carelessness. "I'm not all that good with my hands. Made rather a balls-up of it." In the back of his mind a small voice was trying to tell him he was making a balls-up of this interview. What fence, it was asking? He's going to want to see the fence.

"When?"

The sergeant was writing busily in his notebook. Anthony regarded him thoughtfully. "What?"

"When did you mend the fence?"

"Yesterday, I think. Or the day before. I've been cleaning up a few odd jobs since I've been on my own. You know how it is, there's never enough time when the family's there," said Anthony, generously implying that he and the inspector shared a lifestyle. "It's an opportunity to catch up."

110

"I thought they looked like stabs from bicycle spokes," said Paton, deadpan.

The pause was infinitissimal before Anthony said, "I don't ride a bicycle, Mr Paton. I drive a Ferrari."

"Ben Finlay's old bike was found in Miss Lisamore's hall. Some of the spokes were broken. It could have been done accidentally. It could have been knocked over if there was a scuffle."

Anthony drew a long breath, rose from the table and casually shook his shoulders back. "One cannot imagine," he said, looking down at his long legs, jerking at a dent in the crease of his trousers, "why the milkman's bike would be in Miss Lisamore's hall. If he had wanted to leave it with her I'm sure he could have put it in her garage. She hasn't got – hadn't – a car."

"Did you know her well, Mr Rowsell?"

"In a small village," said Anthony, "it goes without saying that to a greater or lesser degree everyone knows everyone else. I didn't see much of her. As you said, there was this business about no parking outside her cottage. Frankly, Inspector, nobody in the village would have gone along with it. There was no danger. There's very little traffic in Old Wood Lane. None of us like having cars parked outside our houses, but we have to put up with it."

"What did you make of him?" Paton asked as they drove back to Halfpenny Dun.

"Guilty as hell."

"Jumping to conclusions, Sergeant?"

Donovan flushed. "You didn't believe all that baloney about the hole in the fence, did you?"

"No. It looks as though they had a scuffle all right, but that doesn't mean he killed her."

"It's a bit of a long shot, isn't it," Donovan ventured a little brave but diffident sarcasm, "that Paul Street the seducer should come for vengeance right after she's had a set-to with that geezer. I mean, what a busy night!"

"Life's full of long shots," said Paton. "Give me a bit of real evidence, Sergeant."

"He can't account for his time. I mean, nobody saw him. He didn't see anybody."

"You may find half the village won't be able to produce alibis. Try again."

Sergeant Donovan wished he could say, "You're the flipping genius. Have a go yourself." He settled for scratching his head and saying, "I s'pose there isn't any," feeling gormless.

"Right," said Paton as they entered the high street of Halfpenny Dun. "I'm putting you out at the village hall. I want to see how the house-to-house is getting on."

On his return to Badger Cottage Paton said to Charlie Ellis who was standing on guard, "Come in, Mr Ellis. I want to have a word with you." Charlie followed him round the back to the verandah room.

Sergeant Donovan was seated at the table with the little computer on his left, laboriously copying from the screen. He looked up. "We found some bird seed and fed 'im."

Paton walked over to the cage. "My name's Quixote," said the bird, eying his visitor cautiously.

Paton laughed. "I could get fond of him. If nobody wants him after this is over—"

"Shit," said the parrot.

"Maybe not," Paton acceded, recognising that Barbara and her family would not be amused.

Donovan grinned. "I wouldn't mind taking him on myself. He'd be a wow down The Wheatsheaf."

Paton lowered himself on to the sofa, pushing a cushion behind his back. PC Ellis was standing just inside the door.

"Rowsell," he said, addressing the constable. "Tell me about Anthony Rowsell."

"He's very respected, sir. Chairman of the Historical

Society. On the Council. Lives in that big Queen Anne house on the green. Takes an interest in everything in the village. Not the killing type, I'd say, sir."

"What is the killing type, Mr Ellis?" asked Paton, looking interested.

"Don't know, sir," replied Ellis, dismayed at his slip. Sergeant Donovan had warned him the chief inspector did not care for unsolicited opinions.

"Was there anything between him and Miss Lisamore?" He noted the man's hesitation and added, impatiently, "Come on, Mr Ellis. Everyone knows everyone else's affairs in a village like this. Happily married, is he?"

"I've no reason to think otherwise, sir."

"How long's he been married?"

"Five, maybe six years."

"There's a letter on the computer that reads as though Miss Lisamore had it in for him. Can you throw any light on that?"

Sergeant Donovan turned from his contemplation of the computer screen to interject, "One of the teachers at the school came in when Naughton was here. When we were in Castle Manton. Said she'd had a canter with Rowsell before he was married."

Paton looked hard at the constable. "Know about that, Mr Ellis?"

"It was a long time ago, sir." He thought Leslie Hardiman a trouble-making little poofter.

"Okay. Go back to your post."

The sergeant stood up, pen and paper in hand. "That's about it. I've looked at all the disks. There wasn't much. Notes for school work, preparations for lessons, lists of marks given to the children. Exam marks, I expect. Half a dozen letters." He handed the papers to his superior. "There's one file has a name on, and nothing else. Hunter, comma, Bobby. Maybe she was going to write to someone called Bobby Hunter and hadn't got around to it."

"Bobby Hunter," murmured Paton out loud. "Call Constable Ellis back."

He lowered the sheets to his knee as PC Ellis appeared in the doorway. "Know a man called Bobby Hunter, Mr Ellis?"

"There's no one in this village by that name."

"Okay."

Paton glanced down at the papers. "Your handwriting, Sergeant, could do with a bit of improvement."

"Sorry, sir. It's not easy, copying from that screen."

"Why didn't you get Jumping George to show you how to use the printer?"

"It wasn't one he'd had experience of, he said. These machines are all different, he said. You can't just walk in and set about using someone else's printer. That's what he said, anyway."

"Horrible little whippersnapper!" muttered Paton, wishing he had been here to hear Belcher admit to ignorance. "Didn't you point out there must be a manual for the printer in one of the drawers?" he asked, venting his sarcasm.

"I'm not witty like you."

Paton glared, then after all decided Donovan looked innocent, so gave him the benefit of the doubt. "Rowsell was in this cottage last night, there's no doubt in my mind about that. But it would help to know what the victim was writing on the computer when he arrived."

"Or when Paul Street arrived."

"Yeah." The chief inspector gazed at his sergeant without seeing him. One thing at a time, he decided. He could waste a lot of time going up that path. He'd prefer to eliminate Rowsell first.

Chapter 14

Brian Grey, husband of Letitia, settled down in the big drawing room that she had decorated so beautifully with Laura Ashley curtains and wallpaper, antiques inherited from both sides of the family, and rugs brought back from business trips and holidays in the Orient. He loved this house, the glossy manifestation of his success in a company importing Japanese machinery.

Brian was the handsome and talented son of a mother who dutifully chaired charity committees, held garden fêtes to raise money for the local church, entertained shooting parties and served as treasurer of the local Conservative party. His father was an eminent judge, son of an equally eminent QC, now deceased, who was famously known as a formidable opponent and a good man to have on your side. Brian had had a very good start in life.

He had not changed much in eight years of marriage, grown a little meatier, perhaps, on expense-account lunches and drinks, lost a little hair. He considered he had married slightly beneath him, but then he had always been attracted to tarty girls. Though more at ease with his mother's type, he loved the safe unsafeness of Letitia with her flamboyant scarves, her long, sexy legs, her flimsy, high-heeled boots, and her sheer bloody confidence. Early in their engagement, when his mother commented it was hard to believe Letitia had been educated at Roedean he had not protested for he understood she was merely referring to the clothes. Lady Grey saw virtue in shapeless drab.

Now he said comfortingly as he picked up the paper knife and began tackling a week old pile of mail, "Everybody can't have an alibi. Think of all those people who live on their own, lock the doors at supper time and only get the occasional phone call." He abandoned the letters, stretched, yawned and rubbed his eyes. "Damned jet lag! I'm dying of thirst. How about a cuppa?"

She was standing with one foot on the fender, a crooked arm resting on the mantelpiece, staring at her nails. "If you drank water on the flight you wouldn't have jet lag – not nearly so badly, anyway. I'm always telling you that."

"Balls." Brian was not one to turn down free champagne.

"How was business, anyway?" She was still staring at her nails.

He guessed she wanted to know if there had been a big deal that would culminate in the family spending Christmas in the Carribean. Piqued by her criticism of his drinking, he replied, "Very Japanese. Raw fish, and no sleep. I had to concentrate on being grateful. 'If this was Saudi Arabia,' I said to myself, 'it would be sheep's eyes.'" She did not laugh. He looked up, noted her strained expression, and relented. "Business was good, darling. Very good."

She moved over to the window and stood there, looking out. He said to her back, speaking with a touch of impatience, "I can't imagine what you're worrying about, Letty. Why on earth should you be questioned? You didn't have anything to do with the woman. Virtually nothing." He yawned compulsively. "God! I'm tired. I could crash out now, but I'd better keep myself awake until the chicks get home."

Letitia said abruptly, "I'll make you that cup of tea." The kitchen was French. Not that the Greys weren't patriotic and wouldn't prefer to buy British. When British manufacturers turned out cars like the Volvo and the BMW, they told their friends, and kitchens like this one, porcelain bamboo, marble tops and handpainted tiles, then British manufacturers would get their business. While waiting for the electric kettle to boil she stood biting her nails, thinking that someone would almost certainly have seen Anthony in Old Wood Lane or the high street. And what if some interfering cat resurrected his affair with Beryl?

In the drawing room Brian yawned again, closed his eyes, opened them wide, shook himself and wandered into the kitchen. "Put it in a mug, Letty. I'll take it out to the garden. On my feet, I may stay awake. Have you got your stuff ready for the show?"

Letitia adjusted her strained features into a smile. "My dried flower arrangement is in the study. I'm doing the fresh one in the morning. I haven't got much to work with. What with the beastly drought and the hosepipe ban, there's not much in the garden worth having."

"Bloody Water Board," grumbled Brian. He had written long letters to both national and local papers as well as to the Board on the root causes of water shortages in Kent, offering advice on how to terminate them once and for all. His diatribes had set up a scintillating correspondence in the Letters columns, but the Board ignored them. "I'll do some watering tomorrow," he consoled her. "Don't get out the pot. A tea bag will do." Letitia, who deplored the use of tea bags and kept them only for her daily help, did not, this time, protest. Brian picked up the mug and wandered out of the back door.

Standing in the middle of the sloping lawn, sipping his tea, he could see Badger Cottage through the gap in the conifers. Poor old Beryl. He had always thought there was good material there, but she had missed the bus. Who the hell would want to kill her? She was a nobody. He could only think she must have surprised a burglar. Some oaf high on drugs.

His gaze roved over the allotments and came to rest on the paling fence. What on earth was that coming through?

Brambles? He put the empty mug on the grass and strode down the slope to investigate. Yes, brambles they were. It was the council's job to keep this particular footpath clear, but you could wait forever. He decided to bring a spade down and dig them out. Leaning over the fence, assessing the size of the offending root, Brian felt the wood give under his arm. He stood back blinking in surprise as three palings, one after another, slipped sideways and clattered to the ground. What on earth! He picked them up and saw there was a hole in one of them, brown with rust, where a nail had fallen out. But the nails on the other two had been forced, as though someone had tugged at the paling and ripped it off.

"Bloody hell," he muttered, thinking of his defenceless wife and children in the house, and some rabid nut committing murder only a few hundred yards away. He ducked his head and edged through the gap. Something lying in the dry grass caught a sun's ray, glittering. He looked closer, then picked it up. It was a piece of silver. And here, a dark red stone. A few inches away he found a little green scarab. He picked them all up.

These, surely, were part of the necklace that poor old Anthony had given to Beryl and for his pains been forced to look at ever since. Not many people knew that, but Brian did. Anthony had been best man at their wedding. He stared down at the pieces in his palm, greatly disturbed. Had the murderer-thief made his escape through their garden? Why was it broken? Because he had snatched it off Beryl's neck? Or, had the chain caught in his clothes as she fought back, and been brushed off as he climbed through here?

Brian glanced along the track in the opposite direction to Badger Cottage where workmen from the Gas Board had been digging up a pipe, rendering the path impassable with a deep open drain, three or four mounds of earth, cumbersome earth-moving equipment, and several skips. It looked as though the chap couldn't get any further and didn't dare go back, so escaped through their garden! Bloody hell!"

Brian edged back through the fence and ran up the slope. "Letty!" he called urgently, "Letty, come here. Come and see what I've found."

She appeared in the kitchen doorway as he came through the back door.

"What do you make of this? It's a bit of Beryl's necklace, isn't it? It's got to be. I found it on the other side of the back fence. And there are three palings missing."

Letitia could only stare at him.

"I had better report this," said Brian. "Who to? Charlie Ellis, I suppose." He squeezed her shoulder comfortingly as he left her to go to the study telephone. Letitia sat down on the hall chair, feeling ill. She heard Brian asking for the village constable. "Thanks, Denise. I'll ring there. Who did you say is in charge? . . . Paton. Detective Chief Inspector. Yes, thanks. D'you know the number?"

Letitia jumped up and went out of the back door. She stood with arms folded tightly across her chest, shivering. She heard Brian call, "I'm just going to change." A few moments later he came out wearing jeans and T-shirt. "He's going to meet me at the fence. A chap called Paton. Don't worry, darling." He bent and kissed her on the forehead. "Want to come with me?"

She shook her head.

"Perhaps you had better."

"No."

"Are you all right?"

"Yes. Of course I am. A bit—" She couldn't go on.

"I'd better go." He kissed her again.

She watched his tall figure until it disappeared behind the conifers, then hurried inside, head whirling, making for the kitchen telephone.

Anthony answered. "Listen! Anthony! Brian has found a bit of Beryl's necklace at the gap in the fence." She waited, trembling.

"Anthony?"

"So?"

"Did you see her?"

"No," said Anthony, unequivocally.

Letitia's voice rose, shrill and terrified, "It's not true. You did see her. You must have. She was here. You must have met her."

"For God's sake, Letitia. Don't be stupid."

Numbly, Letitia replaced her receiver. She thought of Susan with her rigid, old-fashioned principles. Susan, whose rich father was imminently dying. Was Anthony capable of murdering Beryl if she threatened to expose him? She knew how important the estate was to him, and she knew Susan was capable of divorcing him for infidelity. She stood with her back to the window, shaking.

Brian saw Paton hurrying along between the allotments and the back gardens of the houses in Pieman's Lane. He went to meet him, holding out his hand. "Brian Grey."

"How do you do." Paton looked at the hole in the fence. "Is this where you found the necklace?"

Brian told him about the brambles and the loose palings. Paton's sharp glance took in the deep, open drain and the skips piled high with clay and soil, "Those would have been here yesterday?"

"I dare say. I've been away in Japan on business. They hadn't started the work when I left. It would appear he tore the palings off and came through my garden. He certainly couldn't go any further down the track. What puzzles me," said Brian putting ideas into Paton's head, "was why he stopped to put them back again."

The chief inspector was thinking that Rowsell had told him, unequivocally, that he walked from the high street down the track past the allotments, and emerged in Old Wood Lane. Couple that with the fact that he hadn't seen anyone outside the pub, though Bert Oswhistle had told Donovan there were always customers sitting on the teak garden seats of an evening when the weather was mild, and you got two lies that complemented each other.

"And there's no doubt in your mind that the necklace belonged to Miss Lisamore?" he asked.

"Anyone in the village would vouch for that. She wore it nearly all the time."

The chief inspector held the chain and the gems in the palm of his hand. "Sentimental value, was it?"

Brian shrugged, thinking there was no point to tossing in red herrings, but Paton was remembering the display case of antique jewellery in Rowsell's shop, and the fact that Miss Lisamore was alleged to have had a "canter" with him. He was thinking also of the fact that Grey had been away for a week. And Rowsell's wife was even now away. He was thinking of his summing up of Rowsell: a seducer, rather than a murderer, but all the same, a man who would know how to look after number one.

"Is your wife at home?"

"Yes, she is."

"I'd better have a word with her."

"She's somewhat shocked," Brian said protectively. "And I don't think she'll be able to help you. She didn't hear anything."

"I'd like to speak to her, all the same." Paton was already pushing himself through the hole in the fence, holding his stomach in, finding it a bit of a squeeze. Brian followed, and led him across the lawn, picking up the mug from the grass as he went. Near the top of the slope he turned and looked back, not over the way he had come, but as the crow flies, towards the back windows of Badger Cottage. He noted that if the lonely Rowsell had called on Mrs Grey, Miss Lisamore, who had had "a canter" with him, could have seen him from her bedroom window.

Brian led him round to the front of the big house and in at the open door. Letitia, hearing their voices, came hesitantly into the hall. She was paper white and trembling. Brian introduced them. Paton gave her a shrewd look. Ah yes. Long, sexy legs. Beautiful hair. Hips! Those hips! He concentrated on the eyes and saw raw terror there.

"Do come in." She led the way into the big drawing room and indicated that Paton should sit down, but he went and stationed himself by the window so that he would have the advantage of seeing her face with the light on it.

"Mrs Grey," he came straight to the point, "did you see Mr Rowsell last night?"

Letitia had seated herself in the corner of the sofa. Brian went to stand by the fireplace. "I did – only briefly, though. He called with a message. He was out walking and he called—" her voice faltered, "—with this message. He's on the church—"

"Council," said Brian helpfully, concerned for her.

"Yes. We're having our Harvest Supper shortly." The words came rattling out, one upon the other, "We all contribute. He called to say they wanted me to make a – to make – er – an – er – apple pie."

"I thought that was Marigold Ashendon's job," said Brian, frowning. "Marigold organises the food."

"Oh, Anthony gets into everything." Letitia laughed, a silly ha-ha laugh, without conviction.

The chief inspector looked from wife to husband, then back to the wife. "Would he remove palings from your fence in order to come into the garden to tell you the church – er – Council wanted an apple pie from you at some time in the future?" he asked gravely, as though that was a very reasonable question.

Brian glanced frowningly at the policeman's deadpan face.

Letitia's mind went into a spin. "Oh, I see what you're getting at." Her voice was high and yappy. "Yes, he is a lazy old thing. Yes, if he had come along the track and found the skips blocking the way, he might well have climbed through. That would be fairly typical of Anthony, wouldn't it Brian," she turned glazed eyes on her husband, "taking matters into his own hands, I mean. Though he didn't mention it to me."

She noted the stillness of Brian's face, and added, the words jumping and dancing, "I wouldn't be at all surprised if that was what he did. Took a short-cut through the garden . . . thought I might have seen him . . . banged at the door and brought out the bit about the apple pie. Yes, of course it's Marigold's job. I should have remembered." She caught her breath, put a hand to either side of her face, felt her eyes swivelling, fought for calm. "He would know, about the pie, I mean, from the committee meeting."

What committee meeting? Brian wondered. Wasn't the food organised by a women's committee?

"It doesn't account for Miss Lisamore's necklace lying in the grass by the hole in the fence," said the chief inspector.

"Maybe she saw him passing and walked with him along the track. Maybe they took the palings off together, as you say, when they realised the skips were blocking the way," suggested Paton encouragingly. "The chain might have caught in a wire – or something – as she bent over."

Letitia looked hard at the nails of her left hand.

"Wouldn't he have mentioned to you that he had met Miss Lisamore? That he had left her looking for her necklace in the grass?"

Suddenly it was all too much, the chief inspector's teasing, Brian's hard, suspicious eyes. Letitia could no longer cope and what was the point for she knew Anthony was going to do the dirty on her. He wouldn't hesitate to use her as an alibi to get himself out of . . . Her thoughts stilled, frozen with fear. Out of what? Killing Beryl? Brian knew she and Anthony had been in bed, she could see it in the way he stood, feet planted firmly apart, arms folded, chin jutting. Letitia covered her face with her hands in order to shut out the very worst of it, not her husband and the policeman standing in judgment, but the knowledge that she may have had a murderer in her bed.

The two men watched her, Paton waiting, for he had seen enough people crack to know what was going to happen next. Her hands dropped to her sides and she said, pleading, though more to God than to the inspector, "Anthony wouldn't murder her, Mr Paton. He's not a murderer." She bit her trembling lips, thinking she wouldn't be surprised if he was.

"What time did he leave, Mrs Grey?"

"I don't know." Letitia burst into tears.

"Did he go out the back way?"

"Letitia," said Brian coldly, "the inspector is asking you a question."

She snatched a tissue out of her pocket and mopped at her eyes.

"He asked you what time Anthony left, and if he went out the back way."

"Yes, he went out the back way. About ten, or half past." The tears had ceased. She spoke with a weary sort of despair.

"Thank you, Mrs Grey."

The two men left the room. She could hear them talking in the hall, the adieus, and the back door slamming, violently. Then Brian came and stood in the doorway. "You made a proper balls-up of that," he said venomously. "What a little shit you are. Having it off with Anthony. Anthony, of all people!"

Letitia came defensively alive. "I'll bet you fuck the geishas."

"Geishas are tea-ladies," Brian retorted ambiguously. "And I don't fuck anyone in Japan. I eat raw bloody fish and wish I was at home with you and the children."

She could see he spoke the truth and was doubly frightened. She made a conscious decision to try guile. "It was just a little naughtiness," she pleaded, tearfully, prettily.

"What . . . did . . . you . . . say?" He crossed the

room and stood in front of her. "What . . . did . . . you . . . say?"

"Everyone—"

"You're not everyone," he shouted. "You're my wife. And I've got a position to keep up in this village."

She swung to her feet, tossing her beautiful blonde hair, the woman he loved who had gone so easily, in his absence, to someone else. "Oh pooh! Don't be so pompous. I was bored, and Anthony was bored. We didn't do any harm."

"Didn't you? Didn't you?" The terrible rage in him burst through the boundaries of conscience and he slapped her hard across the face. "You little scrubber. Doyen of Meals-on-wheels, are you? Women's Institute and all that." He slapped her again, harder this time, the retribution in his fingertips taking some of the pain. Ducking to avoid the blow, she fell over the coffee table. Appalled, he looked down at her, lying on her back on the rug with her pretty face screwed up and tears on her cheeks. Overcome with remorse, he dropped to his knees beside her. "Letty, I'm sorry. Oh Letty, I'm sorry. I didn't mean to do it." He buried his face in her hair.

She put an arm round his shoulders and turned his face, kissing him, frantic little wet kisses, desperate-for-forgiveness kisses, all over his cheeks, his chin, his high forehead, into his receding hair.

"I'm sorry," agonised Brian. "It's just that I love you." She hugged him so tightly that she could scarcely breathe. She wriggled her hips under him, felt his warm weight on top of her.

"I know. And I love you."

He fumbled with his zip. "Letty, take off your pants."

She was adept at removing them in a clinch on the floor. As she pulled up her skirt she was conscious of broad daylight and open curtains. Her mind scurried with excited dread over the possibility of the gardener turning up to mow the lawn, or the vicar, nosing around after a cup of tea. Then she settled for the greatest priority, appeasing Brian.

Afterwards, all sin purged, as they lay gazing at the ceiling Letitia ventured the problem uppermost in her mind, "She might have threatened to expose him. He might accidentally have killed her. I mean – could you accidentally strangle someone? Fury and panic . . . You know . . . I mean, if he was shaking her, in exasperation, or something like that?"

Brian was still thinking of a suitably cryptic reply when the telephone rang. Letitia gasped, "The children! My God, the children! Penny Webster was to pick them up from school and take them home to tea. I was supposed to collect them at six." She leapt to her feet.

"Don't forget your pants," said her husband sleepily, and irrevocably overtaken by jet lag, closed his eyes.

Chapter 15

Enid and Mac Lawley were semi-retired New Zealand sheepfarmers on a caravan tour of the British Isles. They had come to Halfpenny Dun this Friday afternoon primarily in search of a free bath, Enid having decided yesterday that after three weeks of washing in a plastic basin she had had enough. Being on a shoestring budget, for New Zealand had its own recession, they did not wish to book into an hotel. They hoped Emma Nesbett, whom they had known during her unfortunate soujourn in New Zealand, would offer this facility. Enid's friend Rosalie, who had befriended Emma and stood by her before and after the court case, had given the Lawleys her English address and asked them to call. Rosalie was anxious to hear how things had turned out for Emma back home.

Mac and Enid came with mixed feelings, for they had made their own judgments on Emma. Unlike their friend, they were not into caring. Not, anyway, what they thought of as indiscriminate caring. If someone committed a sin, and in spite of the jury's decision to the contrary they held their own views as to Emma's guilt, it was right that she should be punished. Enid, who regularly attended church, believed the Lord thy God was a vengeful God and that poor child, snatched from its parents' arms, should be revenged. However, they weren't averse to using the girl's bath.

Driving slowly down the high street, keeping a sharp lookout for a little cottage called Park View where they believed the erstwhile au pair and farm help to be domiciled, they missed the nameplate on the Ashenden's rather grand Georgian house. Coming abreast of The Fox and Hounds with its Car Park sign, Mac suggested they turn in, have a drink and make enquiries. The high street was not wide enough park a car towing a caravan with safety.

Bert Oswhistle was polishing glasses behind the bar. He looked up as the door swung, bringing into the saloon a boney little woman wearing a print dress, and behind her a small man, weather beaten except for a white band lying across the top of his forehead. Bert recognised it as a legacy from a life spent out of doors wearing a hat.

"What can I get you, sir?" he asked, courteous and smiling.

"Two gin and tonics, please."

"Australian?"

"New Zealanders," said Enid, looking upset. Mac grunted. He was baffled by people's inability to distinguish a New Zealand accent from an Australian one.

"I could tell you were Australians or New Zealanders or something like that," said Bert, radiating goodwill.

"Passing through, are you?" asked Dolly graciously as she wiped some spilled beer from the counter. Dolly said of herself that she was sensitive to vibes. She made a mental note to tell Bert that in their business they had to remember such things as New Zealanders didn't like being taken for Australians, any more than Canadians liked being taken for Americans. She had seen Crococile Dundee three times and thought Australians were terrific. Come to think of it, Emma Nesbett, who had been to New Zealand, didn't have a good word to say for the people. And some Canadians who had stayed in The Fox were pretty boring. She thought Americans were always fun. She cursed the Gulf war for putting them off.

"We're looking for a girl by the name of Emma Nesbett," said Mac. "Lives in the high street here, we're told."

"Au pair at the Ashendens," beamed Dolly. "Met her in New Zealand, did you? She worked out there a year or so ago." Dolly sighed. "The young do have it good these days, no doubt about it."

Enid and Mac exchanged glances. "We thought she lived in her own place," said Enid, cast down with disappointment as she saw her free clean-up sliding out of reach.

"No, no. She lives with the Ashendens. They got three little ones."

Enid picked up the glasses, Mac the tonic. He put the bottles down on a table close by. The saloon was empty except for an elderly man sipping a beer in the corner. Enid turned back. "How old are they?" she asked. "The children."

Dolly, who was sharper than her husband, saw the man shoot his wife a warning look. "The youngest is five months. The eldest eight."

"Staying long?" asked Bert conversationally.

Mac said they were moving around. "Do you happen to know if there's a caravan park anywhere near?"

"Not hereabouts. You'll have to go down near the coast." He hoped they wouldn't ask to stay in his car park. People did ask sometimes, and then they wanted the use of the toilets. He didn't like saying No, but start something like that and you drive your regulars away.

"We've got accommodation," offered Dolly, bright-faced and warmly welcoming. "We do a full dinner in the dining room for residents. Would you like to see the rooms?" She picked up a bunch of keys, smiling, anxious to make the booking before locals started coming in and frightened them away with talk of Beryl Lisamore's murder. Business had been slack this summer. It wasn't only the Americans who had stayed away. Because of the recession Londoners had cut back on weekends in the country.

"All right," agreed Mac grudgingly. They certainly

couldn't ask an au pair for the use of her employer's bath.

Back in the caravan, gathering up their night wear and a change of clothes, Mac said worriedly, "It's none of our business, Enid."

"Five months, the woman said. The baby's only five months."

"It's not our place," he argued.

"You'd never forgive yourself if—"

"Shelve it, Enid. I said, it's none of our business." Mac was wishing they hadn't come. "Let's move on. I've paid for the drinks. We don't have to go back."

Enid was prepared to argue. "What shall I say to Rosalie? I promised I'd look Emma up."

"We don't have to. Just because she asked us to, it doesn't mean we have to." They sat down on the sofa bed side-by-side, considering the matter.

"I'd never forgive myself," said Enid. "I don't know about you, but I'd never forgive myself."

"You're just annoyed because that joker took you for an Aussie. Come on, snap out of it."

She sniffed. "I wouldn't be so petty."

The creases in Mac's ageing face deepened. Once his wife got her teeth into something she was like a terrier with a bone. "It's not like you to make trouble, Enid," he said, sycophantic in his determination to change her mind.

"I'm thinking of the baby. Five months old." She stared down at the face flannel and soap box she held in her hands.

Mac tried again, "What's to be will be. That's what you say. You're always saying it. What's to be will be."

"Five months old," repeated his wife, stubbornly. "You don't understand, Mac, because you're not a mother. The judge said she should never again take a job with young children."

"Tell you what," said Mac, meeting her, as he saw it, half way, "let's give her a friendly warning. That way there'll be no harm done. Let's remind her about what the judge said. We could say we're going to ring this woman Mrs Ashenden next week, and if she's still employed there, then we'll put her pot on. Give her a week's grace, Enid. Go on."

"All right." Enid reluctantly agreed.

They booked in, then wandered back along the high street. "Three hundred years," marvelled Mac standing hands in pockets before Zelda Beard's pretty cottage with 1687 carved in stone over the door. "You wouldn't credit its still standing up, would you? Can't help laughing, can you," Mac was not laughing, he was awed, "when you think about Sadie refusing to live in the old farmhouse when she got married because it had been up for twenty-five years."

"Like daughter, like mother." Enid reminded him she had had her little triumphs, too. Sammy Smeed grinned at them from the doorway of Foundry Cottage, one hand covering the wart on his cheek. "They're pretty, but they're probably full of cockroaches. That must be the village idiot."

Marigold Ashenden answered the door and the Lawleys recognised with pleasure a stereotype English rose, though disappointingly dressed in a pair of denim jeans, T-shirt, and a bra that had lost its shape.

Enid explained their mission. "She stayed with a friend of ours. She asked us to look her up. I hope it's not inconvenient."

"Do come in," said Marigold warmly. "Please don't apologise. Emma will be delighted to see you, I'm sure." She led the way into an eau-de-nil drawing room. "I'll go and find her. I think she's out in the garden with the baby. Do sit down."

Mac made for a corded and tasselled sofa. "Knole," he said, *sotto voce*. "I remember seeing it in that antiques book of yours."

Enid tiptoed to the Adam fireplace and swiftly read

the invitations on the mantel, then her eyes roved over the ancestor portraits, the leather-bound books in polished mahogany bookcases, the heavy, swagged curtains, the jewel coloured Persian carpet, and all the time she was remembering what the judge had said in his summing-up, about the haves and the have-nots. About envy. The Ashendens represented an English version of Emma's New Zealand employees, fifth-generation catholic sheep farmers whose aristocratic ancestors had fled the old country on one of the early passenger boats in order to escape the straight jacket of religious oppression.

Marigold re-entered the room, wreathed in smiles, and as though offering a trophy, led forward an ungainly girl wearing jeans, a cotton blouse, and tennis shoes.

"Here she is." Then, to Emma, "That's your surprise, dear."

Emma's face went still.

"Hello, Emma," said Enid awkwardly. "Remember us?" When the girl did not reply she added, "Rosalie Winter was anxious for news of you."

Emma opened her mouth like a trap. "She could write." The trap snapped shut.

"Well," said Marigold, bravely smiling, "shall I leave you to talk over old times? Perhaps you'd like to give your friends tea, dear." Receiving no response, she went hastily out of the room.

Emma spoke with anger and despair, "I know it's an old New Zealand custom to drop in on people without bothering to telephone," she said, "but it won't do here. People expect to be warned. And more especially since this isn't my house."

"Rosalie gave us the address. She thought it was your house."

"This! This house, mine! How d'you think I'd come by a house like this?"

Enid retaliated defensively, "We didn't expect it to be

a house like this. In New Zealand anyone whose address was the high street would be living over a shop."

"You're not in New Zealand, now. Hadn't you noticed?" Two red spots appeared in Enid's cheeks. "We're only a couple of hundred yards down the road, at The Fox and Hounds. It would have been ridiculous to telephone."

"Yes, that's how you think, isn't it? Don't telephone. They might say No. Just barge in." Emma was more distressed now than angry, but they heard only the insults.

Mac turned towards the door. "I think we should go, Enid." They had both forgotten about issuing a warning that Emma must adhere to the judge's ruling.

She herded them out into the hall, beat them to the front door, opened it and stood aside, eyes cast down, waiting for them to leave.

Mac hesitated apologetically on the doorstep. "It's just that the Winters were anxious to know."

"So you said. I'll write to them."

"Sorry," Mac muttered. "Sorry."

"Well!" said his wife as the front door clicked shut behind them, "I've never been so humiliated in the whole of my life! Never!"

Marigold, looking puzzled, came from the kitchen. "What's the matter, dear? You were a little hard on them, weren't you?"

"Serves them right. Bloody New Zealanders. They all do it." Emma was distraught.

"Do what, dear?"

"Walk in on people. Don't bother to ring up. Think they're welcome anywhere, any time. You'd think they didn't know about biros and telephones," said Emma bitterly. "Cheek!" She began to cry.

Marigold put a consoling arm round her shoulders. "Oh come, it's not such a sin."

"What's the matter?" A childish voice spoke from the back of the hall and they turned to see the children looking up at them, round-eyed. Hunter, aged eight, came forward. "Why were you scared of them, Emma?"

"Don't be stupid," snapped Emma, wiping her eyes. "I wasn't scared of them."

"You're scared of dragons," said India, diffusing the danger. "You told me. And ghosts," she added. "You said you were scared of ghosts."

Their mother shooed them back to the garden. "Emma will get your tea in a moment." She said busily, as though nothing untoward had happened, "Now Emma, would you like to change the baby while I see if the seed cake's cooked? I've still got to do my flower arrangement and get the children's plasticine animals boxed up."

Emma set one foot on the bottom tread, looked back at her employer, seemed about to say something, then went on up the stairs. Marigold watched her back with puzzled eyes.

Chapter 16

Chief Inspector Paton pushed open the heavy door and went into the saloon bar followed by his sergeant.

"How are things?" asked Bert as he pulled their pints. "Getting anywhere?"

Paton shrugged non-committedly. "Any ham sandwiches?"

Dolly cast her eye over the selection of lunch leftovers. "I could make you one in a jiffy. Or there's quiche, or I could heat these up," she added, indicating the cold leftovers from luncheon.

"If you wouldn't mind," said Paton, "a ham sandwich." He had to remember his mother-in-law would have a meal ready for him later. "How about you, Sergeant?"

Donovan said yes, he would take the quiche, and was warmed by a sunny beam from Dolly's round blue eyes. They took their ale and seated themselves on either side of a table in a window bay where an enormous cat lay curled up asleep on the cushion.

"Get along, mog," said Donovan, shoving at it with his thigh. The cat rose, stretched, yawned, wound into the far corner, licked one paw and closed its eyes again. A Great Dane that had given every appearance of being asleep under the table, opened his eyes, raised his head, sniffed Paton's ankles, then settled down again. People were starting to come in, a trickle that turned within ten minutes into a steady stream. "Don't look now," Bert was saying to men in navy blue suits on their way home from work, "but those chaps in the far bay are police." No one came to claim the spare seats. Nor would they.

"Who could have done it?"

"God knows, and he won't tell."

"Anyone seen Charlie Ellis? He'll have the dirt."

"My wife was on the phone to Denise . . ."

Bert Oswhistle saw his two residents approaching and said cheerily, "That didn't take long. Was she out, then?"

"Yes," said Enid, unwilling to face further humiliation. She noted with misery that the table where they had sat before was now taken. She looked round hopelessly for a seat.

"I'll get us a couple of drinks," said Mac comfortingly. "You see if you can find a table." Enid, pushing her way through the crowd, fighting the temptation to go to her room and lick her wounds, saw two vacant places at a table for four and resigned herself to staying. Mac had insisted a drink would do them both good.

The two occupants were engrossed in conversation. She heard the older man say, "She's just a baby, after all."

Enid broke in, "Do you mind if my husband and I sit here?"

"Please do," said Paton and then asked amiably, "Do I recognise a New Zealand accent?"

Enid beamed.

"I spent several years there," Paton told her. "Lovely country."

Donovan pushed the cat. It gripped the cushion with its claws. "Get off, cat. We need the space." Heartlessly, for he knew cats, knew they nearly always got away with the best life had to offer, he upended it, pushing until it eventually lost the battle for balance and slipped over the edge on to the floor.

"What were you doing?" Enid asked as she settled herself beside Donovan.

"I'm in the police. I did an exchange."

"But you came back." She was easily slighted.

"We came back because my job was waiting for me. But I've sometimes thought I'd like to retire there one day." He had wondered if that could be the answer to his marital problems, to make a new start in late middle age.

"This is a nice village." Enid was mollified into returning his compliment. "Do you live here?"

"No," said Paton. "We're here on a job."

"A job? A crime, you mean?"

He nodded.

She sat up straight, startled. "A murder?" The word that had been balancing on her tongue for the past hour, tripped off.

"'fraid so."

"I heard you mention a baby. There hasn't by any chance been a baby murdered?"

"No," said Paton, failing to recognise that she had overheard his reference to Goldie Montrose.

Enid looked down at her hands that were resting on the table, then back at the chief inspector. It was meant, she decided, resigning herself to the inexorability of fate. Why else would the only vacant seats in the room be at this table? And I have got a social conscience, she told herself defensively, even if Mac hasn't.

"There's a bit of a rush on," Bert was saying apologetically to Mac at the bar. "People coming home from work. It's because the Horticultural Society's annual show is tomorrow," he said, hoping his guest wouldn't talk to locals and hear the truth. "It raises a whole lot of excitement in the village. Same again? Want to take a menu with you? It's early, but you might like to look at it."

Mac put the card under his arm, picked up the glasses in one hand, the tonic in the other, and turned. The regulars drifted apart to provide the stranger with a passage through. As he approached the table Enid was saying, "Everyone believed she was guilty, even the judge, else why would he say she wasn't to work with children again? And here she is, working with children."

"Enid!" remonstrated Mac weakly as he put the glasses and bottles down on the table.

"These men are police," said his wife defensively. "When I discovered that, I knew I had been given a second chance to do what was right. I wouldn't be able to live with myself if it happened again," she said earnestly to Paton, "knowing we had had the opportunity to stop it, I mean."

As Mac settled into his seat beside the chief inspector and handed Enid her gin he told himself not to get rattled. Now that there was the added motive of revenge nothing short of a bolt of lightning would have stopped his wife. He lifted a bottle of tonic and held it above her glass, wishing he could tip it all over her. "Say when, dear."

"We had better have a look at this girl," said Paton as they left the pub.

Donovan looked mystified. "What's it got to do with us, her killing someone in another country?"

"Nothing. I'm glad you noticed. Look at that garden. Bloody marvellous," said the chief inspector leaning on the Tate's wrought iron gate, admiring a bed of chrysanthemums and late roses. "But in my experience, Sergeant, the incidence of unlikely chance meetings is damn high. Never underrate chance."

"No, sir." Kelly Donovan missed the comforting pressure of the comic he hadn't had time to read and patting his back pocket realised it must have slipped out on to the seat in the pub.

"What's wrong? Lost something?"

"No. It's all right. What were you saying, sir?"

"You've lost your bloody comic. I saw it on the seat. It's time you graduated to books, Sergeant. What do you think that rubbish is doing to your mind?"

Donovan's long face turned a slow red. "It's relaxation,

sir," he protested feebly. "I can't study police manuals all day."

"Nobody ever asked you to. Want to hear about the laws of chance, or not?"

"Yes, sir."

"Those people, the Lawleys, came here by chance at the time of a murder, and by chance sat at our table. It's not impossible that Miss Lisamore talked, also by chance, to someone from New Zealand. The case would have made headlines there. Any murder would. It's not like here where we've got millions of people. There are more sheep than human beings in New Zealand."

He paused and Donovan, anxious to get back into the inspector's good books suggested, "Could be every New Zealand tourist passing through Kent knows about it."

"Brilliant! Keep it up, boy."

Donovan sneaked a look at his superior's face, hoping he was laughing, but he wasn't. They covered the rest of the way in silence.

Marigold Ashenden held the door wide. She had been warned about the door-to-door enquiries and was prepared to be questioned. "My husband has just returned from work. He's putting the car away. Come into the drawing room and I'll call him." She was open and friendly. Anxious to help.

Donovan went to stand by the window, looking out into the street. Paton looked round the elegant room, seeing it differently from the way the Lawleys saw it. He noticed the antiques were scuffed here and there by a child's shoe, marked by a puppy's teeth. He recognised an eighteen-year-old Mrs Ashenden in the blue-eyed silky blonde girl wearing jodhpurs in the painting over the fireplace. He decided he had a nose for houses. He had known when he came through the front door that people had been happy here, not just this family but over the generations. He wondered if dwellings could affect a marriage. Would he and Barbara have hit it off better if—

They came through the door together, a tall, dark haired man in a business suit, clean-shaven, pleasant-faced, momentarily grave. "Hal Ashenden. Good evening. This is a bad business." He strode forward and shook hands with both men.

"I'm Chief Inspector Paton, and this is Sergeant Donovan."

"So, you want to know what we were up to last night?" Hal held his hands steepled, eyes raised ceilingwards. "Let me think. I made two long phone calls after supper. If you want the names of the clients I spoke to I can give them to you. I'm a solicitor. Then, the box." He said amiably, "I can give you a detailed account of the documentary I saw. BBC2 from nine to ten-thirty. Then we went to bed."

"Thank you, Mr Ashenden. That's very straightforward."

Marigold said, "I was getting my entries ready for the show. I didn't watch TV. I was mainly in the kitchen."

"Did either of you see anything untoward in the village that day? Any strangers?"

"I was at work. What about you, Marigold?"

She shrugged. "Nothing unusual. No."

"And your au pair? I believe you have an au pair called Emma Nesbett."

"Oh yes," remembered Hal, "that's something I forgot." He slapped a hand to his forehead, looking dismayed. "I didn't go directly to bed after the TV. Emma went to Castle Manton to the cinema. I met her off the bus. One has to these days, you know. Even in a little village like this, one can't have young girls walking around alone." His mouth twisted wryly. "We have the proof, haven't we."

"Could I have a word with her?"

Marigold hesitated.

"If you don't mind." When she still looked uncertain, he asked, "Is there any reason?"

"No, no. It's just that, she couldn't possibly be connected with the murder. I mean, as my husband said, he brought her in off the Castle Manton bus, and then we locked up, and the burglar alarm was on, so she couldn't go out again."

"Just a word, if you don't mind, Mrs Ashenden."

"Be gentle with her then, please. She's had a little upset this evening."

Paton nodded and she went out into the hall. They heard her call from the foot of the stairs. "Emma, dear, could you come down, please?" There was a muffled reply and Marigold said, "No dear. It's not."

Emma came and stood in the doorway, a dejected lump of a girl, her face blotched with tears. She recognised Paton as one of the men she had seen coming and going at Badger Cottage when she was in the Post Office Stores, clapped both hands to her face, and screamed.

Still screaming, she swung round sharply, collided with Marigold in the doorway and rushed back upstairs. A door banged, and a baby began to cry.

"What on earth!" Hal strode out of the room and took the stairs two at a time, with Paton and Donovan in pursuit. On the landing he grasped a door handle, rattling it. "Emma! Unlock this door!" he demanded. "Unlock it, instantly."

The baby's screams increased in volume. Paton said urgently, "Force it. We'll have to force it." Donovan stepped forward but Paton pushed him aside. He was strong, but too light for the job. Hal launched himself against the door, with Paton beside him. The door groaned. Marigold, uncomprehending, rigid with fear, was joined on the stairs by the two older children, pop-eyed and silent. She shooed them back. "Go to the kitchen. Hunter, India, go to the kitchen." She ran up to the landing. The children stopped but they did not turn back.

A sullen voice said, "I'll unlock it."

They came hesitantly upright, waiting. Then the key

turned. Emma stood back. Marigold rushed past and picked the screaming baby out of his cot.

Paton asked, "Is he all right?"

"As if I'd hurt him," said the girl contemptuously. "He woke up when I banged the door."

Marigold looked bewilderedly from the inspector to Emma, and back at Emma again. "What is all this about?"

"If it wasn't so fucking tragic—"

"Mind your language." That was Hal, upset and angry.

"—I could laugh," Emma finished her sentence on a shout. "I could bloody laugh. So I didn't tell you. D'you think I don't need to start my life again?"

Marigold, calm again, asked, quietly, "What has happened? You didn't kill Beryl, you couldn't have."

Paton said, "I came about—"

"I know," broke in Emma. "I know what you came about. Bloody interfering spiteful Lawleys told you because I didn't want to talk to them. If I tell you, you'll at least have the facts right." The baby had stopped crying. In a bitter voice, Emma went on, looking from Marigold to Hal, "In New Zealand I was tried for allegedly—" she repeated the word, "allegedly", then a third time, "for allegedly killing a baby. They couldn't pin it on me for the pure and simple reason that I didn't do it. But they couldn't find out who did, so they managed to trump up a theft charge. They were determined to get me, one way or another. They put me inside for four months. Okay?" She swung round violently to address Paton. "I hope you're satisfied. And I hope those Lawleys roast in hell. Some people are vile and evil. Tell them that from me, will you? They're vile and evil, and I hope they roast in hell."

"They had a duty, on behalf of your employers." The chief inspector felt uncomfortable saying it.

Emma turned back to the Ashendens, head high, tears streaming down her face. "Don't worry. You won't have to sack me. I'll go."

They went out of the room. Marigold hesitated in the doorway. "I'm sorry, dear." Emma turned her back.

The men had reached the hall, propelling the startled children before them. "Why did she shout, Daddy?" asked the boy.

Marigold, carrying the baby, joined them. "Ssh, dear. Come and have your tea." She hustled them in to the kitchen and closed the door. Hal led the way back into the drawing room.

"There's still the matter of what she was doing last night," said Paton, clearing up the loose ends, though convinced in his own mind now that the girl had nothing to do with Beryl's murder.

"The bus goes to Castle Manton four times a day. She was certainly on it, for I saw her. I happened to look out of the window as it passed, and caught a glimpse of her. And as I said, I met her off it about ten-thirty. Then I locked up and put on the alarm, so she couldn't have gone out again."

"Can she turn it off? The alarm?"

Ashenden hesitated. "I suppose so. She sees me do it all the time. But why should she kill Beryl?"

"Did she know her?"

"Yes, she would know her. Of course. I believe Emma's a good girl," he said as though trying to convince himself. "She's been with us for eighteen months."

"What are you going to do about her?"

"It's for my wife to decide." Hal wiped a hand across his brow. "I need a drink. Mr Paton, Sergeant, I'd like to offer you one."

"I'm just going home, actually. No, thank you. Better not. I'm driving."

"You're sure? No? Sergeant?"

Donovan shook his head. Hell no. Not when the chief inspector was turning it down. Pity.

They walked swiftly along the high street. "I'll give you a lift back to London," said Paton.

"Thanks."

They had both forgotten the inspector was supposed to have dinner with his wife's parents, and bring Barbara home afterwards.

Hal poured a large vodka and took it to the kitchen. Marigold was standing with her back to the sink, cuddling the baby, and watching the older children eating their tea. The little collection of exhibits for the Horticultural Show stood on a bench: a pot of home-made marmalade, the seed cake and a dried flower arrangement. He wondered if, in the end, their sordid little village drama would put paid to the show.

Marigold's lips trembled. "You had better give her a month's wages. More. Perhaps we could get her in at The Fox for the night. No one would know why. We can't drive her out of the village. She might want to stay. But I can't have her here. I don't want to be unkind—" she bit her lips and looked away, blinking hard, feeling the shock all over again, "it is unkind, I know, but I couldn't risk it." Her arms tightened around the baby. "You do understand, don't you?"

He supposed he did. "It's condemning her out of hand. I'll like to have a talk with her."

"I can't, Hal." Marigold gazed down into the baby's face. "I can't take the risk. I'm sure she's innocent, but . . ." She looked up and met his concerned eyes. "I really can't. Not with my darling baby. I can't."

Upstairs, Hal knocked on Emma's door. When there was no reply he opened it. The room was empty. He stood on the landing and called. He knocked on the bathroom door, then opened that. Empty. He opened those leading to the other bedrooms, then hurried downstairs.

The door to the saloon bar at The Fox and Hounds swung inwards and Emma Nesbett catapaulted into the crowded room. Someone said, "Hello, Emma. The whole village will be here soon."

At the bar Bert Oswhistle was telephoning Sid Jenkins,

who had the bicycle shop, and sometimes helped out in a jam. "Like greased lightning, Sid," he was saying. "Dolly's got a couple of meals to prepare and I can't cope, now, on my own. What with the murder and the Horticultural Show, damn near the whole village is here."

Emma fought her way to the bar. "Hello, Bert. I believe you've got some New Zealanders staying here."

"Over there." The harassed landlord waved a vague hand towards the window bay.

Emma slipped through the crowd. Enid saw her, too late for escape. Emma lurched forward, both arms extended. Enid leapt to her feet, screaming. Emma's hands came away clutching brown curls, flecked with grey. She looked down at the bald patch, first with shock, then with a kind of startled satisfaction. Mac, protectively half way to his feet, rocked backwards, struck dumb.

"God will punish you, I hope," said Emma. Her voice went echoing round the suddenly silent room. "But just in case he doesn't—" Her voice broke, she looked down at the hair clutched in her hands, then turned and made her way towards the door. The crowd, inarticulate with horror, moved aside to allow her through.

She went up the high street, walking all the way to the T-junction where Old Wood Lane came in, then turned left and kept going. Outside Cobblers she paused, opened the gate, and went up the path.

Romy Childs opened the door and cried, "My dear! What on earth has happened?"

"Some people came and put my pot on." Emma stumbled over the doorstep.

"Oh Emma! Oh Emma, my dear!" She put her arms round the girl and held her. Emma sobbed bitterly. When she calmed a little Romy led her into the room. "Sit down and let's talk. You know, if they hurt you, they hurt themselves. It's Karma." She saw the hair clutched in Emma's hands and gaped. "What's that? What on earth is that?"

"I couldn't wait for Karma," said Emma, staring down at her hands. "I pulled her hair out. May God forgive me."

Romy tried to identify the grey/blonde curls, and failed. At least they didn't, thank God, belong to nice Marigold Ashenden.

"He probably will," she said, meaning God.

Chapter 17

At number seven Church Lane, Old Purford, Oxfordshire, Joan Lisamore settled at the table in the breakfast room, picked up a pot exuberantly decorated with flaming poppies and poured out the coffee. Vinegary scents seeping through the hatch from the kitchen came from a batch of apple chutney destined for the church shop.

Joan's sister-in-law Beryl, had she been invited to number seven, would have thought the floral wallpaper vulgar, the draylon chairs, at best suburban, at worst, tasteless, the patterned wall-to-wall carpet barbarous, and the frilly curtains offensive. Beryl drank her coffee from hand-made pottery mugs. She would have been astonished at the screaming poppies on Joan's fine china cups and coffee pot.

Good taste was not one of Joan's virtues. The prints on the walls had been bought with an eye to the space available. The built-in shelves with their mass-produced ornaments were the end product of her on-going seduction by advertisements in glossy magazines. A series of thimbles were displayed on their own stand. There were china plates commemorating royal marriages. The appearance of an advertisement, "Limited edition of five hundred. Pay by instalments, £30.99 a month for three months, plus £3.99 for postage and packing", and Joan was hypnotised.

In magazines she found stretch covers, clothes for the larger woman, plastic garden furniture and seeds "carefully chosen by our expert for a splendid spring display". Her mail-order buying was not a bargain, but as she would say to her helpers in the church shop, it saved her feet.

"Brown or white?" she asked looking across the table at her husband. Noel's large, pale eyes lifted from the letter he was reading. The dome of his head shone in the sunlight pouring through the picture window behind him. His face, like his body, was broad at the top, and long. Skull-shaped, Beryl had thought when she saw him last, but then her mind had been on death, and rejection had made her unkind. Joan, an uncomplicated woman, was not normally critical, but she did wish he had not lost his hair so early. Noel wished she wasn't so fat. They might have been closer if they had discussed such matters.

"One of each." Joan decided for him and dropped two slices of bread into the toaster. "How did the PCC meeting go last night?"

"PCC?" he echoed vaguely, speaking as though his mind was a long way off.

"Yes. Wasn't last night the Parochial Church Council?"

"No." He put the letter back into its envelope and laid it on top of the pile. "That was Wednesday," he said, drumming his fingers on the table. "PCC Wednesday. Last night was Village Hall Committee. Where's the coffee?"

"It's in front of you, Noel. Look. In front of you. I've poured it out."

"Oh." He hadn't seen it, nor even smelt it. "Sugar?" He sipped.

"Look, there's the sugar. Surely you don't expect me to put it in for you? What's the matter with you? She leaned across the table, forehead crinkled, eyes puzzled.

He reached for the basin and helped himself. "It's hot in here," he said.

Obligingly, she rose and opened a window. Outside, a neat lawn flanked by regimented, well-weeded beds spread across the half acre block on either side to the tall wooden fence that ensured their privacy from the house next door. It was all very tidy. The two sycamores were trimmed annually. They would never be allowed to grow big, for Noel liked even the trees to be neat. In October when they began to shed their leaves the gardener would come every morning to sweep them up, then he would take them away in plastic bags.

"Have you got the money for the new kitchen?" she asked. Recent government legislation had made it necessary for village-hall kitchens to reach certain standards of hygiene.

The toast popped up and Noel helped himself. "We're going to start a fund and we'll expect the better-heeled residents . . ." He looked down at the letter he had replaced on the pile, and dried up.

Joan regarded him with dismay. "Are you all right?" In the past she would have reached out and taken his hand. She was not unloving, but the natural gestures of warmth she had brought to their marriage had long ago lost first their spontaneity and then their impetus, for Noel neither understood, nor knew how to respond. She had wondered during the last week if he was working too hard. He had never said that his job was too taxing, but with the added burden of his voluntary community work he seldom had a moment to himself. Or, for that matter, for her.

"I'm tired." With an abrupt movement, he towered to his feet.

He had said that too often in recent days. She was worried about him. "Noel, you've eaten nothing," she protested. "Heaven knows, you don't need to lose weight." He was no advertisement for her cooking. It was one of the many disappointments of her life that he showed little interest in, or appreciation for, her food. She slumped back in her seat, an overweight woman foxed by the trivia of every day life.

Not Alzheimers, she said to herself, she who frequently consulted the Reader's Digest Family Medical Adviser.

How could it be, he's not much over fifty, although, having gone bald early, maybe he'll do other things early. She had sometimes wondered about impotence. He hadn't been into her bed for some time. She returned to the matter of the village hall kitchen, "Why did you say—"

He cut her off. "Let it go, Joan."

Meekly accepting her role of discarded helpmate, she stared absorbedly at the toaster, her little world filled with marmalade, butter and bread. Food was her greatest comfort. When she had spread her toast she opened the paper, folded it so that she could hold it comfortably in her left hand, and continued with her breakfast as she read. Noel sipped his coffee, absorbed in his thoughts.

"Noel!" The paper came down. Joan thrust it under his nose. "Look at this! Noel, look at this! It's about your sister," she said, gazing up into his face. "Noel. Oh, Noel," her voice broke, "the poor thing's been murdered. It's there. That paragraph. Look, I'm pointing at it."

Noel's lips parted, then closed again.

"I'll read it to you," she offered kindly. She turned the paper round, scanned the lines, then looked up again. Her eyes were enormous, full of excitement, and awe. "That child she had, it's a film star! It's Goldie Montrose!" She waited for a reaction. "Noel, did you hear what I said? Your sister – Look, I think you should read it for yourself."

Noel covered his eyes with his hands.

She waited. When he remained like that she said querulously, "It's not as though you were close. In fact, you don't really know her. I can't imagine why you should be so shocked."

He took the paper. He was reading the paragraph, trying to read, when Joan said, still uncharacteristically critical, "If you'd had her to stay and treated her like a sister, that would be another matter. But you didn't." In her voice he read the tabloid headlines: "Lonely schoolteacher dies violently. Prosperous Civil Servant brother says he has seen her only once since . . ." He remembered the sour triumph of their mother's funeral when his head and his withered heart were full of the fact that now she would know what it was like to be alone. She, who had split the family down the centre leaving him with their cold, introverted father, taking his mother, the core of his life. He had not seen her again. "Choose," his father had told him bleakly when he protested. "You can be my heir or you can go back to your mother and sister." He had chosen the money. He felt it would pay for the disruption in his life. Now he visualised articles in the tabloids written by vultures searching for something to write about; some reputation to shred. "Whatever became of the English family? We talk of caring, and yet this woman . . ."

Joan was thinking, too, that her reputation as a good church worker could be irretrievably damaged. "You should have kept in touch," she said, emboldened by Noel's surprising collapse.

"You could have invited her," he burst out, losing control, for he knew full well she could not have invited Beryl without his assent. "It's as much your house as mine," he said, though that was not so. "You never suggested it."

"Beryl wasn't my sister. I wouldn't have treated a sister of mine like that." She was angry with herself, as well as with him, for in some part of her she acknowledged a share of guilt. She could have extended a hand to her sister-in-law when they met at the mother's funeral, but she took the easy way out because she felt guilty, on Noel's behalf, about the money. So let him receive the brick-bats, she said to herself now, he to whom the money came. He had the distribution of it. "Everyone knows who wears the trousers in this house," she said resentfully, astounding him, for he had never heard her speak like this before.

"We had better get in the car and go," she added, pushing back her chair and rising from the table. "I'll see Mrs Langtry about coming in to feed the cat, and we must let the vicar know, in case we don't get back tomorrow.

You're down to read the lesson." She cringed, thinking that the vicar could be very forthright.

"If they want us, they'll get in touch," said Noel.

"They? Who's they?"

"The police."

She blinked. "You can't – you really can't be so callous!" She watched him, waiting for a reply, and when it did not come said with slowly dawning surprise, "You do feel guilty, don't you? You actually do."

"I don't. I have no reason to." Beryl the schoolgirl slut had ruined his life.

"No you don't," she agreed, her voice hardening in a wholly unfamiliar and frightening way, "You're cornered. That's what it is. You're caught out, and you're sticking your head in the sand like an ostrich. Well," she said, allowing herself a small satisfaction tinged with triumph as she thought of the friendship she had been denied, "you'll have to deal with her effects. Someone has to sell her house. Wind up her affairs. You're her only relative."

"There's the film star," he said, though knowing an adopted child had no claim, that the house would come to him. Joan wouldn't know that. Her level of general knowledge was abysmal. The air between them throbbed with their animosity.

The telephone rang and Joan went to answer it.

"Yes, vicar. Yes, Noel's sister. You didn't? It's true, she doesn't visit often, but then we all lead such busy lives. She particularly," Joan added, after all blaming Beryl who could not be embarrassed in death. "Yes, we're going, just as soon as we can get away. How kind, but Mrs Langtry will feed it. She knows where the key's hidden. Thank you, I would be grateful." She came back into the room. "People are so generous," she told Noel, smiling her way back into her role of exemplary church worker and dutiful wife. "I've nothing to do, now. Everything is being done for me."

Noel, chin in his cupped hands, elbows on the table,

saw for the first time the petty vengeance of their father's excluding his sister from the will. Too late, far, far too late, he recognised that he had been offered the opportunity to rectify a wrong. That was what Beryl's begging letter was about. He saw it now in the blinding light of this new and terrible reality as less of a request for help, than an offer of redemption.

He went out to the garage, unrolled the hose and connected it to the outside tap, then ran the car into the drive. He took a chamois leather from a shelf in the garage. He was proud of his car. Cleaning it comforted him now. It hadn't been his decision to leave Beryl to her own resources, he decided, justifying his behaviour as he wiped the chamois back and forth, polishing the car windows. He had merely carried on as their father decreed. It was his father's fault for decreeing it. "She made a mess of my life, and she'll make a mess of yours," he had said, and Noel had not stopped to consider whether that was true or false. The prediction was coming true. She was going to make a mess of his life now, wreaking vengeance from beyond the grave.

Joan came out. "You're cleaning the car!" She stated the obvious with exasperation and bewilderment. "Cleaning the car! What for? It's not dirty!"

He rolled up the hose in silence.

"Are you all right?" Joan asked again.

"No," he snapped, "I am not all right. I am in a daze."

Baffled, Joan went back inside.

He lifted the bonnet and tinkered with the engine, filling in time, not wanting to talk to Joan, this new Joan who had become his conscience.

Noel was not a God-fearing man. His work with the church had little to do with Him. It was to do with standing tall in the aisles, gravely accepting the offerings of the congregation, looking and feeling important. It had to do with the enormous satisfaction of handing over a cheque to pay for the replacement of the old boiler that was always breaking down. With being able to say, magnanimously, "No, no, make it anonymous," knowing full well that word of his generosity would get round. He needed the goodwill of the world. Not Joan's goodwill, she didn't count. Noel had lost touch with individuals when the family broke up and the lonely life began.

He would not go to Halfpenny Dun and lay himself open to questions about his private life that had nothing to do with the police or the media, he told himself. He would simply refuse.

Joan was sitting at the kitchen table drinking coffee when he went back inside. He stood in the doorway. She glanced up, helped herself to the two last chocolate biscuits lying on a plate beside her cup, and defiantly stuffed them both into her mouth. His eyes registered his disgust.

"I'm not going to Halfpenny Dun," he said. "Not unless the police insist, though I can't think why they would since, as you pointed out yourself, I've played no part in Beryl's life."

His wife said fiercely, "I've got news for you." She broke off, moving the half chewed biscuit round her tongue, swallowing. "Chief Inspector Paton or maybe Pattern, has been on the phone." She swallowed again and wiped the chocolate from her mouth. "He wants to talk to us. "I've told him we'll be leaving shortly, and I've packed overnight bags." She rose and with an air of bitter triumph replaced the lid on the biscuit barrel.

"You're enjoying this. You rather like the thought of me being in a fix."

"Yes," she said defiantly, "if you want to know I am delighted you've been caught out," and before he could recover from the shock of her admission she rushed on, "Do you realise that you sail through life looking straight ahead, never to right or left, never thinking of me?" The words swept across her tongue in a flood tide of bitter emotion, "Have you any idea what a boring life I lead, chained to that ghastly church shop and all those boring people, keeping up my end, and what is it for except to bolster your conceit, while you go off to your meetings and your boring job? What do I get out of it? Nothing.

"You're a boring man," she flared. "And now, when there's this happening you don't want to go—" she broke off and began to cry, thinking she was making it sound as though poor Beryl's death was an excitement, which was not at all what she had intended. In the midst of confusion and dismay other resentments leapt to the surface and she shouted, "We've got no children – you don't even care about that, though we still could have, if you ever had time to get into bed with me."

He glared at her.

"It's true. You hop on me every now and again—"
"Joan!"

But the waves of long-stored bitterness and disappointment, once broken loose, could not be stemmed. "And when I don't get pregnant you decide I'm barren and— Do you know what I think?" she screamed at him, "I think you're the one who's barren. I think your sperm is made of minutes from annual general meetings. Did you ever ask me if I wanted to be the wife of a pompous, important man? I would rather have had a sister," she said, her voice breaking. "I would have liked to know Beryl."

It was a moment before he recovered. "Why didn't you say so?" He spoke as though her loss was her own fault.

"I wanted to, when your mother died, but don't you remember, you wouldn't risk offending that bitter, twisted father of yours. You wanted his money. You knew he was capable of giving it to a cats' home."

He hit back, "If you hadn't wanted the money, you would have stuck to your guns. You didn't take much persuading."

She began to cry again, from frustration as well as misery, because it wasn't true. There had been no getting through to him, Noel the brick wall. "I tried again when he died, you know that, you must remember," she sobbed. "I hoped you would have a conscience about taking all that money when Beryl had none, but you didn't." She paused, became calmer, and wiped her eyes. "I didn't keep on about it because I could see there could be no brother and sister relationship, your having taken everything. It was a wicked and spiteful thing your father did. No good could ever come of it."

As if he didn't know that, now. But, "My father's misdemeanours are not my affair," he said, brittle with hurt from her insults, staggered at the strength of her passion.

"Oh God!" She dragged the top off the barrel and snatched two more chocolate covered biscuits, fat with marzipan, and stuffed them into her mouth.

"Thou shalt not take the Lord thy God's name in vain."

Choking over the biscuits, she screamed, "You pious sod!" Chocolate flakes spattered out on to the table and her lap. "You pious, empty, cold-blooded twerp!"

"Do you hate me?" he asked, suddenly nervous.

"I didn't," she whimpered, choking, swallowing, talking over the top of the half-chewed food, "I loved you, you know that. I hate what you've done to our marriage, that could have been so good. It could have been, if you were the person I thought you were. The person you show to other people, that you showed to me before we were married. It seems as though you can't be nice to anyone who's close to you."

There was a long silence. Shocked, he realised that she spoke the truth. He had been nice to his family once, and they rejected him. He had been afraid to risk rejection from her. These were the things Joan did not know, and he could not tell her now. It was too late.

Joan lumbered to her feet, wiped her eyes with her

table napkin, and said, "The least we can do now is go to Halfpenny Dun and see if we can help."

Yes. He recognised that. There was no way out of it.

"What's the matter?" she asked when he did not move.

He wanted to tell her he thought he deserved the money as compensation for the long evenings he spent alone while Beryl was with his mother in a real home. He wanted to say he would like to begin again. But it was too late, for he had no experience of sharing. His father had shared nothing with him, wanted nothing from him, not even his company.

He took the way he knew. "It's going to be very embarrassing," he said stiffly.

"Yes," she replied and blew her nose on the napkin. "Yes, I dare say it is."

Chapter 18

At nine o'clock on Saturday morning the village of Halfpenny Dun was awash with hurrying humanity. They brought their exhibits in baskets attached to the front of their bicycles, in Mercedes, Volvos and Minis, as well as on foot. Old Paddy Knight, retired railway porter, came wheeling the enormous yellow pumpkin that annually afforded him a moment of fame. In spite of the tragedy, the show was to go on.

In the marquee trestle tables, laid out by the committee the night before, displayed the exhibits.

Section one. A dish of five white potatoes, any variety.

A dish of twelve runner beans.

Five onions grown from sets. Five onions grown from seed.

Over on the apple display: Five cookers, five dessert.

Denise Ellis, gripping the handle of the baby's push chair with one hand, balancing a plate of six sausage rolls pinned down with microfilm in the other, was bewailing her luck. "What chance had I?" she demanded of a group keeping close to her in the hope that she had some special knowledge to impart, "Bert did 'is best, and 'e did get the washing machine going in the end, but it meant I had to stop me cooking, and what with carting buckets for him, because the beastly thing had to be emptied by hand, and keeping the children out of his way, I didn't get back to the baking. Didn't get my dried flower arrangement finished, either. This is all I've got. One miserable plate of sausage rolls. Break your heart, it would. Dunno why she had to get herself murdered this week," Denise grumbled naughtily.

Her mother-in-law, stumping along with her stick because of a recent hip operation (waited nine months for a bed on the National Health), said in a confidential whisper to Mrs Potter, "I tell Denise she's no right to talk like that in public. In a manner of speaking, as Charlie's wife, she's got a position to uphold. Bother Miss Lisamore, she says. It don't show much respect for the dead."

Betty Potter nodded. "You can't talk to the young these days. They've got all the answers."

"Dahlias over here," called Tony Adamson, one of the organising committee, waving both arms in the air so that people could pinpoint him in the milling crowd. "Section four, jams and cakes in the centre, and the miniature arrangements down at the far end." Judging began at eleven. Any exhibits not in place by then would automatically be disqualified. For the chronically late it was a race against time.

Lord Oaks, fresh from his walk in the park with the black labradors, stood in the entrance to the tent, knuckles resting on his hips, long legs set apart, feet in green Wellington boots wet from the morning dew. "How are things going?" he asked Geoff Tate, Hon. Secretary, who was crossing off names as the competitors arrived.

"Fine. We've got more exhibits than last year, which is surprising, considering the drought."

"My new gardener has produced an amazing show of chrysanthemums," offered his lordship. "And potatoes. Never seen anything like them. That Miss Childs, know who I mean, from Old Wood Lane, put him on to what she calls environmentally friendly fertiliser. It works wonders."

"She waves a magic wand," said Geoff with a twinkle.

"Magic wand. Hmn." His lordship twinkled back. "Crystals, isn't it? Oh well, there's more things in heaven and earth, according to Shakespeare, and we're enjoying the potatoes. It'll cause a rumble or two if we take home the Oaks Cup."

"Why not?"

"Hmn. Any developments on the murder? A bad business, that."

"Not that I know of. They're going from house-to-house asking questions. There's quite a team down at the village hall. Everyone's a bit on edge." He was thinking of his wife Helen, who was jumpy as a cat, he couldn't think why. She had a sound enough alibi. The hospital would vouch for the fact that she worked at their canteen every Thursday evening.

"If there's anything I can do, let me know."

"Remind her ladyship she's to judge the children's fancy dress at 2.15. 2.15, this year. We've decided 2.30's a bit late. We're going to do it by the big chestnut before the official opening. But I'm sure she hasn't forgotten."

Oaks nodded and wandered off with his dogs prancing beside him. Geoff returned to scanning his list. There were still a dozen or so to come. Romy Childs hadn't turned up, she who always had a car load of exhibits and vegetables which, as a Friend of the Earth, she grew organically; and queer flower arrangements glittering with crystals that were nearly always disqualified, though she never took offence.

"The eye only registers what the mind perceives," she would say, obscurely criticising the judges as she took her flashy stuff away. Once, Geoff suggested diffidently she may have her quote the wrong way round. She smiled, the vastly irritating smile of one who knows but doesn't choose to tell. "Think about it, Geoff." He did think about it and came up with the same conclusion, that she had it the wrong way round.

And where was Helen? He checked her entry form. One tapestry article. Six chocolate eclairs. Dish of twelve pickling shallots, and a flower arrangement in a teapot,

15 inches by 15 inches for all round effect. It wasn't like Helen to be late.

Helen was on her way. As she hurried past The Fox and Hounds carrying a basket containing her exhibits she narrowly missed being run down by a car pulling out in a hurry with a caravan in tow. Her basket went flying, flowers, chocolate éclairs and shallots dancing dementedly ahead. The little china teapot that was the base for her flower arrangement shattered against the tar macadam.

An angry woman in a headscarf screeched from the passenger seat, "Look where you're going," then the car moved on, the caravan swinging out after it. Helen stoically picked up the pieces, put them back into her basket and made her way home, telling herself to keep things in proportion. Far, far worse things were liable to happen to her today.

George King drove a six-year-old Citroen which he had had converted to use unleaded petrol. Normally a cautious driver, this morning he had come along the motorway in the fast lane. His wife Mollie held the map on her lap.

"I think you should put that right out of your mind," he said. "Lisa can be silly, God knows, but she has never been violent."

Mollie took the morning paper out from under the map and read again, for the umpteenth time, the paragraph about Beryl Lisamore's murder. The tears were very close. "Lisa never thought of herself as our child," she said. "And yet, she was only two days old when we took her home. What makes these thing happen?"

Her husband shrugged. "God knows."

"All that love. Where did it go?"

"Everybody has trouble with their children." He took one hand off the wheel to squeeze hers, comfortingly. "Lisa was only different in that she had something to attach her rebellion to. Most teenagers merely rebel. Think of what she's done as natural curiosity."

"I can't help feeling we failed her."

"I thought we settled that at breakfast." Then, he had been explosive. "We did not fail her. We gave her everything. What she has done is nothing to do with us. It is something within her."

They entered the village from the north. A large sign proclaimed "Halfpenny Dun, 30 mph" and "Please Drive Carefully Through the Village". They knew the address. For all her waywardness, Lisa kept in touch. Last week she had sent a postcard with a picture of The Fox and Hounds. "Filming has stopped for the moment, and I'm having a few days in a darling little cottage, all by myself. Real Hansel and Gretel stuff. I'll send you a snap," she wrote cheerfully, and the address was written in the top right-hand corner.

Her father drove slowly looking for Old Wood Lane and found it at the beginning of the high street, where three police cars were parked outside a pretty Tudor cottage. They stared, but neither spoke as he swung round into the lane. Both felt a sense of shock. There were two cottages ahead on the right hand side. They noted the name of the first, Cobblers, and cruised slowly past. "Here's Wayside." They climbed out in silence and in silence went up the path.

Lisa answered the door wearing a flimsy gown that barely touched her knees. Her legs and feet were bare. Her eyes flew wide with astonishment when she saw her parents and quick as a flash, she slammed the door in their faces. Immediately, she pulled it open again. Her father was already turning away, shoulders hunched. Her mother was staring at the door with tears in her eyes.

"Sorry," Lisa apologised, floundering backwards into the room. "Sorry, sorry. I didn't mean to. It was a reflex action. You didn't have to come," she said resentfully, gesturing to them to enter.

They crossed over the doorstep, George, who was a tall man, ducking his head to avoid the arm of a queen post where it curved upwards in support of the ceiling. "We wanted to. You are our daughter," said Molly emotionally.

"I am not your daughter. My mother is dead." Lisa was equally emotional.

"Yes, dear. We know." Mollie hid her hurt. "Did you meet her?"

"Yes. She's – was – a cold bitch." Lisa swallowed and looked down at the floor. "But she was my mother." They guessed at her rejection and even in their bewilderment, grieved for her.

Her father said, looking round the oak-beamed living room to avoid the shadow of pubic hair and the pink nipples that showed through the thin material of Lisa's gown, "Don't you think it would be a good idea, ducky, if you put a few clothes on?"

Without a word she swung round and went up the narrow stairs. They waited, standing, two awkward, uninvited guests, wanting to comfort and cherish, fearful of that one false move that could get them thrown out. They did not speak, and nor did they exchange looks. The situation was too delicate to risk any hint of collusion. They wanted Lisa to know they were individually, as well as collectively, on her side.

They blindly surveyed the room, not seeing its brightness, the great yellow vase on the square oak table, full of wild grasses and leaves turned golden at the edges, the big chairs draped in loose covers and patterned with roses, the goatskin rugs, fluffy islands on black oak floorboards, the polished horse brasses ranged round an enormous brick fireplace; the copper cauldron filled with logs. Their minds and eyes registered nothing, their ears listened to the sounds from upstairs, the rattle and gurgle of water in old pipes, the light slam of a cupboard door. She came back dressed in a green cotton jump suit. Her feet were bare.

"That's my girl," said her father, allowing a little tentative warmth to show.

Lisa, reacting with insult, went over to the fireplace and took down a framed picture. "This is my father," she said, "at least I still have a father of my own," making his rejection absolute.

He was not a man to indulge in self-pity. He conjectured shrewdly that a woman who kept a framed newspaper picture of a man was unlikely to be living with him. There would therefore have been no happy home from which Lisa could claim exclusion.

Her mother asked, "Have you met him, dear?"

"No. But I will. They want to interview everyone, so they'll get around to him. "That's a newspaper cutting so I expect he's famous."

Her father, who was not famous, went to look through the window into the silver birches at the side of the house. Behind him Lisa said bitterly,

"If you had helped me find her, this would never have happened."

Moved to dangerous intolerance, he said, still with his back turned, "This cold bitch?"

The wilful child in Lisa hit out, "You knew, all the time, who she was. When I wanted to find her you talked me out of it. You said no good could come of it. It could cause an upset in her life, you said. And all the time you knew her name. Can't you understand how I feel? Betrayed!" said Lisa passionately. "Maybe you even knew she lived here."

"No."

"Well, you could have told me her name. You even called me Lisa, short for Lisamore. Why did you do that?"

"It was something we could give you." Molly spoke apologetically, "A little heritage, we thought."

"Heritage!" Lisa spat the word out. "Is that what you call it?" She spoke directly to her father, "I found an envelope in your desk. Nothing written on it. Sealed down. I held it up to the light. Just a scrap of paper inside. I had a presentiment about it, so I steamed it open."

"We knew, dear," said her mother, "you didn't stick the envelope down again."

"Steamed it open," echoed her father mildly. "I thought we brought you up with standards."

"If you're not honest with me I don't have to be honest with you," she retorted. "When I wanted to go about finding her the proper way you pretended you knew nothing. Yet you had her name. Why did you keep it? The name. You were hardly likely to forget it, were you? There might have been some point if her address was there, too."

"We thought, if anything happened to us—"

"What do you mean, 'anything happened'? If you were killed? Is that what you mean?" she asked, brutal in her need to punish them.

"Yes, dear."

"We came here to offer support," said her father, carefully keeping his voice neutral. "Your postcard had a picture on it of a pub. We'll go there. We'll be on hand if you need us."

"You don't have to," she said, her eyes dark, her face sullen.

"We'd like to take you home with us, if you're not needed here." Molly waited, hoping without hope that Lisa would invite them to stay.

"No."

Molly said, "I'm sorry, dear," meaning she understood that in Lisa's eyes they had failed her. Lisa stood leaning against the bannister with eyes cast down. They waited, then went out of the door. Two fat wood pigeons looked up at them from the path, then flapped noisily into the air. They walked in silence down the path, listening, hoping Lisa would call or run after them. He opened the passenger door and held it while his wife stepped in. Behind the wheel again, he stared straight ahead through the windscreen, seeing their journey as fruitless, wanting to protect his wife, to take her home. "What do you think, darling?"

"We had better stay."

"I don't like to see you treated like this." "Think of her," said Mollie. "Only think of her." She choked. He put a hand over hers. The tears broke away then, and rained down her cheeks.

Chapter 19

Susan Rowsell sped along the road to Halfpenny Dun, past the arable fields brown with wheat stubble, past the little wood where she and the children wandered in the afternoons picking bluebells and primroses in spring, where they dashed, shrieking, through the fallen leaves in autumn holding Ginger the corgi on a leash lest he chase pheasants happy in ignorance that before the winter they would be sacrificed to the guns. Poor things, Susan would say. Such wickedness, to breed for the mindless satisfaction of killing, but Anthony, puffed up by virtue of an occasional invitation to join Lord Oaks' shoot, told her she was too sentimental by half.

"Nearly there, darlings," she sang to Matthew and Jane, strapped securely into their car seats in the back. Though loving her father dearly, she was relieved to be free once again of the stuffy sick room.

At the 30 mph sign a placard had been erected to advertise the Halfpenny Dun Horticultural Show. She did not notice Charlie Ellis' car outside Badger Cottage, and if she had would have thought nothing of it, assuming he was in the Post Office Stores, but she did see a uniformed policeman in front of the village hall, standing hands behind his back, looking bored. Police to control traffic for the show? Surely it hadn't come to that!

She waved to Mrs Alberry, her daily help, then to Helen Tate who did not see because she was scurrying along with her head down, clutching an enormous basket. Running home to get something she had forgotten for the show, no doubt, Susan thought. She hoped Anthony had remembered her entry form.

She swung round and sped up the side of the green past the two enormous chestnuts and the Victorian almshouses that were being tidied up, as an unsightly placard proclaimed, by W. Westridge & Sons, Builders and Decorators.

And there was home, warm red brick with big, square, white painted windows, smiling a benign welcome in the morning sunshine. She turned into the drive, switched off the engine and prepared to jump out, a diminutive figure in white T-shirt and jeans with caramel-coloured curls caught on top of her head, the wisps that had broken away framing her forehead. With one foot in the car, one on the drive and her face raised, Susan drew in long breaths of flower-scented Halfpenny Dun air. "Wonderful!" she exclaimed. "Wonderful! Here we are, chicks."

"Lemme out! Lemme out!" Four-year-old Jane battled with the seat belt.

"Out!" echoed Matthew imperiously. "Daddy! Daddy!"

Anthony, who had been standing unhappily at his study window, hurried to the front door, strode down the brick path between the lavender bushes and clasped bright-eyed Susan in his arms while the children continued to shout for release. "My darlings!" He was emotionally overwhelmed.

Susan grimaced. "It was no fun."

"Poor pet." He leaned into the car, kissing the children as he released them, lifting Matthew out. "Kiss Daddy." But Matthew only wanted to rush inside and find the dog. On the path they collided and Matthew tumbled over backwards into the lavender with the puppy on top, ecstatically licking his face.

Jane shouted, "Look what I got!" indicating her scarlet tracksuit. "Mummy bought this in Kids-Clothes." She added importantly, "Grandad's going to die, and the old devil's terrified about what he'll find on the other side."

"Jane! Jane!"

"Nurse did say." She skipped up the path, excited at having shocked the grown-ups.

"Stop that dog! He shouldn't be licking Matthew's face."

Anthony snatched up the three year old. Jane said, "The lady thinks I'm—"

"I'll get the bags, darling. You hold Matthew." Anthony thrust the child into his mother's arms. The corgi set up a frenzied barking and the cat, showing off, leapt over the lavender and rubbed herself, purring, against Jane's ankles. Jane picked her up and diverted, forgot what she was going to say.

Susan went through the front door, dumped Matthew on the sofa in the hall, and looked round with pleasure. "I feel as though I've been away a month. How lovely," she said, "how perfectly lovely to be home."

"It feels like a year," said Anthony, holding his guilt and his misery at bay, kissing her again, and again.

Lightheartedly, she pushed him away. "What an old smoothie you are." She stood off, looking up at him, tossing the crown curls, looking flattered and pleased. Then she saw his hands. "Anthony! What on earth!"

"I was mending the fence, I mean the rabbit hutch, with a bit of chicken wire." There was no fence, only a hedge. It was one of the matters keeping him awake, the fact that he had told the chief inspector he was mending a fence.

"What happened to the rabbit hutch?"

"Nothing much. I had to cut some chicken wire and – never mind about my hands," he interrupted himself, feeling sick at the thought of what a mess he was making of everything, loving his family, feeling the riches in his life with which he had so lightly gambled, sliding out of reach.

"So, what fantastic developments have occurred in

crazy, exciting Halfpenny Dun during the past week?" asked Susan jauntily, putting aside the puzzle of the rabbit hutch that was perfectly sound last time she saw it. "You may think it's quiet, but it's one up on sitting by a dying man with the curtains drawn."

"Poor pet. How is he?" Anthony was showing unaccustomed concern.

"Low. Sad, isn't it, that people don't want to die?"

Anthony shivered, then abruptly turning, gathered the bags together. "I'll take these upstairs."

"I've been racing to get here in time to deliver my dried flower arrangement and the marmalade." Susan chattered happily in his wake. "Did you put in my entry form? Better say yes, you've had nothing else to do all week, except cook your meals, and you probably didn't bother. Went out to restaurants, didn't you! I rang you half a dozen times – when was it – Monday night, Wednesday night, and Thursday. No answer. Where did you eat?"

He paused on the landing and she looked up at him, bright-eyed and lovely. He bent to kiss her, his heart like lead.

"Great to be appreciated." She laughed warmly. "I say, you must have been awfully bored!"

Anthony dumped the big case in their bedroom, took the holdalls into the childrens' rooms and trailed back. She was sitting at the dressing table. She had released her pretty hair and was combing it down over her shoulders. He steeled himself. "Something has happened in Halfpenny Dun in your absence," he said.

"Go on. Tell me." Her big grey eyes shone from the mirror. "At last! At last! Dynamite, is it?"

"Beryl Lisamore has been murdered."

The face in the mirror went blank. "We don't do anything often," Susan said in a small, shocked voice, "but when we do, we certainly do it properly." She swung slowly round on the stool and stared down at pink-painted toenails peeping through the sandal straps, not seeing them, trying to come to terms with what she had heard. "Poor Beryl. A burglar, was it? She disturbed a burglar? She couldn't have that kind of enemy. I mean, who would?"

He sat down on the edge of the big four poster, one of his lucky acquisitions, picked up at auction when a crumbling manor house came on the market. "You obviously haven't seen today's paper," he said.

She leapt up. "Where is it?"

"On the kitchen table still."

She ran down the stairs. He followed her. When he reached the kitchen she was waving the paper over the sink, shaking away the toast crumbs he had dropped as he ate breakfast. He stood in the doorway while she read the paragraph. She looked up,

"Poor Beryl. I've always felt guilty about her." Their eyes met. "You never told me, did you? It was a long time before I found out. Poor Beryl," she repeated.

The doorbell rang. Anthony, glad to get away, went to answer it. Chief Inspector Paton was standing on the doorstep, looking grave. Sergeant Donovan stood behind him.

"Good morning, Mr Rowsell. Could I have a word with you?"

Anthony said, "It's not very convenient, Inspector. My family have just arrived home. As you know, they've been away for a week with my wife's father. I could come down to Badger Cottage, or the village hall in, say, half an hour."

"If you don't mind, I'd like to speak to you now."

Anthony, recognising that Paton was going to speak to him now whether he minded or not, backed into the hall. The two men stepped over the threshold and with an anxious glance towards the kitchen, Anthony ushered them swiftly into the study. Turning to close the door, he saw his wife coming. "Won't be a moment, darling," he said in a loud, cheerful voice. Susan kept coming. Panicking, he closed the door in her face.

She opened it. Paton was surprised. He had imagined Rowsell married to a plainish woman, a safe woman who would be grateful and home-loving; reticent with her questions. He was not prepared for a pretty little kitten in tight jeans. Without waiting to be introduced, the kitten asked straightforwardly, "Are you a policeman?"

"Detective Chief Inspector Paton, Mrs Rowsell. And this is Sergeant Donovan."

"Do sit down."

He saw then that the grey eyes were telling him his first impression was incorrect. This was no kitten. He took a seat in a wing chair beneath a brass stand on which stood a flower arrangement that must have been spectacularly beautiful a week ago but which was now wilting. He thought this small, pretty, very able-looking wife, wanting the house to look lived-in in her absence, might have set it up for her husband before going to visit her father. The room was expensively furnished, suitable, he thought, for the provider of the 318i BMW parked outside. Donovan sat on a straight backed chair by the fireplace.

"Susan," said Anthony, regaining a little of his normal aplomb, "I think the chief inspector would like to speak to me alone."

As though he had not spoken, Susan went to the single square-paned window that looked out on lawn and colourful flower beds. The little girl came peddling fast round the side of the house, the puppy bouncing beside her tricycle, barking happily, making little forays at the tyres, teeth bared, teasing. The little boy ran after her with a ball, tripped, and the dog was on him, nuzzling him into a wrestling bout. The cat streaked across the lawn, leapt, landed briefly on the boy's raised rump as he was clambering to his feet, and streaked off again.

Susan said, "Go and play somewhere else, darlings," and closed the window. She went to a blue velvet chair and sat down with her hands spread along the arms. "You've come about Beryl's murder," she said, addressing both men. "If you're questioning my husband, I would like to be present."

Paton thought fast. He didn't want to be the cause of trouble between husband and wife, not yet, anyway, so he took a short-cut, jumping over the business of the palings, the necklace, and Letitia Grey. "Would you mind being fingerprinted, Mr Rowsell? I have to tell you that you have a right to refuse."

"Then I refuse." Anthony carefully chose a big wing chair and with a grave and thoughtful smile at his wife, took his seat. Paton thought that was the sort of smile he might use in the showroom when asking an outrageous price for a piece of furniture.

Susan did not move. She might have been a statue, or a Madame Tussauds wax model, thought Donovan, fascinated.

"There were fingerprints on the coffee mugs," said Paton, omitting to add that they had been on walls and floor as well. "It's a matter of eliminating you."

"I did not have coffee with Beryl on Thursday night," said Anthony very, very distinctly.

"There are a number of discrepancies to be sorted out," the chief inspector said. "The path you say you took from the high streeet to Old Wood Lane is blocked behind The Red House."

"I am aware of that. But it was possible, that evening, to clamber over. The situation may have changed since," said Anthony, lying carefully and very, very firmly, "for I dare say there were workmen there on Friday, but on Thursday evening it was possible to pass."

"Mr Grey found some palings missing from his back fence, and part of Miss Lisamore's necklace was found there. Mrs Grey has admitted you visited her that evening. Perhaps you could—"

"I did not visit Mrs Grey on Thursday evening or any other evening," said Anthony unequivocally. "If she said that, then she's lying. Maybe she's got something to cover up, and is using me. And I did not see Beryl Lisamore. You're wasting your time, Mr Paton." He rose to his feet, a confident, steely man, not at all frightened by having his back to the wall.

There was a long silence, then Paton and Donovan rose. "Thank you," said the inspector. "We'll no doubt be in touch."

Chapter 20

"He's lying," said Donovan as they crossed the narrow feed road that served the school, the doctor's surgery, the cricket pavilion and the half dozen houses on the green.

"Yeah." Paton hunched his shoulders and pushed his hands deep down into his pockets. He wished he didn't feel sorry for Rowsell. Outside of the possibility that he had murdered Miss Lisamore, the man was a shit, but no more so than a million others with red corpuscles in their blood and a way with women. He saw that pretty wife and the children, the dog, the cat, the house ideally placed to look out over this leafy green as a load of privilege that nobody in his right mind would risk losing. And yet, Rowsell had. It must all have come too easily, the inspector opined. He wondered if, with The Cedars as a part of his own background, his marriage would be on the rocks now.

"He knows we know he's lying," Donovan ventured into his thoughts.

"Yeah. Go on ahead, Sergeant," he said. "I need a moment to myself." He paused at the big stone trough with 1618 carved into the side and looked back at The Cedars, queen of the green, basking in the sunshine, wondering what was going on there now. The little girl opened the wrought iron gate and came running through with the dog at her heels. The little boy followed, shrieking. The puppy rushed between his legs and sent him flying. Paton felt angry that such a life should be wantonly put at risk, and angry with himself for being upset about it. Why? It wasn't like him to mirror himself into other people's lives. Was he getting soft? He looked back at the children, seeing their potential in a marriage, wishing, all those years ago, they had adopted a child.

And have her turn out like that little twit Goldie Montrose? Come on! Stay cynical. It's a damn sight more comfortable.

He rested his hands on the trough, thinking of fluffy-footed cart horses, coach horses, the fast steeds of highway men and smugglers watering here over the centuries. He recognised that he had been seduced by the village. It would be easy to believe, standing here with the sun warm on his balding head, that the privileged folk who lived in Halfpenny Dun were as perfect as their surroundings. But they weren't. They were the same old human beings who erred in the same way as the barrow boys in Hackney, the stockbrokers in their Thameside maisonettes, the waiters in posh hotels, the furled umbrella brigade in Whitehall. All descended from apes, he said to himself, and wondered if apes made a better job of things.

He walked diagonally across the green and into the high street. If there had been some rough stuff in the hall, if Rowsell had hit her, and they had both fallen over the bike . . .? He could not imagine any woman making coffee for a man who had hit her. He wondered if Rowsell, for the moment penitent, had waited on her. "I'm sorry. I'll make you a coffee, and let's talk over this business of the double yellow lines." But they hadn't agreed. She had threatened to expose him to his wife. That had lead to violent blows and strangulation. Donovan's words hung in the air, "He knows we know he's lying." In his experience people only told obvious lies when they needed to gain time, or when they had nothing more to lose.

He mustn't jump to conclusions. He'd be down on his sergeant like a ton of bricks if he started making the sort of assumptions that were running through his mind at this point.

There was a Mercedes 500 SL convertible parked outside Badger Cottage. Who was this, then? Donovan met him as he crossed the lawn. "Her brother's here, Chief."

"Right." They went together into the verandah room. A tall man rose to greet him, a cold, clean-looking man, shinily bald. In his presence the inspector felt fleshy, and self-indulgent. "I'm Noel Lisamore," he said. "I'm Beryl's brother. This is my wife." He gestured towards a large woman who had seated herself on the sofa. She wore a floral dress that reminded Paton, on a Harrods level, of Mrs Finlay's curtains. Her mouse-coloured hair was stiffly corrugated and arranged neatly round a large, worried face. She nodded to him, then, as though after all she decided she would rise, edged forward clutching her skirt against fat thighs.

Paton, who knew well enough her predicament, told her not to get up. He made a point of avoiding the low sofa, now. "Do sit down," he said to Noel, then hesitated, wondering if, in the circumstances that brother and sister were said to have no contact, he should offer condolences. He decided against and settled for, "An unfortunate business."

Donovan brought out his notebook.

"When did you last see your sister, Mr Lisamore?"

"At our mother's funeral. Three years ago. I don't see how we can help you. We couldn't possibly know if she had any enemies. Or even throw any light on her movements."

Paton nodded. "There are a few questions I'd like to ask, all the same. "Was there ill-feeling in the family?"

"No. How could there be? We had no contact."

Joan explained, with a conciliatory glance at her husband, "There was a divorce, more than twenty years ago. Noel went with his father. Beryl and the mother stayed together."

"Tell me about that." Without waiting for a reply, he said, "Get some coffee, Sergeant. Will you have a cup,

Mrs Lisamore?" Joan said eagerly that was just what she would like, after the long drive.

"Mr Lisamore?" asked Donovan, hesitating in the doorway.

"Yes. All right. Yes." He turned to Paton. "There's nothing to tell. The family, as my wife said, split down the centre."

"You didn't correspond?"

"No. She wrote after seeing our father's death notice in the—"

"Shit!" said Quixote.

Joan gasped. Noel blinked.

"Sorry about that," said Paton, keeping a straight face. "Your sister's parrot."

Joan made a silent, distraught looking appeal to her husband who asked stiffly, "Can you remove it?"

"I'm afraid not." Paton spoke apologetically. "We're hoping he might come up with something useful. He was here at the time of the murder, you see. Sorry. You were saying – the death notice? You saw her at your father's funeral, then?"

"No."

The inspector had taken one of the upright chairs standing near the door leading into the house, so that he formed the apex of a triangle from which he could watch the faces of both husband and wife.

"She could have come," Noel said and Paton wondered if he imagined a faintly defensive note. "She chose not to."

"You invited her, then?"

"I am not aware that people are invited to funerals. I did not 'invite' anybody." Noel avoided eye contact.

Joan leaned forward to catch Paton's attention. "Their father blamed Beryl for the break-up of the marriage, you see. She had the child. You will know that. Goldie Montrose." She looked pleased, and at the same time faintly embarrassed, that the child had turned out to be Goldie Montrose.

"I belong to Beryl." They all turned to look at Quixote. Though Paton had heard the words before, only now did they strike him as particularly poignant. He was getting a picture of a very lonely woman.

The sergeant came in with the coffee. "Sugar? Milk?" They took the mugs in silence. Paton drank his meditatively. Silence, he had long ago learned, created tension; often unnerved people. He wasn't sure, but he thought there was something bothering this chap. He pulled a question out of the hat, one of those instinctive curiosities that came apparently pointlessly, and only occasionally made sense, "So presumably your sister did not inherit anything from her father?" he asked.

"Why should she?" Now Noel was indeed defensive. "She had been the cause of the family break-up."

Ah! He thought he saw what the chap was bothered about. "So you inherited everything?" he asked mildly.

"I don't see that my father's estate bears any relation to this enquiry."

"On the contrary, everything bears relation to it. I was wondering why your sister got in touch. You have said she didn't attend the funeral."

"I said, she had seen the death notice."

"Was she hoping for a reconciliation, now that your father was dead?"

Noel gave the faintest of shrugs.

"Did she ask about money? If your father had left anything to her?" He was thinking that Beryl was a woman who felt strongly about her rights.

"No, she didn't ask. I couldn't have answered if she had. I hadn't seen the will."

Paton wondered if she had tentatively extended the hand of friendship, and been rebuffed. That shrug could have meant anything. He repeated the question. "So you inherited the whole of your father's estate?"

Noel was staring at the parrot. "I got the house, naturally."

"Was that all?"

"There were a few stocks and shares."

The inspector, who was experienced at spotting economical truths, glanced at his sergeant who made a note to get a copy of the will. Paton was thinking Beryl wouldn't have stood a chance if she had taken her brother to court for her share of the inheritance. She had a good job. She was not overtly in need. That was the way the law stood. The father had had no contact with her. The brother, on the face of it, had no reason to kill her. And he was a cold bugger, anyway. The murderers whom he had known commit the crime within families had all been capable of passion. He felt there was precious little, if any, passion in this man.

"Where were you on Thursday?" he asked.

"I went to work as usual."

"By car?"

"No. I use public transport."

"You leave the car at the station?"

"Y-es."

Paton wondered if he detected a faint hesitation, and decided he imagined it. "You drove straight home from the station?"

"Home? No. I was late that night. I went straight on to a village hall meeting. I'd had a substantial lunch at my club. I had a cup of tea on the train."

"What time did you eventually get home?"

Noel looked towards Joan, his eyes vague. "Eleven, maybe."

"It's usually about eleven," said Joan who had fallen asleep the moment her head hit the pillow.

"You heard him come in?"

"Yes," said Joan for he always came in about eleven and she could see no point in producing red herrings that would waste the time of the police. Anyone at the meeting would vouch for his presence there.

"And you?" Paton asked.

"I was at the church shop all day. Four of us were there, having a tidy-up. I went home about five."

"Did you see anyone after that?"

"You mean I have to produce an alibi?" Her face crumpled. "Why would I want to kill Beryl? I didn't even know her."

Paton smiled apologetically. "We ask these questions of everybody, Mrs Lisamore."

"Sorry. I'm sorry. I'm not used to—" She smiled nervously and he was aware of deep unhappiness behind the smile. Again she said, "Sorry." The word slid out easily, as from frequent use. "I remember," she said, anxious again. "I did speak to my next door neighbour. That would be about seven – or maybe eight."

"Were there any telephone calls?"

"Yes." Her big face cleared. "I remember the vicar rang about – I don't know – nineish. I went to bed at ten."

Paton rose. "Thank you. I won't keep you, then," he said. "We've got your address and telephone number."

Using her hands to hold her skirt close against her thighs, Joan edged off the sofa and staggered to her feet. "The girl, Goldie Montrose. I think we ought to—" she glanced at her husband, met a cold stare, then resumed with nervous defiance, "My husband doesn't think – but I think—"

"She has taken Wayside Cottage," said Paton perfunctorily, not wishing to be drawn on the matter of righting old wrongs. "You'll find it a little way up the lane that runs beside this cottage."

"That parrot." Noel nodded in the direction of the cage, "will need a home."

His wife gasped. "No, no, Noel. Really, no."

He said, speaking to her directly, "Beryl's affairs are our responsibility, now."

Sergeant Donovan's face darkened. "I'm looking after it," he said, openly possessive. "Besides, as the inspector said, it might be useful. It might repeat something that was said at the time of the murder."

Noel's pale eyes widened. "You can't be serious, Inspector. You can't use parrot talk as evidence!"

Quixote, noting their interest in him, swung upside down on his perch. "Bugger to you, too," he said.

Joan flushed. "I certainly wouldn't give it house room," she said. She felt a little light-headed, having for the second time today stood up to her husband. It just went to show, she thought, if you felt strongly enough, you could do anything. Imagine that bird, and the vicar!

"It will remain here for the moment." Paton rose. He went with them to the front gate. That was some car! He looked at the number plate. Three years old. The father had died three years ago. He thought of Beryl's bicycle, in an otherwise empty garage. As he climbed into his modest Cortina he wondered what Goldie Montrose would make of the Lisamores. He drove along the high street thinking that some people got a raw deal from life. Beryl – he found himself calling her Beryl now – seemed to have had more than her share of misfortune. The monstrous father who had not included her in his will, Paul Street, the brother who took all the money and didn't get in touch even to say their father had died. And Rowsell. Lord love me. He cast his eyes heavenwards, hoping the mother had been all right.

Passing the green, he looked across at The Cedars. There were other matters to clear up. Bobby Hunter, for instance. Who the hell was he that his name should be on the computer disk? Maybe the Horticultural Show would throw up something.

And then, Paul Street. On Thursday evening not only did he have a very good reason for killing the woman whom he had seduced as a child over twenty years ago, but he would know there was nothing, absolutely nothing, to link him with her murder. Beryl was hardly likely to have told him she had consigned his picture to the kitchen bin where there was a very real possibility of its being found by investigating police.

Chapter 21

Romy Childs saw the car drive away from Wayside Cottage, saw at the driving wheel a baldish man and by his side a handsome, grey-haired woman dabbing at her eyes. Who else could they be but Lisa's parents driven out by their over-emotional, ungrateful, misguided little twit of a daughter? Romy knew a lot about people. She could sum them up with a fair degree of accuracy on very short acquaintance. She went to the utility room and extricated a pair of leather sandals from the jumble of boots and shoes she kept there, buckled them on her brown feet, then shouted upstairs to Emma, "I'm going along to Wayside Cottage. Won't be long."

Emma raced to the top of the stairs, her lumpiness disguised by a frail and magnificent Edwardian nightshirt that her hostess had bought at a jumble sale years ago for sixpence, old money. "You know her! Don't tell me you know her! Goldie Montrose!"

"I know everybody," said the white witch immodestly, tossing her rough black hair and setting her crystal earrings dancing.

"Golly! Can I come?" Emma's eyes were circular, her mouth open as though waiting for the answer to drop in.

"Not now, love. You have a rest." Romy straightened her blouse, adjusted the saucy neckline so as to bare the curve of her breasts, hitched at the black skirt until the sunburst so decoratively stitched on the front was precisely dead centre, and left.

Offended by the rebuff, Emma slouched back to her

room, caught a glimpse of herself in the mirror and stuck out her tongue. "If you had been born with Goldie Montrose's looks none of this would have happened to you," she said, hating her round blob of a face, her dull skin, her mousey hair, and especially her figure. Food makes you fat, she said to herself three times a day before meals, and ate them anyway.

There was no footpath between Cobblers and Wayside Cottage. Larch, birch, chestnut and beech hugged the road, shading it. Romy loved living on the edge of the forest for she was by instinct a forest person. She talked to the birds as she talked to her plants. When others claimed they also talked to their plants, though no one had admitted to talking to wild birds, she would confound them by asking, head on one side, eyes dark and secretive (the cultivated gypsy look), "Ah, but do you listen to their answers?" She enjoyed her unique position in the village, only halfway respectable, but never ignored.

The front door of Wayside Cottage was open. She stepped over the threshold into the pretty oak-beamed living room. Lisa, spreadeagled on a divan, was indulging her confusion and guilt in a torment of sobbing. Romy sat down on the rocking chair by the vast brick fireplace, spread her skirt round her and removed the pear-shaped crystal from her neck. It caught the light, sending a rainbow darting across the room and speeding up the opposite wall. Lisa, sensing another presence, tentatively lifted her head, saw Romy and swung her feet to the floor.

"Do you always walk into people's houses without knocking?" Lisa asked resentfully.

"I did knock. You didn't hear it through that awful cacophony." Romy presented her insults with such winsome charm that often one only recognised them in retrospect. "I came because I saw your parents leaving."

"They're not my parents," snapped Lisa childishly.

"Oh, but they are, dear. And you drove them out! No wonder you're in a state. Consciences are hell."

Lisa sniffed.

"Do blow your nose."

"They could have told me about Beryl," she said emotionally. "They knew her name. They actually called me after her. But didn't tell me. Lisa – more." She found a tissue in her pocket and blew her nose loudly. "It was written on a bit of paper in an envelope in my fa—in George King's desk." She used the name defiantly. "If they had told me before, Beryl wouldn't be dead now."

"You're an expert on God and the mysterious workings of the universe, then?"

"What are you saying? I don't understand." The white witch smiled. Lisa waited, but she remained infuriatingly silent. Lisa said, "God didn't have anything to do with it. He doesn't shuffle babies round from pillar to post, creating disasters. God sent me to Beryl. If I had been with her she would have been different. It's enough to make anyone kinky, having your baby taken away from you," said Lisa, loving Beryl now, forgiving her the vile-tongued parrot.

Romy had slipped the chain over her wrist. The crystal began to move in slow circles. She watched it with dreamy eyes. "So, you're finding fault with her! What was she to you? Some sort of imaginary doll that you had dressed up in pretty clothes and stuffed with ideal mothering virtues?"

Lisa blinked.

"Well?"

"Do you know how old my par— George and Molly King are? They were forty-two and forty when they adopted me," Lisa said resentfully. "They could be my grandparents. Why are you swinging that thing?"

"I'm not swinging it. Look, my hand is still. It's speaking to me. Crystals are a part of the infinite. Tap into them and you will get all the answers."

"What do you mean? What answers? Are you asking it questions about me? What is it telling you?" Lisa was suspicious, apprehensive of revelation.

"Do you not know that babies go to the people they're meant for?" Romy adopted her practised, wise-gypsy look.

"Sucks to your old crystal. I was meant for Beryl. And this man." Lisa rose and went in that long-legged, elegant way she had of moving to the mantelpiece, and picked up the newspaper cutting of Paul Street. "This is my father." She held it close to her chest, gazing at it with absorbed pride. "I'm going to find him, now. I'm going to have a father, anyway." Romy held out her hand. Lisa passed the picture over. "Can't you see the likeness?"

In an instant, Romy knew she had seen that face before. "You were not only meant for the family King," she said, holding the picture at arm's length, frowning at it, "but you chose to come to them. I dare say there was some sound medical problem that caused you to come via Beryl. You're wrong when you say God doesn't shuffle babies around. Sometimes he has to."

"Honestly! The things you say!" Lisa laughed on a high, astonished note. "Don't you see the likeness? Romy, are you listening to me? Don't you see the likeness?"

Romy thoughtfully examined Lisa's features, then returned her eyes to the picture. "Where did you get this?"

"Beryl had it. They found it in the cottage. Anyway," Lisa said, flopping bonelessly down on the sofa, "I can't go back. I've burnt my boats. I've been foul to them since I was about thirteen."

"Why?" Romy put the picture down on the table in front of her.

"I don't know, except that nobody likes the idea of being a charity. I mean, a charitable gesture. I mean—" Lisa looked near to tears. "You don't understand. Nobody who hasn't been adopted would understand."

"You were no charitable gesture," said the white witch, gentle now, reverting to Englishness. "You were greatly wanted. And deeply loved."

"How do you know?"

"I told you. Crystals speak."

"Well," said Lisa, partially seduced, "ask it why this has happened to me."

"Nothing has happened to you, dear. You've been a victim of your own wrong thinking. I expect you came to your adoptive mother to repay her for something you did to her in a former life." Romy was heavily into reincarnation.

"Oh, honestly! D'you want a coffee?"

"Only if you're having one."

Lisa went out to the kitchen. Romy picked up the picture again, examining the wide-set, attractive eyes, the straight nose, the faintly cynical mouth. The man did indeed appear to bear a resemblance to Lisa. No, she decided, she did not know him. But she was convinced she had recently seen his picture somewhere.

Lisa came to the kitchen doorway. "I've put the jug on. What did I do to them in a former life? Do you know? Did the crystal tell you?" The mockery was not much in evidence now. She looked and sounded subdued.

"You might not like it."

Lisa went back to the kitchen.

Romy relaxed against the chair back, gazing at the picture of Paul Street. Lisa returned carefully carrying two mugs. She paused in the middle of the room. "What happens if I don't repay?"

"You'll have to come back again, and again, until you do. It's karma."

Lisa stood looking down at her guest, an odd expression on her face as though laughter, or tears, were just below the surface. "Are you serious?"

Romy smiled her secret, gypsy smile.

"You interfere in people's lives, don't you?" A little of the coffee splashed out of a mug on to the floor. Lisa scuffed at it with a bare foot.

"Sometimes. If I think I can help them."

"I don't think I need help." Lisa gave Romy her mug and sat down. They drank the coffee in silence.

"I must go," said Romy, rising to her feet, slipping the chain off her wrist and clasping it once again round her neck. "I have to take my entries down to the marquee. I presume you'll be at the show this afternoon?"

Lisa rose also. "It wouldn't be decent," she said piously.

"Oh, come." For the first time the white witch allowed herself to show a little impatience. "You could hardly be said to be bereaved. Give the locals a treat. There's swimming in the lake. I'll put word round the village that you're going to appear in a bikini. That'll bring in a record crowd."

"I don't swim. I can't swim." Lisa looked embarrassed.

"Why not? Why can't you swim?" Romy turned back from the door. "What are you going to do if you get a film part that calls for swimming?"

"If you must know, I get scared in the water. Maybe I got drowned in my last life." Lisa resorted to ridicule.

"Maybe you saved yourself at someone else's expense. Maybe you know this at soul level but your ego doesn't want you to atone and manifests itself in a fear of water."

Lisa looked at the white witch with big eyes.

"Maybe that's why you've been foul, as you say, to your mother," Romy continued, "because you can't bear the fact that every time you look at her an inner voice reminds you of the fact that you left her to drown."

Lisa looked angry and upset. "It's a lot of rot, that crystal stuff." She waved a hand, dismissively. "Does anyone listen to it? In the village, I mean."

"You'd be surprised how many people listen to it. They come after dark," Romy tiptoed forward, whispering conspiratorially, "praying they won't run into anyone they know."

"Honestly, you are dramatic." Lisa was prepared to be tolerant, even amused. "Who comes? Did Beryl?"

"You shouldn't be on your own at this time," Romy said, ignoring the question. "Why don't you come with me to Cobblers? There's someone there I'd like you to meet." She thought it might do Lisa no harm at all to talk to a girl who had been through troubles that were not of her own making. A girl without looks, money, or a job. "You can keep her company while I take my entries over to the marquee."

Lisa hesitated.

"Come on. Get some shoes."

Surprisingly subdued and obedient, Lisa found a pair of sandals and followed. She locked the door behind them, then stooped to slide the key under the mat.

"Do you think that's wise?"

She grinned. "Dad – George King says burglars don't expect it of intelligent people. Besides, this one is too big to cart around. It would go right through my pocket."

Romy noted the word Dad with cautious interest.

As they entered the front door of Cobblers Emma jumped up from her chair, her plain face alight, her eyes shy. "Gosh!"

"Now here's my friend Emma," said Romy, introducing the two girls. "While you've been becoming a great success she's done a lot of travelling. She's been all round the world. I'm sure you could learn a lot from each other." She left them bright-eyed, summing each other up. In the kitchen, with one hand on the latch of the broom cupboard, she glanced at her watch. There wasn't really time to go through the old papers now. She picked up a box from the floor and packed her show entries, then glanced again at her watch. The hands seemed not to have moved. She assumed then that her higher self, for whom time did not exist, was telling her to look in the papers, now. She lifted them on to the sink and began methodically searching. There it was:

"Paul Street, headmaster of Brockley Martin Abbey, the famous boys' public school in Wiltshire . . . paternity

. . . 'I am innocent,' he said when charged. 'I never touched the girl. Would I be such a fool, in my position?'"

Who was to say, Romy wondered cynically, knowing what she knew about men, she who had become rich over the years in the knowledge of what makes human beings tick. She tore the article out and without premeditation went through to the sitting room.

"I've got to go," she said, addressing both girls. She handed the piece of newspaper to Lisa. "You might like to talk to Emma about this," she said, then went back to the kitchen, picked up her box and left by the back door.

Chapter 22

On her return Romy saw a large woman limp out of Lisa's gateway and start up Old Wood Lane. She waited until the stranger was within speaking distance then asked, "Were you looking for Goldie Montrose?"

"I was, but she's not there. I've left a note." Joan eyed Romy uncertainly. "I'm Beryl Lisamore's sister-in-law."

Romy politely introduced herself, effectively hiding her surprise, and her fear for the Kings. "I think Lisa may have gone off with her parents," she said, offering up a little prayer that she would not choose that moment to lean out of a window.

"Oh." Joan looked momentarily nonplussed, then, as though making time to consider what to do or say next, she lifted the hem of her skirt and tenderly brushed some dirt and fine gravel from her plump knees that were showing through an enormous hole in her tights. Her shins were dusty and there were pieces of metal caught in the nylon. Trickles of blood had begun to dry on their way down her leg.

Romy bit back automatic expressions of sympathy and fought a stern battle with her conscience. There was a well-equipped First Aid box in her bathroom cupboard. Had this woman been anyone other than Lisa's aunt she would have been hustled up the garden path with the greatest goodwill. "I doubt if she'll be back today," she said, lying for the greatest good. Joan seemed about to speak but affecting to believe the exchange was at an end, Romy returned to the car and pretended to be absorbed in cleaning the windscreen. Immediately Joan had limped out of sight round the corner of the high street she ran, in a whirl of skirts, down the lane to Wayside Cottage.

"Thank God for Mr King's quirky view of burglars," she said to herself as she took the key from under the mat and unlocked the door. A used envelope from which the contents had been removed, lay on the floor. She picked it up and read the message on the back. "Noel and Joan Lisamore send their love and sympathy. We would be pleased if you would get in touch at this address." A series of little arrows pointed to the edge of the envelope and continued round to the front. She had added a telephone number. Romy put the envelope into her pocket, went into the living room and took the photo of Paul Street down from the mantelpiece, then left the cottage, locking the door behind her and replacing the key beneath the mat.

Emma, looking downcast, met her at the door. "Lisa rushed off, Romy."

"Rushed off where?" Romy was faintly alarmed.

"She said her parents had gone to The Fox. She went to join them."

Romy breathed a sigh of relief.

"Did you know they were here? Her parents?"

Romy said, "Yes."

"Why are you looking so smug?" Emma asked querulously. "What was in the paper? She wouldn't show it to me. She said it was about some dirty old man molesting schoolgirls, and she tore it up. She seemed angry with you. It wasn't, was it? I mean, why would you – I wouldn't have thought . . ." Her voice tailed off. People laughed gently about the white witch, but they hesitated to criticise. "Anyway, you did tell her to show that cutting to me. Was there a reason?"

"It doesn't hurt, when you think you're in trouble, to learn that other people have problems too. I thought she might like to talk things over with you. You might have both got something out of it."

Emma was exasperated. "Out of a story about a dirty old man molesting schoolgirls?" She waved her arms despairingly in the air. "I give up." Romy tucked the photo under one arm, took the envelope from her pocket and tore it into very small strips, then went through to the kitchen. Emma followed, watching with puzzled eyes as she tossed everything into the bin.

"What are you up to now?"

"Finishing the job."

With an air of martyred resignation, Emma leaned on the sink. "I saw you talking to that fat woman who went down to Wayside. Who's she? She's not Lisa's mother, is she?"

"No. Let's have some lunch. Then I'm going off to persuade Marigold Ashenden to take you back."

"I'm not sure I want to go back to the Ashendens," Emma said as they stood at the bench making sandwiches with organically grown lettuce and tomatoes.

"You have to. For their sakes. They have to be considered, too."

"What do you mean?" When the white witch smiled she assumed it was something she was expected to know.

Pulling into the car park behind The Fox and Hounds, Paton was not surprised to see a television van spewing out men carrying cameras. He hurried in through the back entrance, ordered a pork pie and chips, and sat down at the same table in the window bay where Enid had found him the night before with such disastrous consequences.

There were not many people at the bar, three or four men in jeans who looked like locals, and four hikers in T-shirts with satchels on their backs and graffiti streaming across their chests: "Keep England green". "I'm looking for someone to love". "I am that man".

There was a young couple eating, and at another table a greyhaired, sadlooking man and woman gazing into their drinks, not talking. He thrust his hands into his pockets, slid down in his seat and gazed at the beamed ceiling, thinking about the various dramas of the day before: Forgetting to pick Barbara up. That was the worst. Better not think about it. Not until this job was over. He'd have to face it then, his neglect, as she said. His obsession with his work.

He came back to the present with a jerk as the door to the Saloon Bar swung open. A slender, leaf-green girl stood silhouetted against the dark wood. The chatter at the bar ceased. Goldie Montrose glanced round, theatrically aware of her audience, then spotting her quarry, tossed her mane of silky blonde hair back over her shoulders, first the right side, then the left, lifted her chin for the greatest effect, and proceeded to make her elegant way across the room. Paton watched her with puzzled eyes. She approached the silent, middle-aged couple, and paused.

The woman lifted her head. The man's features softened. Goldie Montrose pulled out a chair, sat down, then reaching across the table lifted first the man's hand, then the woman's, and raised them to her lips.

Well, he thought, just as the television crew burst in, I wonder what that was about.

Noel, having moved the Mercedes convertible fifty yards further along the street so that now his back was turned to Badger Cottage and the people coming and going at the Post Office Stores, was fuming behind the wheel. With his back to Old Wood Lane he was not aware of Joan approaching until the off-side door opened and she edged herself awkwardly into the passenger seat, tenderly favouring her right knee. Noel looked at her with dislike.

"I didn't see her," Joan said. "Apparently her parents

are here. I left our address and a note asking her to get in touch." She lifted the hem of her skirt to show him her wounded knee. "That was cruel of you, Noel."

"Fasten your seat belt."

She rummaged in her handbag among a litter of keys, lipsticks, old letters and reminder notes, found a tissue and dabbed at the wound, suffering. "Look," she said, "there's gravel in it." Tenderly, she drew the edge of the torn tights away from the wound, dampened the tissue with saliva and gently attempted to clean the surrounding skin.

"If you hadn't jumped out of the car when it was moving, it wouldn't have happened," said Noel impatiently. "Do up your seat belt."

"I didn't jump out when it was moving." Joan was unaccustomedly indignant. "I told you if you wouldn't drive me I would walk, and you said you wouldn't, and you saw me open the door. You knew I was getting out. You started off deliberately."

"Joan! I can't start. Will you please do up your seat belt!" He put the car into gear and moved off fast while she was still struggling with the strap.

She said sullenly, "The speed limit here is 30 miles an hour." The sullenness gave way to distress as the needle went up, 50, 60. They passed the deregulation sign and she relaxed a little. "It's not necessary to drive so fast." The car kept its pace.

"I don't know what's come over you," Noel said. "Beryl and her affairs have nothing whatsoever to do with you. You've no right to meddle. You're not even a relation."

"I am a relation. I am." She was passionate.

"By marriage, only. To someone you didn't know."

"Noel! It's you who are behaving in an extraordinary manner."

"How would you expect a man to behave when his sister has been murdered?" he asked, thinking with terror of the computer he had seen on the table, knowing it could hold evidence of that terrible accident in Soho Square.

Obviously the police had not discovered it yet, but they would. Or had they? Was that why they had sent for him? Maybe they hadn't. Had Joan, wanting to go, lied in order to get him there? He was filled with rage at the thought that she may have tricked him, putting Beryl and her affairs before his. He wanted to ask her, but he was afraid of his own feelings. Keep calm. A car is a lethal weapon. You ought to know, you who have already killed a man at the wheel. Maybe Beryl hadn't written her letter on the machine. Maybe she had cleared the disk. Maybe he was safe. Stop worrying.

The car sped past cultivated fields, heading for the motorway. Noel said angrily because he was angry with her, thinking she had lied to him to get him to Halfpenny Dun, "I have things on my mind."

"What things? What could be more important than that your sister's been murdered, even if you didn't love her – didn't know her – and didn't want to?" Joan said boldly, "I'm going to ask her daughter to visit us."

"Perhaps you've forgotten that the house is mine," he said coldly. "People don't come if I don't want them." He never would have Beryl's illegitimate child to stay, she who was was the cause of everything that had gone wrong for him.

"As a matter of fact, it's only half your house," the new Joan, born that morning, slid the rug from under his feet. "And if we were divorced I'd get half. That's the law."

He could scarcely believe his ears. Divorce! What on earth had made her think of divorce? This born-again Joan, this newly treacherous wife, would divorce him, he could see that now, if the police found a copy of that cryptic note from Beryl suggesting she knew about Soho Square, and followed it up. She wouldn't stay with a convicted criminal, how could she, she would say, not with the vicar coming to tea, and her voluntary work in the church shop. His mind skittered haphazardly, picking up little bits of the future. Joan, sitting in the courtroom, watching him in the dock, thinking it served him right – this Joan who had accused him of denying her a sister-in-law would think it served him right – when he was convicted and sent to jail for life.

He saw a narrow bed in a bleak prison cell. His room in his father's cold, silent, unfriendly house had not been unlike a prison cell. He had been alone there, too, for his friends never came more than once. They didn't like the silence, and the cold.

Without realising what he was doing, he pressed his foot on the accelerator. They sped up and over a hump-backed bridge where an enormous sign bellowed SLOW. The car took off and landed again with a soft thump, then whirled dangerously round a sharp bend, crossing the centre line as though out of control. Was it out of control? He wasn't sure. He didn't care.

The stranger next to him cried shrilly, "If we meet a bus we'll both be killed." She watched the needle with terrified eyes as the speedometer crept up, 70, 75, 80. "You're driving dangerously!"

The voice was full of terror now. He enjoyed it. Serve her right. They whirled round another sharp corner, hit the grassy verge, swayed, straightened.

"Noel! Stop!"

He had frightened himself. He lifted his foot and the needle began to come down.

Neither spoke again, Joan because she was praying, he because what he wanted to say could not be said to this newly defiant wife.

He pretended to agree with her, thinking it would be easy to reneg when all was well again. "Maybe we should take the girl on," he said.

She turned to look up at him, her face bright and forgiving. "I'm so glad. There's something I want to say, Noel. I don't want you to lay claim to Beryl's estate. You've no right to it. I'm sorry," she said, reverting to the wife that was familiar to him, the one who played second fiddle and was contrite in error, "but that's how I feel. I wish you would talk to me about this. There's so much to talk about. We shouldn't be going home now. Let's turn back. I don't like walking out on poor Beryl before the murder's been solved. If you think about it you'll realise it is our concern."

He felt certain she had the vicar on her mind. She was worried about his reaction. There was more to it than that, if she only knew. What was the vicar going to say when his sidesman and most respected member of the PCC was arrested on a charge of hit-and-run driving? He thought about all that he had built up. His reputation. His job. He would be a nobody again, at the mercy of people with power, as he had been at the mercy of his father all those years.

"Your mother doesn't want you."

"Pass your exams, then you can thumb your nose at the world." He hadn't wanted to thumb his nose at the world, only to have its esteem. To have what, in the end, he did have, that money and a good job had brought to him. And now he could lose it. Joan, in Beryl's hands, Beryl reaching out from the great beyond, had insisted he go to Halfpenny Dun to be taunted by the computer with its terrible potential.

He felt the panic rising up again, setting his head spinning. The car swerved into the path of an oncoming lorry, swerved fast back again. The lorry went rumbling on. He braked, pulled into the side of the road, and turned the engine off. He was sweating.

"Noel!" She was beside herself with fear and shock. "Noel! What is the matter with you?"

Accustomed as he was to blaming others, he said violently, "There's nothing the matter with me. You nearly got us killed, you stupid cow."

Chapter 23

The village street was awash with cars and bicycles crawling at a snail's pace because those in the front had to pause to pay their entrance fees at a booth in the drive. Paton, conscious of the build-up of petrol fumes between the tall laurels, walked swiftly, dodging cyclists who were themselves dodging chattering pedestrians. At the booth, which was set in a gap in the hedge, he too paused,

A ruddy-cheeked man of military bearing said, as though conferring an honour, "Forty pence, please."

"Forty pence!" ejaculated the chief inspector in astonishment. "You're joking!"

"You get good value for money in Halfpenny Dun," the man replied goodhumouredly. He did a double take, "You're—"

Paton, annoyed at being unmasked so easily, said, "Don't flash it around."

"Mum's the word," he said importantly, turning to the next person in the queue. "Forty pence, please."

Paton hurried on his way. The marquee stood directly between the lake and the house. Crossing the gravel forecourt, he paused to look up at the Georgian mansion with that mixture of envy and uncertain disapproval with which he regarded the inheritances of the aristocracy, wondering what it would be like to live in such splendour. The lawn was dotted with white-clothed bridge tables, some placed in the sun, some within the shade of an enormous oak. There were fat men in shorts and T-shirts; plump, permed women in flowered cottons; slender, elegant men in Jermyn Street shirts; busy young mothers escorting well-brushed toddlers; stately ladies who but for their garden hats, or bare heads, might have dropped in on their way to the races.

Down by the water a docile animal drooped between the shafts of a pony cart that bore a sign reading: Rides 20p. Outside the marquee dainty fairies, wobbly clowns, an embarrassed Julius Caesar sucking his thumb, a perambulating birthday cake, a strolling renaissance castle were being judged by an erect and rather beautiful woman in the grande dame style. Lady Oaks? He wandered down to the edge of the lake, then turned and stood looking back at the colourful, sunny scene.

The ring of children in fancy dress disintegrated. The castle went up to collect first prize. People strolling in from the car park put on speed. Those standing around moved in closer. The grande dame's impressive hat suddenly jumped above the heads of the crowd. He strained to hear the few ragged words that the breeze brought his way. "Soap box . . . weight." A ripple of laughter. "Privilege . . . thanks to . . . made all this possible." He saw Sergeant Donovan standing on the periphery of the crowd.

The speech ended, the hat disappeared and the crowd streamed into the marquee. He wandered back up the slope and was accosted by a bright-faced young woman selling raffle tickets. "The prizes are over there." She indicated a small table sheltered from the sun by a striped golf umbrella. "Bottles of wine, chocolate biscuits, all sorts of nice things. Do have a look. How many will you have?" She smiled winningly, separating a sheet with her fingers, "Five for a pound."

He paid. "You're a good saleswoman."

As he handed her the coin she said, "You're—"

"Yes." He went hurriedly to merge with the crowd in the tent. Strolling down a line of trestle tables he cursorily examined plates of circular golden onions, green runner beans a foot long, a group of potatoes marked: 1st prize, Mrs Ledward.

At the flower arrangements three women were volubly discussing the incompetence of the judge who should never have given first prize to an arrangement of roses and cacti set in a clam shell. Ignorant of the niceties of line and form, Paton thought it looked great.

He paused at the children's section. An old hat, decorated. A flower arrangement in a tea-cup, won by Prunella Smith, aged 13. A pig made from vegetables, had won Bobby Wake, aged eight, first prize. A bear cut out of potatoes had won for Hunter Ashenden second prize. A transient memory fled through the inspector's consciousness and flew away, leaving a tiny residue behind.

As he came back down the inside tables admiring the single blooms in vases, pastel pink, orange, vermilion, great mops of snow white cactus dahlias, enormous roses filling the air with perfume, that curious memory came creeping back. He stopped to admire the biggest, reddest dahlia he had ever seen, worrying. More roses. He leant forward, sniffing delicately. Mmn. Like perfumed butter. He smelt them all, filling his nostrils with their fragrance, then thoughtfully retraced his steps to the children's entries. Hunter Ashenden. Bobby Wake. That was it! That was what was bothering him! The juxtaposition of the names that were on Beryl's computer. Not Bobby Hunter, perhaps, but Bobby and Hunter? Were they the two boys whom Beryl said had taught the parrot to swear?

A consciously cultured voice behind him said, "Inspector Paton, I believe." He swung round, jerking his mind back from Beryl Lisamore's computer disks. "I'm Oaks. Glad you could spare the time." His lordship held out a large brown hand.

"Glad to meet you, sir."

"How are things going?"

People were surreptitiously closing in, lingering, listening. Lord Oaks, aware, ushered the inspector towards the entrance, leaving the eavesdroppers behind.

"We're doing our best," he said. "I thought I'd take an hour off and have a look round here. I'm impressed by the children's entries," he said, tentatively playing a wild card, thinking at least the noble lord might be more open in his replies than others. "Particularly by the vegetable pig. Made by a little chap of eight. Bobby Wake. Did you see it? It got first prize."

"My gardener's boy," replied Lord Oaks, innocently supplying an answer. "D'you know, my father had ten gardeners. I've got one full time, one half. We work our fingers to the bone trying to keep things tidy. It's all we can hope to do, these days."

A gardener's son, Paton thought, unfeelingly discarding his lordship's troubles, and the son of a solicitor. What was the connection? He had heard talk of the school run, young wives with large cars collecting up the privileged children and taking them to Castle Manton each morning. A gardener's son was unlikely to be included, but it was possible, he felt, that all the little boys in the village knew one another, regardless of background.

"He's a bright little chap, Bobby Wake," commented his lordship amiably, "and he has the voice of an angel. Sang solo in the carol service last Christmas. That's him over there."

Paton looked and saw a beautiful little boy with a head of pale golden curls. "Looks like an angel, too," he said.

"They're a good-looking family."

Anthony Rowsell, strolling towards the entrance with his daughter, saw the inspector talking to Lord Oaks and turned back. Jane tugged at his hand. "I want to go into the big tent, Daddy."

"Just a minute, darling." The last person Anthony wanted to confront was Detective Chief Inspector Paton. "Wouldn't you like to throw a hoop first?" He urged her towards a trestle table laden with prizes. "Let's see if you can win one of these." She turned reluctantly to look at an array of objects of doubtful attraction to a child. Lucozade. Tomato soup. A nutmeg grater. Patrick Henry, who was running the hoop stall and who lived in Pieman's Lane not a hundred yards from the Greys moved close to Anthony as he handed the hoops over, "Just heard a rumour it was a burglar. Broke down the Grey's fence on his way out. Damn close to home!"

"Best not to listen to rumours." Anthony turned away, handing the hoops to the child. "Try and win something for Mummy, Jane."

"Watch me."

Susan came towards them, carrying Matthew. "I won!" cried Jane, jumping excitedly up and down. "Here's Mummy. Look Mummy, I threw a hoop over a bottle of Rybena. It's for you."

Susan said gravely, "I'm not sure Mummies drink Rybena. You shall have it, darling."

"Come into the tent now. Please come into the tent." Clutching the bottle, Jane tugged at her father's hand.

"Yes," agreed Susan, equally gravely, not looking at her husband. She had scarcely looked at him since their confrontation in the wake of the inspector's visit. "Let's go into the tent and see who has won what."

Sammy Smeed materialised before them in a clean T-shirt and stone-washed jeans. "Hello, Mr Rowsell," he beamed. "I told the inspector I didn't see you on Thursday night." He gyrated directly in Anthony's path, as though he were a puppy waiting for a pat on the head. Anthony closed his eyes. "I told him I didn't see Hunter or Bobby, either," Sammy added virtuously.

"What's that?" Susan was alert, hostile, curious. Her eyes went from Sammy's face to Anthony's, and back to Sammy. "What's that you're saying?"

Anthony grasped her arm and unceremoniously turned her round. "Come on. Let's go into the tent."

Paton, wandering through the crowd, spied Sammy Smeed now standing alone, grinning euphorically, following the departing Rowsell family with his eyes. "Hello, Sam."

The grin faded and Sammy said defensively, "I ain't done nuffin'."

"I didn't suppose you had. I thought you might be able to help me. I was wondering if you knew Bobby Wake and Hunter Ashenden."

Sammy looked confused. "Course I know them. Why d'you think I don't?"

The inspector continued encouragingly, "Did you see them on Thursday night?" The boy edged away, grinning. "Come on, Sam, you can tell me." Sammy moved another step away. "Were they the boys who taught the parrot to swear?"

"Nah. Course they didn't."

"What were they up to on Thursday night, lad?" He made a wild guess. "Had they skipped choir practice?"

Sammy giggled.

Keeping it casual, Paton said, "All little boys get up to tricks. Why wouldn't they skip choir practice?"

Sammy, guffawed, slapped his hand over his mouth and took to his heels.

Paton decided he was wasting his time. Was that Mrs Ashenden carrying the baby? Yes, it was. He hurried and caught up with her as she paused at one of the leaf-shaded tea tables.

"Mind if I join you?" he asked, pulling out a slatted wooden chair for her.

"Not at all, Inspector. Do."

He took the chair opposite. She settled the child on her knee. "I had to abandon the push chair," she said. "A wheel came off half way up the drive. This baby is a terrible weight and I can't find my husband. I thought if I sat here he might find me."

"Your au pair? What happened to her?" He wondered if she knew about the fracas in the pub.

Marigold said, "She left. Ran away. But she's here, in the village. A neighbour telephoned late last night to say she had taken her in."

"What's going to happen to her?"

"I don't know." She looked down at the child. "I can't have her back. I couldn't take the risk."

A lively teenage girl wearing a frilly apron over a print dress came forward, smiling. "Can I get you some tea, Mrs Ashenden?"

"Would you, dear, I'd be so grateful. I'm exhausted."

"Where's Emma? Can't she carry the baby?"

"She's having a day off. Lydia, dear, I think this gentleman would like a cup, too, wouldn't you, Mr Paton?"

He nodded. "But I can get it. There appears to be self-service." He nodded towards the queue by the trestle table.

"No, really," insisted the girl, "I've been recruited as waitress specially to look after mothers with babies. I'll get your tea at the same time. Scones, cakes?"

"How wise of me to choose a mother and baby to sit with. Cakes and scones, thanks."

"That's Lord Oaks' granddaughter," said Marigold, as the girl hurried away. "Isn't she pretty?"

"She is indeed." He felt she was trying to change the subject. "To revert to Emma, Mrs Ashenden. One is innocent until proved guilty."

"I'm sorry, Inspector, but I can't have her back. I am sorry, I really am."

"Do you know if she's trained for anything else?"

"I believe not." Marigold added swiftly, sounding upset, "But how would I know? There were things she didn't tell us. You know that."

The child Lydia returned carrying a tray. "Here you are. Two teas, four scones, and two bits of cake. That will be two pounds, please."

Paton gallantly put his hand in his pocket. The tables round them were filling up. As Lydia moved away he said, "I believe your son Hunter sings in the church choir."

She nodded, sipping her tea.

"Did he know Beryl Lisamore?"

"Come, come, Inspector." Marigold's voice was sharp.

"I believe he was out on Thursday evening."

"Yes, at choir practice."

"What time did he come home?"

"Rather late," Marigold replied, remembering. "About nine. They're supposed to finish at eight, but they seem always to be late when the vicar takes them. I meant to speak to him last week but I was upstairs when they arrived and Hal met them. The vicar has been doubling as choirmaster while John Tewkes, whose job it is, has a hip operation. But we're wandering off the track," she said. "You want to know about Beryl. All right, it's common knowledge in the village that she blamed Hunter and another little boy for teaching her parrot to swear. As if they're ever free to do so! Hunter is driven to and from school. After school, and in the hols, I always know where he is. One has to, these days, there are so many peculiar people around. One simply dare not let them roam as we used to as children."

"Bobby Wake? Is he the other one Miss Lisamore accused?"

Marigold's blue eyes were large and pleading, "I do hope, Inspector, that you're not going to involve these children."

"I hope I won't have to." He finished his delicious scone, licked the cream off his fingers, and rose. "I'd better be on my way. Enjoy your tea."

Sergeant Donovan was standing alone outside the marquee, looking in. "Find out who the children are who sing in the church choir, Sergeant," Paton said. "Don't bother about young Ashenden. I know about him. Get the names of the others, and find out what time they arrived home on Thursday evening." If there was a discrepancy in time, if Bobby and Hunter reached home later than the others, then they had been up to something. He could not imagine where this trail was leading. In one part of his mind he felt he was going up a blind alley, in another part he wondered if there was a thread that tied in, however incongruously, with the murdered woman.

There had to be a reason for those two names being on the computer disk. Donovan would find out. Though he was a bachelor, he had a way with children.

Chapter 24

Down by the lake Lisa, arm-in-arm with her parents, looked out over the water and said, "I do see that Beryl must have gone through a kind of hell. No wonder—" They waited, but she did not immediately continue. Mollie's arm tightened within hers. After a while she said, "Some day I may want to talk about it. But I may not. Would you think I was callous if I just wanted to drop the whole thing?"

Her mother said, "There's nothing anyone can do."

"That photo," said Lisa, looking out over the lake, "I don't believe it is my father. I think I imagined the resemblance."

Molly put "Yes," carefully into the silence. They walked down to the edge of the lake then turned, surveying the crowd.

After a while Lisa said, "I've got news. I've decided to learn to swim."

"I don't believe I'm hearing this," said her father, looking amazed.

Her mother recovered first. "I am so pleased, dear. And what brought about this momentous decision?"

"I've found out that the reason I'm scared of water is because I remember, at soul level, something awful that happened in my past life." She glanced at them under her lashes, first one then the other.

"At what level?"

"According to this white witch who lives in Old Wood Lane, near Wayside," said Lisa solemnly, "one of my sins in a past life was to leave you to drown. So the next time I came on earth I had to make amends. So I was sent back as your daughter. That's why Beryl didn't keep me. I had this job to do with you."

"Oh."

"You couldn't swim, you see." She nudged her mother in the ribs. "You should have learnt to swim, shouldn't you."

"I expect one didn't, in those days." Molly smiled. "When was it, dear? I don't think ladies swam much before this century."

Lisa considered. "It was in the First World War," she decided. "I was a Nightingale nurse, and you were a wounded soldier coming home from the Dardenelles. The ship was sunk by a German U-boat." Her voice gathered speed and her eyes lit up. She gestured with her hands. "I rushed out on deck. It was dead of night. They filled up a lifeboat with wounded soldiers. You were a wounded soldier, Mum. The last in the queue. So, I thought they would need a nurse in their boat. All those wounded chaps, and no one to look after them!"

Her father joined in, "I was limping along in front with my left leg in plaster. You had your first-aid kit in a waterproof packet on a cord round your neck."

"That's right. So, you being the last, Mum, I pushed you aside – sorry, sorry," Lisa acting penitent, planted a kiss on Molly's cheek. "I took your place. As the lifeboat hit the water, the ship went down, and you with it."

"The lifeboat was sucked under with the ship. That's what happens, you know, if a small boat hasn't time to get clear. We were all drowned."

"Daddy! You weren't there," Lisa scolded. "And you're ruining my story. The lifeboat got away."

"A miracle?"

"Yes. And I saved the lives of five of those soldiers. We were three days in the life boat."

Her father clapped his hands, applauding her. "Great. You got a medal from the Queen – King, sorry. George

V, wasn't it? And you went to Buckingham Palace with a feather in your hat. What a hat!"

Lisa slapped his hand gently. "Daddy, Daddy, Daddy!" She rubbed her chin against his shoulder, feline and loving, then squeezed her mother's arm and whispered, "Sorry I've been so foul, Mum. I'll make it up to you."

Her father hugged her. "That's my Lisa. All over now?"

Molly said placidly, "Fancy that. Well, I'm very glad you've got it sorted out, darling. You look lovely in a bikini."

Lisa looked up solemnly into her father's face. "What do you make of it, Daddy, this atonement of souls?"

"Oh, I'm all for it. All for it, ducky."

"It looks like you've got to put up with me while I work out my karma."

"No problem." The laughter went. His eyes were smarting and there was a disconcerting lump in his throat. "There are spin-offs to being related to a film star," he said. "Free cinema tickets. Previews with champers. Lots of fun. We'd probably put up with you though, even if you weren't a film star."

"Cross your heart?"

"Cross my heart." He chuckled. "And your mother's, too."

Lisa giggled. "It was quite an experience, meeting that white witch. Come and have an ice cream. My treat."

Romy, biting into the scone Paton had left, said, "I'm asking you seriously, Marigold, to take Emma back. And you know I wouldn't if she was guilty."

"How can you possibly know?" Marigold scoffed.

"My crystals tell me."

"Oh Romy! You and your crystals!"

"Smile if you must, but they produce answers. Didn't my crystals tell you how to cure India's asthma?"

"And Helen Tate's grandmother told me how to cure my varicose ulcer," retorted Marigold, sipping her tea.

"Now, now, this is no joking matter. It's your Christian duty to do right by that girl."

"Don't ask me to expose my darling children to risks. I will not do it, Romy."

"She's not into killing babies. She's not violent."

"I'd consider her violent if she pulled my hair out," said Marigold slyly.

Lord Oaks' granddaughter intervened. "D'you want a cup of tea, Romy? I've run out of mothers and babies so I'm waiting on everyone."

"That's nice of you, dear. Nothing to eat." Lydia ran back to the tea tent, long hair swinging. Romy turned to Marigold. "Ah! So you heard about that. It was not the reaction of a guilty person. If she had been guilty she'd have slunk away. Found somewhere to hide. Emma's pulling the woman's hair was an act of sheer frustration. She had left her troubles on the other side of the world. Now this wretch turns up and spills the beans. It was an 'Oh no! I can't believe it!' reaction. Believe me, Marigold, I know a lot about human behaviour."

The pretty waitress brought Romy's tea. "Thanks, love."

"Appearing in church and collecting for the Lifeboat Appeal goes for nothing if the next moment you're turning an unfortunate child out on the street," said the white witch.

Marigold's arms tightened round the baby. "Don't make me feel any worse than I feel now," she begged. "I'm glad there are people like you in the world. Thank you for taking her in. I mean that most sincerely. I am grateful."

Romy finished her tea and prepared to rise from her chair. "I'm offering you redemption," she said.

Marigold ignored her.

Romy pushed her chair in. "I'll be on my way." She leaned forward and said in a low voice, "Just a word of warning, Marigold. If you wilfully treat an innocent person as guilty you weaken your karma and lower your resistance to evil forces."

"Don't put a spell on us, Romy." Marigold's voice was sharp through her laughter. "If you want to take Emma in and find her another job, it's up to you, and it's your responsibility. My responsibility is to my children. I will not expose them to known risks. Tell Emma she can come and pick up her things tomorrow."

"I don't need to."

"What d'you mean, you don't need to?" Marigold frowned.

"I don't need to put a spell on you," said Romy who heard only what she wished to hear. "The forces of nature know how to equalise things. They don't need any help from me."

Marigold watched the white witch's back as she strolled across the lawn, swinging her hips, the flamboyant red and black of her clothes and her mane of dark hair conspicuous among the pastels. Then she disappeared. Marigold shivered, picked up a scone, hesitated, then put it back on the plate.

Sergeant Donovan spied the inspector standing alone. "Eight o'clock," he said. "Choir practice finishes at eight. There's one, the little Wake boy, who wouldn't talk. And he looked guilty as hell."

Paton said with satisfaction, "We have to find out what young Ashenden and young Wake were doing between eight and nine."

"What's on your mind, sir?"

The inspector shrugged. "A red herring, I dare say. But I'll talk to the Ashenden's, all the same."

"There are plenty of them swimming around." Shoals, bloody shoals, Donovan said to himself as he wandered off. He thought personally that his superior was wasting his time. He knew damn well who did the murder. Rowsell, or, as an outsider, Paul Street. But the inspector was like that. On every case when they had been together, he had gone for what he began by calling a red herring. The elimination process, he called it. Get rid of the trees and then you can see the wood, he would say. Donovan knew that to be back to front but had not dared to question him. Ah well! He looked up at the sun, feeling it warm on his face. This wasn't a bad way to fill in an afternoon. He wished he hadn't lost his comic.

Paton stationed himself where he could see at a glance if the rest of the Ashenden family came to join the mother. The dark complexioned woman who had taken his place at the table had gone on her way. A few minutes later Hal Ashenden, accompanied by the two older children, emerged from the marquee. The family found extra chairs and they sat down together. Paton went across.

"No, no," he said as the father rose and offered his chair. "I'm not staying." He looked across at the eldest child. He had scarcely taken note of the children in the turmoil of the night before. Now he saw they were a good-looking bunch. Hunter was particularly beautiful, though a trifle girlish, with large blue eyes and soft brown hair curling round his ears. "You're Hunter," he said. The boy nodded.

"And this is India," said Marigold, determined not to recognise his special interest. "Bernie the baby you have already met."

Paton addressed the elder boy genially, "I believe you've got a good voice, Hunter."

The boy smiled bashfully and looked at his mother.

"He sings in the church choir," said Hal.

"Do you mind if I ask him a question?"

Marigold looked annoyed. Hal looked momentarily uncertain, then nodded.

"You can ask me a question," offered India.

Paton smiled at her. "Your turn next time." He addressed the boy, "When the others left choir practice last Thursday evening, where did you and Bobby Wake go?"

Hunter answered straightforwardly, "Nowhere."

"It seems the others arrived home at ten past eight. You were much later."

The child leaned towards his mother, his blue eyes vague. "I didn't go anywhere."

"But darling," protested Marigold, looking distressed, "you didn't come home. You weren't home until nine."

The boy sidled behind his mother's chair, head lowered, and stood kicking the wooden leg. She looked up at Paton with worried eyes. Hunter put his arms round her neck and hid his face in her shoulder. She took his hand and drew him gently round to face her. "Darling, you must tell the inspector what you did between choir practice and coming home. It's important." She put two fingers beneath his chin and lifted his face.

"He doesn't want to tell you," said India. "I'll tell you what I was doing."

"Hush, dear."

"Nothing," muttered the boy.

Marigold asked in a shocked voice, "You surely weren't down at Miss Lisamore's talking to her parrot!"

"No," retorted the child, coming violently to life. "She's a liar. I never talked to her parrot."

"You're not supposed to say liar. You have to say untroofs," the irrepressible India admonished him.

"Please, dear, we're talking to Hunter."

They all looked at the boy. Hal asked, "What were you doing, son?"

There was a long silence. Hunter again sidled round the back of his mother's chair and put his arms round her neck. She signed to her husband to relieve her of the baby. "Whisper," she said, giving her full attention to the boy. "Whisper in my ear."

They waited, in silence.

Marigold stood up. "We're going off to have a little talk," she said. They watched with varying degrees of apprehension while mother and son crossed the lawn hand-in-hand.

"Do sit down," said Hal to Paton, indicating his wife's vacant chair.

"Thanks. I'll come back later." He rose and wandered back towards the marquee.

Sergeant Donovan accosted him outside. "That's Mrs Tate from Spring House over there," he said, indicating by a nod a slim, dark-haired woman with one child in a push-chair and two older children standing by. "She's the one who's been lying about where she was on Thursday night."

Paton looked across at Helen with narrowed eyes. Slim, upright, finely boned, prettily dressed. Not the type to sneak out and strangle the local schoolmistress, he thought whimsically. "All right. I'll speak to her. You go back to the cottage. I'll come as soon as I've dealt with this business of the boys."

"What about Trent and Farlow? They're wandering round somewhere."

"Leave them." He went off round the lake, admiring the silver birches, the graceful willows, the banks of dark green rhododendrons, imagining them flaring with colour in the spring. He had a feeling his wife would fit in here, baking cakes, making jam, chatting with the local grandees. He wondered if he could work from a country village. He'd always told her adamantly he had to live in London. He resolved to think about it when he had the time. He crossed a little stone bridge, and then another, stood watching while a gaggle of geese took off, honking and cackling, to disappear beyond the trees. Then he went back to find out what Hunter Ashenden had been up to between eight and nine on Thursday evening.

The table was deserted.

Chapter 25

Paton rubbed his chin and looked up at the parrot from the depths of the lumpy sofa. "You're the bugger that knows," he growled. Quixote lifted a leisurely claw and scratched behind his ear. Donovan grinned. The inspector staggered to his feet and looked back at the sofa with dislike. "Stop me sitting in that damn thing. That's an order." He crossed to the telephone, intending to ring his wife, dreading having to say he was going to be late again.

"I'll try, sir, but I'm not experienced at ordering round detective chief inspectors."

Paton gave him a sharp look. He wasn't sure he liked his sergeant being funny. Not, anyway, in his present mood of frustration. He was annoyed with the Ashendens for going off without a word when they knew damn well he was waiting to hear what they had found out from the boy. He was also disturbed. What if young Hunter did hold the key to the murder? What would a father do, in these circumstances?

Disappear with him? Ashenden was a solicitor. He knew the law. But Paton knew people, knew how illogical they could be under stress.

How could a child of eight be involved in a murder?

He stared at the telephone, not thinking of Barbara, only of Ashenden. He, or his wife, could be at Gatwick in half an hour and on the first plane that had spare seats. He was letting his imagination run amok. No, he wasn't. In his job he had seen odder things happen.

Kelly Donovan wandered over to the cage. "I'm going to like having you living with me," he said to the parrot. Quixote turned a full circle on his perch, moving his claws delicately and with precision, then settled down again.

Paton picked up the handpiece and dialled. He counted ten rings then replaced the receiver and turned to face the room, thumbs in his trousers pockets, chin stuck out, frowning. "Thinking of getting married, Sergeant?"

"No. I'll be quite happy with this old Quixote. He won't expect me back for meals."

"I'm sure you're wise." Paton also went to stand by the cage, looking down at the bird.

"You're not going to let that brother of hers have him, are you?" Donovan was anxious.

"I don't think he was serious. Couldn't be, with that pious wife. She made it clear she wouldn't have a dirty-minded parrot in the house."

"This chap is valuable."

"Yeah. That's probably it. He's a greedy bastard. That we know."

Donovan extended a finger and held it close to the wire. "I'd like to stroke him. You don't suppose he'd take my finger off, do you?"

"Don't!" shrieked Quixote.

The two men froze. Quixote walked the length of his perch and back.

"Miss Lisamore wouldn't be likely to teach him to shout 'Don't', would she?" asked Donovan, the first to find his voice.

Paton shook his head thoughtfully. "I wouldn't think so."

"Could I take him home with me tonight, sir? He might come up with something more."

"Yeah. You take him home." The inspector looked at his watch. Even if the Ashendens had returned to the show for the prizegiving they should be back by now. "I'm going along to Park View. Stick around till I get back."

Halfway along Old Wood Lane Marigold Ashenden's Rover pulled up outside Cobblers. Marigold jumped out, ran up the path and rang the bell. Emma came to the door. Marigold looked at her with tears in her eyes. "Emma, dear, I've come to take you back."

Emma backed away. "You're a little late," she said ungraciously. "I've already had a message that I should come and collect my things."

"Please, Emma. Please." Marigold reached out and took the girl's hands in hers. Romy came forward, her fingers on the crystal at her throat. Marigold looked at her with open dislike, then her eyes slid away. Speaking directly to Emma she said, "You were upset last night, dear. It was better that you should stay away. None of us was responsible, really. I'm sorry for what happened. Please come with me now."

Emma turned to Romy for support.

Marigold let go of her hands, turned abruptly on her heel, and went back to the car. "I'll wait for you," she said.

"What did you mean when you said I have to go back for their sakes?" asked Emma of her hostess.

Romy smiled gently, indicating the door. "Go with the flow," she said.

It wasn't far up the high street to the imposing Queen Anne house. Paton walked, hands in his pockets, head down, passing groups of chattering locals who fell silent as he approached. Cyclists pedalled slowly past carrying exhibits in baskets attached to their handlebars. Ahead, cars were still turning out into the high street from the Crumford Place drive. As he opened the little wrought-iron gate of Park View and went up the path a car entered the drive and glancing up he was surprised to see Marigold Ashenden at the wheel with Emma, her erstwhile au pair in the passenger seat. They were both looking ahead, deliberately ignoring him.

Puzzled, he moved across the tiny pebbled forecourt and looking down the drive saw Emma slip out of the passenger seat and open the door leading to the stable block. The car disappeared inside and the girl followed. He waited a moment, long enough for Marigold to lock up and emerge. When neither appeared he turned uncertainly towards the front door, and it was then he saw a piece of white paper sellotaped to the brass knocker. He could see his name printed on it in large letters: Detective Chief Inspector Paton. With a feeling of foreboding he jerked it free and unfolded the single sheet.

> Dear Mr Paton. There is nothing we can tell you that would be of any help in solving the mystery of Miss Lisamore's murder. If you are not satisfied, then see the vicar. His name is Cecil Penn. The vicarage is next door to the church, nearly opposite the entrance to Pieman's Lane.

The note was signed, HA.

Paton pushed it into his pocket and went back down the path. As he crossed the drive he saw the two women emerge and keeping their backs turned, close the door. Puzzled, he continued on his way up the high street, past Spring House, home of the innocent-looking Mrs Tate who lacked an alibi, past The Fox and Hounds and the mock Tudor estate dwellings with their treeless gardens whimsically named Plane Cottage, Sycamore and Oak. At the edge of the green he paused, looking across to the cricket club where men in white were pulling up stumps and getting into their cars, an indication that the all-important horticultural show nonetheless did not take precedence over cricket.

The vicarage was Georgian, an elegant building built of mellow red brick contrasting oddly with the ancient grey stone of the Norman church that stood next door. Paton went up the drive. Ahead lay an ugly modern garage built in front of the original coach-houses that had been converted into two cottages fronting on to and sharing the vicarage drive. The doors of the garage were propped open and an old Rover was parked in front, the lid of its boot raised. Two suitcases and a wooden box stood on the gravel. As Paton headed towards the front door a small woman with straight dark hair, smooth as a cap, and wearing a floppy beige cardigan over a beige dress came running out from behind the garage and headed for the box. Paton turned back.

She heard his footsteps and looked up. "Oh!" she said, and stopped dead. "It's you." Then she added, her expression showing a mixture of hostility and triumph, "That didn't take you long."

"Let me do this." Paton bent down and raising the box with some difficulty, placed it in the boot. "You shouldn't be attempting to lift such a heavy weight," he admonished her.

"I had no choice." She sounded angry. "Thank you, anyway."

He indicated the cases standing on the ground. "Can I put these in for you, too?"

"I'd be grateful." She stood aside while he fitted them in with the box. "Are you Mrs Penn?" he asked.

"It's the vicar you want," she said. "I've got nothing to do with this. Nothing whatsoever. I knew nothing about it until Hal Ashenden appeared."

"Mrs Penn—" He uncertainly assumed she must be the vicar's wife.

"I don't need to talk to you," she broke in. "I'm leaving, as you see." She ran a hand distractedly across her forehead. "You'll find him in the front room on the right. The door's open. Go right in. Don't bother to ring."

"Mrs Penn—" But she had slipped into the driving seat and slammed the door. He stepped back swiftly as she started the engine and began to reverse fast down the drive. Concerned for her safety, he hurried out into the road and signalled that all was clear. Without a glance in his direction she swung the car round and made off along the Castle Manton road.

He stood on the pavement as the car raced on its way, scratching his head, frowning. What the hell was going on! She couldn't be the vicar's wife. Maybe she was the housekeeper, walking out in a huff. He went back up the drive and paused halfway, eying the empty, single-car garage while readjusting his thoughts. She must be the vicar's wife. That must be his car, for there was no accommodation for a second one. He went to the front door and stood looking at the bell, remembering her instruction to walk in, feeling uncomfortable about taking her at her word.

He peered round the door. A rather beautiful staircase covered with shabby carpet ran to the upper floor. There were several dark Victorian portraits on walls stained here and there with damp. The only piece of furniture was an antique table on which stood a telephone, and across which was spread a shambles of papers. He stepped over the threshold. The door on the right, the woman had said, would be open. He crossed to it and stood looking in.

Mud-coloured curtains, dark panelled wood, a threadbare Turkey carpet, shabby chairs and a tortoiseshell cat curled up in the corner of the sofa. There were books on the wide mantelpiece and more dark portraits on the walls. It was a moment before he realised there was a man crouched in a chair between a tall bookcase and the window. Paton cleared his throat and the man looked up. His right eye was barely visible through a slit in bruised flesh. His upper lip was split and a trickle of blood had congealed on his chin. Appalled, the chief inspector hurried forward.

The damaged face was plump and very pale, the hair around it fine, fair, and thinning towards the crown. "He certainly didn't waste any time getting to you. You've come to arrest me, I suppose," Cecil Penn the vicar said. "Well," he added, pathetically defiant, "I'm not guilty."

"Who? Who didn't waste time?" Even as he spoke Paton's mind had gone into overdrive. He remembered the pretty boys, Hunter and Bobby, who had been late home when the vicar took choir practice. Jes-us! Was this Hal Ashenden's work?

The vicar tenderly patted his bleeding lip, then with his handkerchief indicated the sofa. Paton was glad to sit down. "Beryl Lisamore," he said, battling to keep censure and distaste out of his voice. "I'm investigating the murder. That's what I'm here for. What had the boys to do with her?"

Penn sank deeper into the big chair. "She came sneaking around the church one night after choir practice," he said resentfully. "Said she wanted to remove the dead flowers on the altar. She's – was – on the flowerarranging roster. The boys were there. That's what the parrot's swearing was about."

Paton said, "Would you mind taking your handkerchief away from your mouth so that I can hear what you're saying?" The cat, taking fright at his tone, leapt off the sofa and streaked out of the room.

Penn obeyed. The blood began once again to trickle over his lip.

God! What a mess! Paton could almost, but not quite, feel sympathy for him. "Could we start at the beginning? What's this about the parrot?"

"She said the boys taught the parrot to swear."

"Yes. But why?"

"Well, I don't know," Penn said resentfully, "I suppose she thought people would watch out for them and trace . . ." He broke off, put a finger to his lip, stared at the blood, and covered his mouth once again with the handkerchief.

"So you murdered her?"

"I did not." The hunched figure jerked untidily upright, glaring horribly through the swollen flesh. "You're not going to pin that on me as well. I didn't have anything to do with the murder. Nothing. Absolutely nothing."

Paton hadn't thought he had, but there had been sour satisfaction in asking. He rose, wanting to get out of the house and into the clean fresh air. "Paederasty is an actionable offence, as you well know," he said.

"It's my word against theirs," Penn muttered through his bloodied handkerchief. "Anyway," he added with another effort at defiance, "the boys are too young to give evidence."

"In the circumstances that I'm investigating the murder it's not my domain," Paton replied, "but I shall have to report you. I assume you won't be leaving the village. The parents may wish to lay charges."

The vicar gave a mirthless laugh that came from his throat and did not touch his torn and swollen lips. "Don't worry. I haven't the means to go far. My wife's left, taking my car."

The chief inspector did not offer sympathy.

Walking back down the high street he felt he had had a long day. And yet, he was not ready to go home.

He paused outside Spring House where the Tates lived. Better find out why this woman didn't have an alibi.

Geoff Tate, who had been standing at the front window brooding, saw Paton come down the street. He went into the hall, picked up a piece of paper from the table, wrote something on it and met him at the door.

Before the inspector could open his mouth, he said, "You've come to check my wife's alibi. She was at this address on the night in question." Paton looked down at the paper and read, "Hamberly, Sentry Park, Pinmartin". He raised his head. Geoff Tate was looking at him with angry eyes. "Pinmartin is about five miles the other side of Castle Manton. The staff will confirm it."

The door began to close. Paton felt certain as he walked

back down the street that whatever they found out about Mrs Tate's movements on the night in question, it would prove to be none of their business. He regretted that he was obliged to send Ellis to check.

Chapter 26

Halfpenny Dun had settled back into its normal stride. The marquee was being dismantled, the children were at school and a supply teacher had been brought in to take Beryl Lisamore's place. Bert Oswhistle had done a masterly repair on Denise Ellis' washing machine and she was urging everyone not to pay these company sharks who wanted a small fortune just for stepping over the doorstep, but merely to call in Bert.

This morning the girl assistant at Anthony Rowsell Antiques in Castle Manton had opened the shop. At The Cedars Susan was re-packing her bags for a return to Buckinghamshire and he was sitting on their bed desperately trying to dissuade her from going.

"Just tell everyone Daddy's taken a turn for the worse," she said, "and I've had to rush back. I'm sure you'll easily make them believe you." She added, cruel to cover her hurt, "One thing you're really good at is lying."

Anthony told himself he had not known she had this iron in her soul, but he had.

"What made you think you could whore around with the neighbours' wives and hold on to my affections and loyalty?"

"One neighbour's wife, Susan," he beseeched her, "and I've said over and over again that I'm sorry."

"I suppose you've always lied to me."

He tried the old-fashioned approach, "If you loved me—" but she broke in scornfully.

"I'd forgive you a few male peccadilloes? Wake up,

Anthony. This is 1992. Women have rights. I don't have to forgive you anything, just on account of your being a man. I can cast you out, just as women have been cast out, all through history, for adultery. The bible," said Susan with evident satisfaction, "is now out of date." She folded a silky blue nightdress and laid it on top of a pile of delicate underwear in the suitcase. Anthony followed her movements with his eyes, suffering.

"Forsaking all others," she said fiercely. "That's what you promised in church. You forsook that poor Beryl Lisamore, all right. She didn't have as much potential as me, did she? Did you kill her because she threatened to tell me what you were up to?"

He lifted his haggard face. "Susie, how could you!"

"I could because of what you've done. Because we had a wonderful marriage and you've ruined it." She stood back from her side of the bed, a diminutive, utterly desirable woman in a blue blouse with her curls tied on top of her head, knuckles on her slender, jean-clad hips, and spat like a cat, "I idolised you, did you know that? I thought – I didn't think you were perfect – but you were perfect for me. I don't give a damn if you killed Beryl," shouted Susan with tears running down her face. "It's not as important to me as what you've done to our marriage. D'you know what I can see all the time? That Letitia Grey flat on her back with her legs in the air and you panting all over her. That's all I can see," howled his wife, searching desperately in her sleeves, her bosom and her pockets, then tugging at the hem of her blouse and using it to mop her eyes. "I'll take that picture to my grave."

Matthew came running in with the dog and stopped, little face lifted, staring. "Why you crying, Mummy?" She snatched him up and hugged him fiercely, filling him with the love that her hurt pride would not allow her to give to her husband.

"We're going back to stay with Grandad," she said, speaking into his soft little shoulder, choking.

"I want to take Ginger and Fluffy."

"We can take Ginger this time, but cats like to stay in their own houses."

"I want to stay in my own house." Matthew struggled out of her arms and ran out to the landing with the dog barking at his heels.

"Don't," pleaded Anthony, his face drawn with distress. "Don't take them away again."

"Just because you're their father that doesn't mean you're a suitable person to look after them," she retorted, fierce again. "Why don't you go to work? You're only upsetting me by staying here." He rose, went round the foot of the bed, and tried to kiss her, but she pushed him away. "Don't bother," she said, dismissing him.

She stood at the window watching the Ferrari as it left the drive and crawled along the slip road at the side of the green. She waited until it turned the corner into the high street and sped off towards Castle Manton, then with tears streaming down her face she closed the suitcase, carried it downstairs, picked up the keys of the BMW and went to the converted stable block behind the house where cars and garden implements were kept. When her tears had stopped and she could see properly, she brought the car up level with the house.

There was a big Volvo pulling in directly across the drive, blocking her. She stepped out, shut the car door, and stood absolutely still, waiting. "You've got a nerve," she said as Letitia approached.

"I suppose you could say that," Letitia agreed tolerantly, looking glum. "Can we go inside and have a little talk?"

"There's no point," snapped Susan. "Besides, I really don't want to talk to you."

"We've got to live together," Letitia pointed out. "Come on, Sue, let's have a coffee and talk it over." She bent down and lifted the bag. "You're not going anywhere." Carting the luggage with her, she led the way across the lawn towards the front door.

Susan stayed where she was.

"Come *on*," said Letitia impatiently, turning at the door. "Come on."

Susan put the keys in her pocket, passed Letitia in the hall as she paused to put the bag down, and went into the kitchen, head high, curls bobbing. "I can't imagine," she said, reaching with a kind of violence for the electric kettle, "what you think this will achieve."

Letitia pulled out a chair and sat down at the kitchen table. "We're two grown women, Sue, and we've been friends for a long time. I'm sorry for what I did. God, how sorry! Of course I shouldn't have done it. I'm very, very, very sorry. Does that satisfy you?"

"No, it doesn't, as a matter of fact, since you're only sorry because you've been caught out. And what has Brian got to say?" Susan thumped two mugs down on the table.

Letitia stared down at the quarry tiles between her feet. "Men," she said philosophically, "stick it anywhere they can get in, you know that. He's in no position to object."

"Does he screw around?" Susan was defiant, but interested.

"I dare say. He's not going to tell me, is he? Honestly, Sue, this is such a little thing by comparison with – well, think of it – Bosnia, Lloyds crash, all these people being made redundant in the recession. Honestly, you're so darned privileged you don't know you're alive. We've both got smashing chaps, good looking, and successful. We're not affected by the recession. Well, maybe Anthony is a bit," she allowed, "but look what you've got. Do you want to be a pathetic little one-parent family just because that silly cow Beryl Lisamore got herself murdered?"

Susan looked stoney. "I get the impression Anthony is the number-one suspect."

Letitia went still.

"And he refused to have his fingerprints taken."

"Why?"

"Your guess."

"I mean," Letitia, trying not to show fear, asked, "Why did they want to fingerprint him? I haven't heard of anyone else—"

"That's just the point."

They stared at each other. "Well," said Letitia at last, exuding false calm, "I think he's very sensible. "I think I'd hold off, if they asked me. One would be doing them a good turn, stopping them from going up a blind alley, I mean. Besides, imagine the rumours! The village saying, 'Hsst! Did you hear, they've fingerprinted Anthony Rowsell!' Very sensible," said Letitia again, making a determined effort to convince herself.

Susan drooped against the central unit, looking distressed.

Letitia jumped up. "Where is it? Oh, I know. This cupboard." She put a jar of Nescafé down on the bench and pulled out the silver drawer, rattling the teaspoons noisily with her fingers. "Have you heard about Cecil Penn interfering with little boys?" Her light, yappy voice took over, "Hunter and the Wake boy. In the vestry, after choir practice. Sylvia's scarpered with the car and Hal's smashed Cecil's face in. Got any brown sugar? I'm on a health kick. That was something Beryl did for the village on the way out. Got the police on to Cecil. D'you think the church will stand bail?"

"You're unbelievable!"

"Sure. If you don't laugh, you cry." Letitia put her mug down on the table and dropped back into her chair.

Susan brought a bottle of milk from the frig.

"Kiss and make up?" asked Letitia, looking up winsomely as Susan slopped milk into her mug.

"Oh God! Letty, you're so – so—" Susan choked.

Letitia shrugged.

They drank their coffee in silence. Susan's intransigence had, in the end, taken the wind out of Letitia's sails. "Well,

I'll be going," she said rising from her chair. "You'll want to have a quiet little think."

"Letitia—"

She waved a hand dismissively. "Just think about things. Have a good old think." Without saying goodbye, she left by the front door, feeling spent.

Chapter 27

It was Emma who answered the bell at Park House. "Come in," said the au pair looking very much her familiar calm and stolid self. "Marigold's in the garden. Shall I call her, or—"

"Don't bother. I'll find her." Letitia hid her surprise behind a chatter of goodwill. "Nice day, Emma. It's time I got on to some gardening, too." She went out of the door at the back of the hall and continued across the lawn to where Marigold, dressed in dirty jeans with her hair tied back, was standing in the bright morning sunshine raking slime out of the lily pond.

"Hello, Letty." She smiled wanly, leaning on the rake. They stood side-by-side looking down into the water.

"What's happened to the fish?"

"A heron got them. On Saturday. Saturday was not a good day."

"What a weekend!"

Marigold pushed her rake into the water and straightened a basket of waterlilies that had slipped sideways.

Letitia said, tentatively, "There's a rumour running amok that Anthony did it." She waited, breath held, to see how Marigold was going to react. Marigold simply stared at her. She began to tremble. When she spoke again it was in a panicky rush, her head full of the implications of Anthony's guilt, "I've been up to see Sue. To show support. To stop her running away. We've got to stand together."

"Yes."

"Sylvia's scarpered."

Marigold said, her face working, "Hal made a terrible mess of Cecil."

"Yes, well . . . why not?"

"I went up to see him this morning."

"How bloody Christian of you."

Marigold looked weary. "How could I not? Afterwards, I went to see old Doc Wykham and asked him to call. Cecil wouldn't have anyone from the practice. Absolutely refused. I felt he'd rather die than face them. The old Doc remembered Cecil borrowed a spade from him ages ago, just after he retired. He's going to use it as an excuse. He's going to drop in casually and ask for it back. He'll be able to see if the damage needs medical attention."

Letitia said, dryly, "Okay, I'll recommend you for sainthood."

Marigold's weary calm went and her face began to work, the muscles pulling, out of control. "It wasn't saintly. I actually wanted to see the damage. I—" She could not go on.

"Ah, yes. Yes, I understand."

Marigold recovered herself and said fiercely, "What do you think it's done to Hunter? Turned him into a queer? Started him masturbating? I can tell you, I didn't feel much like a saint when I looked at Cecil. Do you know what I thought, seeing all that blood and the bruises – you should have seen his face, Letty – I thought, good. I'm glad Sylvia's left him. I'm glad Hal's done this. I'll be very glad if he goes to jail and gets drummed out of the church. I thought, good, good, good." Marigold dropped the rake and began to cry.

Letitia did not feel like comforting her. All her strength had gone into the confrontation at The Cedars. Now, in the wake of Marigold's ambiguous reaction to Anthony's predicament, she was in need of comfort and reassurance herself. She went on staring into the water. "What's happened to the fish?"

"I told you," sobbed Marigold, "a heron got them. Didn't you hear me? I told you a heron got them."

Letitia felt like crying herself. "What's going to happen to Hal?" she asked bleakly. "Cecil could bring charges."

"He wouldn't dare!" Marigold wiped her face with a grubby tissue and pushed it back into the pocket of her jeans.

Letitia clasped her hands above her head, entwining her fingers, tugging, trying to loosen the knots in her shoulders. "God! What a mess! What a hornet's nest that wretched Beryl stirred up." She glanced across the lawn towards the house. "I see Emma's back."

"Yes." Letitia picked up the rake and began once again, with useless little stabbing movements, to attempt to get hold of the slime lying just below the water level. "It's not that much of a sin, causing a furore in a pub."

Letitia, who would have liked to discuss the matter, let it go.

"D' you want a coffee?"

"No, thanks. I forced one out of Susan. Go and see her, Marigold. She's got to be brought to terms with what's happening. I've stopped her from running. I think I've stopped her, but go along and do your bit. What happened to Helen?" She had remembered in the night Helen's strange telephone call on the morning of the murder when she had slammed down the receiver, feeling her privacy was being invaded. "None of her exhibits was in the show."

"The woman who caused the trouble – the hair – you know," said Marigold vaguely, "was driving out of the pub car park – her husband was driving out, and Helen – maybe she was day-dreaming, she nearly got hit, and her basket of exhibits went for a Burton. Bits all over the road. And now Geoff's left."

"What do you mean, Geoff's left?" Letitia blinked.

"He got drunk in The Fox and Dolly put him to bed. And now he's gone. So Dolly says. I mean, it's a rumour going round the village. Anyway, Dolly started it."

"But Geoff scarcely drinks at all!" Geoff and Helen were thought to have a near perfect marriage.

"Apparently he didn't scarcely drink at all on Saturday night," said Marigold ungramatically, poking at the waterlilies with her rake.

"Have you been to see Helen?"

"No."

"Why not, if you knew?" Letitia spoke sharply.

"I can't spread myself any further. That's why. And you must deal with Susan, Letty. She's your responsibility." Marigold looked at her friend with something approaching despair and began again to weep.

Letitia waited for her to calm.

"You may as well go," said Marigold wiping her blotched face with a soaked tissue. "I'm not feeling very sociable."

Letitia trailed slowly across the lawn and exited via the drive. She climbed behind the wheel of the Volvo and stared unhappily through the windscreen, looking down the deserted street. After a few moments she got out again, locked the doors, and made her way along the high street to Spring House.

June Tate, widowed mother of Geoff and mother-in-law to Helen, a neat, smart woman with delicately tinted auburn hair and a pretty face, was not normally to be seen in Halfpenny Dun on week days. She owned and managed a gift shop in Haverstocke, a town thirty miles distant, tempting those who already had everything with expensive china, crystal and a variety of beautiful and fascinating baubles. In answer to Letitia's ring she opened the door wearing an apron and looking uncharacteristically in command, for she had always been careful to take a back seat in the homes of her children.

"June!" Letitia greeted her with swiftly repressed dismay. "How nice!"

"Good morning, Letitia. What can I do for you?"

Letitia stepped into the hall.

"I – er – I came to see Helen. To apologise, actually. I owe her an apology."

"I sent her away. She's gone to her sister for a day or two. Geoffrey has been behaving very badly. I don't have to tell you that men can be difficult," said June whose late husband's reputation as a Lothario had been an ongoing embarrassment to her children and the root cause of Geoff's total fidelity in marriage. "Would you care for a sherry?"

"Thanks." Letitia apprehensively went ahead into the familiar blue drawing room and sat down in an ageing armchair decorated with an artistically slung Turkey rug. Geoff's mother crossed to a cupboard in the corner, opened the door and looked in at an array of bottles. "Dry," she said, staring at the Amontillado, which was the only sherry in evidence. "This Dolly woman at The Fox, is she discreet?"

"Not particularly. No, I'm afraid not."

"Could you shut her up?" June took out the Amontillado and stared at it critically.

"I think," said Letitia after a moment's nervous consideration, "she would probably exacerbate things by telling people that I tried to." She added, "If it's any comfort to you, her heart's in the right place."

"It's Amontillado. Sorry."

"That'll be fine. Thanks." Letitia took the glass and put it down on an occasional table by the arm of her chair.

Geoff's mother settled, very upright, in a low chair by the window, frowning. "I know what you've come about," she said looking at Letitia critically. "If you had provided Helen with an alibi a great deal of trouble would have been avoided."

Letitia recognised she was under attack and began to wish she had not come.

"She rang you on Friday."

"Yes. But—"

June waved her uncertain protest aside. "Helen," she said as though delivering a treatise, "as you will know, is a very moral woman."

"Of course. Yes. Yes, of course." Letitia felt out of her depth.

"As moral as you and me. Her marriage is as rock solid as yours. She would no more think of being unfaithful to Geoffrey than you would think of being unfaithful to your husband."

Letitia's insides jumped. She took a gulp of the sherry.

"On the other hand," went on Geoff's mother, fingering her glass, "nearly everybody of your age, indeed of mine, has committed the odd indiscretion before marriage. I mean, of course, warm-hearted people, and one would not wish one's relatives to be otherwise. But there is no need to be self-indulgent about a slip from grace."

"No. Er – No." Absurdly – she knew it was absurd to care at all – Letitia felt depressed at the thought that the perfect Helen had a past.

"What I am saying is that there is nothing to be gained by spilling the beans. It's sheer selfishness to risk rocking the boat in order to clear one's own conscience."

"Yes. Yes, I agree. Absolutely," agreed Letitia, flustered and more than ever confused.

"It's a pity," Geoff's mother said critically, "that you were unable to provide Helen with an alibi, because all this might have been so easily avoided."

"I'm sorry. I—" Letitia looked helplessly across at her hostess.

June waited, relentlessly. Letitia looked down into her glass. With a sharp sigh the older woman rose, leaving her drink untouched. "When one's children are grown up and one can no longer chastise them," she said, apparently including Letitia in her criticism, "one still has to pick up the pieces." She began to undo her apron ties. "I think

I'll go down to The Fox and see this woman. I'm quite good with people. Quite experienced." She folded the apron carefully and laid it on the back of her chair. "I don't want to push you out, my dear—"

"I'll go," said Letitia, hurriedly emptying her glass. "Look, I want to say, I'm sorry. Tell Helen I'm awfully, awfully sorry."

When she found herself out in the street she felt as though she had been swept there.

Sammy Smeed wandered through the back gate of Badger Cottage and up the path, glanced in, and failing to see Paton, entered.

"Do you always walk into other people's houses when you see an open door?" asked the chief inspector who had watched his approach.

"Only sometimes." Sammy was not sensitive to sarcasm. "I was wondering, now Miss Lisamore's dead, if I could use her computer."

Paton looked at him speculatively. "Do you know how to use a computer?"

"I used that one." Sammy nodded towards the machine.

The inspector frowned and rose from his chair. "When? When did you use it?"

"That night Miss Lisamore got murdered."

"You were here, with her?"

Sammy shook his head. "Not with her. There was only me." He added defensively, "I wouldn't've come in if the door hadn't been open. Mr Rowsell left it open."

"Rowsell?" Paton reacted sharply.

"He come out," said Sammy innocently.

Donovan, hearing voices, came from the kitchen where he had been making coffee and stood leaning against the door post.

"What time was that, Sammy?"

"Dunno."

"Did you speak to Mr Rowsell?"

At that moment Sam remembered he had promised not to tell a soul about the meeting. He clapped a hand to his treacherous mouth, then removed it in order to add, "I didn't see him. I never saw him, all night."

"I dare say he asked you not to tell anyone you had seen him," said Paton, reading Sammy like a book.

The boy nodded, and smiled uncertainly.

"So, what did he say?"

"He didn't say Miss Lisamore had been killed," said Sammy.

Both men frowned, looking for some obscure meaning in the boy's words.

"God's honour," said Sammy unhelpfully.

"Where did you meet him? In the street, or in here?"

"At the back gate. No, I didn't. I didn't see him," Sam amended in a rush.

"And you talked?" Paton led him firmly on and Sammy gave up.

"Only a bit. About the rubbish."

"What rubbish?"

"Dunno. There weren't any."

The two men exchanged glances. Paton shrugged. "So, what did you do?"

"I used the computer. The light was on," said the boy, as though the fact of the light being on made his use of the computer acceptable.

Paton went over to the table. "Come here." Sammy followed. Paton lifted the lid. "Show me what you did."

He looked down at the machine. "There's no lights," he said, disappointed.

"No, well, its not turned on. Do you know how to turn it on?"

"I could try." He was anxious to help.

"Try, then." Paton moved aside and Sammy stood in his place. He tentatively pressed one key, then another. "It's died," he said mournfully. "When I was here before there was lights, and printing on that." He pointed to the screen. Losing interest, he backed, turned, and went over to the parrot. "Hello, Quixote," he said.

An idea surfaced in Paton's brain. "The reason you can't use the machine, Sam," he said, "is because there's something missing. Come here. Come with me." He crossed the floor, took the boy's arm, led him back to the table, opened a drawer and took out a disk. "See this? If you had two of these, you could use this computer. The lights would come on."

"Honest?" The boy's eyes opened wide.

"Did you take two disks away, Sam?"

Sammy looked confused.

"What a pity you didn't," said Paton slyly, "because if you were to bring them back now you could have a lot of fun with that computer."

"I got two," said Sammy, falling for the trick.

"Right." Paton turned him briskly towards the door. "You go with the sergeant and get them." He stood with hands in his pockets looking after the two figures as they crossed the lawn. No, he said to himself, holding a rush of excitement at bay, it couldn't be as easy as that.

"Disks?" repeated Elsie Smeed moving out of the doorway to allow her son and the policeman through. "What do you mean? Disks? I never heard of no disks."

"They was in my jeans pocket and you washed them."

"I didn't see no disks in your pockets. Round things? There weren't no round things in your pockets."

"Square," supplied Donovan, "with a silver tab on the side."

"I threw them out," said Elsie, remembering.

Sammy uttered a wail of terrible distress.

"I called you to come and pick up your rubbish," she said defensively, "and when you didn't come I threw them out."

"Where's the rubbish?" asked Donovan, fearfully remembering the smelly mess in which he had finally found the photograph of Paul Street.

"Outside."

"Would you mind showing me?"

"I don't know what he's got to complain about," said Elsie, leading Donovan past the tiny kitchen and out into the sleazy little yard. "I did call 'im. 'Come and get your rubbish,' I said, but did he? It's always the same. He collects these things then forgets about them. 'Come and get your rubbish.'" Elsie Smeed dwelt morbidly on the root of her problem. "I could say it a thousand times and he wouldn't take no notice."

Donovan stood in the back doorway looking over the tiny yard and recognised with relief that this was what Sam's mother was referring to when she said "rubbish". Rampant ivy, brambles weighted with berries, broken sheets of iron, and enough miscellaneous, unidentifiable junk to fill several skips. A single spray of blue flowers rose bravely from a plumbago plant clinging to life behind a tangle of barbed wire against the far wall.

Sam distractedly kicked stones and broken bricks out of the way, all the time exuding a low-pitched, anxious whimper like that of a distressed puppy. Donovan began to search, kicking at stinging nettles and carefully parting self-sown feverfew with its yellow-centred daisies. He picked up a stick and poked it among pieces of glass, bottle tops, an old sock, some broken tiles. Hell, he thought, it could take a week to sort through this lot.

He turned to address the boy's mother, "How far did you throw them?"

Elsie Smeed extended her right arm for inspection. "I can't throw all that far, Constable. I broke me arm."

"Sergeant."

She giggled coyly. "Sorry. I'm not to know, am I? I broke it, you see, and its never been that strong since.

So I couldn't throw it right over there, like." She pointed to the wall.

"Yes," said Donovan patiently, "but how far do you think they might have gone?"

"I wasn't looking, was I? I just threw them out the window."

Sam turned on her savagely, "You lost them! It's your fault. It's all your fault. You no right to throw my things away. I told you—"

Donovan, concerned at the turn events were taking, broke in, "Mrs Smeed, why don't you go back into the kitchen and throw something out?" He picked up two pieces of tile and handed them to her. As she went obediently through the door into the house he took a long, sober look at her son. Wouldn't hurt a fly, eh? Was that the village closing ranks? Maybe the locals knew just how far to go with this lad. What about Beryl Lisamore? A schoolmistress who had taught him might feel more free to show impatience, or anger, when she found him on the premises, using her computer. He jumped as a piece of tile flew through the air, missing him by a hair's breadth. Elsie Smeed's arm was not useless, by any means. He went swiftly to the spot from which a clink had emerged. Another tile landed.

"There's one," shouted Sam, behind him. "There it is. There it is. Look! Look! I got it. I got it," he yelled, diving on the prize which was several yards distant from where either of the pieces of tile had fallen.

Donovan held out his hand. "Give it to me, Sam."

"It's mine." The boy pressed the disk against his chest.

"Yes, it is yours," Donovan agreed, "but I need to look at it. You won't be able to use it if it's damaged. Just let me check it, boy."

Sammy reluctantly handed over the disk. So far as Donovan could see it was undamaged. He read the words on the label. Universal Micro Floppydisk. WORDSORT. "Damn!" This was the program disk. The one Belcher had replaced. "We've got to find the other one. Keep looking, Sammy. You've done a good job. You can keep that one for yourself, but you can't use it until you find the other one."

Beaming, the boy tucked the disk into the pocket of his jeans. Donovan returned to the spot where the first tile had fallen.

"I could have thrown it different," said Mrs Smeed unhelpfully, speaking through the kitchen window. "You know how it is when you chuck things. You just chuck them."

Sinking to his knees among the rubble, Donovan carefully parted docks, dried grass, and one forlorn ox-eye daisy, working his way in a straight line towards the back wall. And there it was, its silver tab catching the sunlight. He picked it up carefully in his fingers and blew some crumbs of soil away. "Got it! Here we are, Sammy. The search is over. I've got it." He stood up and slipped it into his pocket.

"That's mine," shouted the boy, his face scarlet with indignation.

"If everyone had their rights, it belongs to Miss Lisamore."

"She's dead. She don't want it. She can't use it. It's mine. Finders keepers," said Sammy angrily.

"In that case," said Donovan, "it's mine."

The boy leapt at his mother, both arms raised, his face contorted with fury. "It's all your fault," he shrieked.

Donovan grasped his wrist and swung him round. "Enough of that," he said. "Nothing is your mother's fault. You stole the discs. People go to jail for stealing."

A look of blank incomprehension showed in the boy's face. He turned towards his mother, childlike now, and only faintly aggrieved.

Elsie put an arm round him. "Don't worry, Sammy," she said, "I won't let you go to jail."

As Donovan left by the front door he turned to ask, "Is he often like that? Violent?"

"Never," replied his mother with absolute conviction. "Never. Ask anyone in the village. 'e's never been violent in 'is life."

Donovan went off thoughtfully down the street.

Chapter 28

At Badger Cottage Anthony Rowsell was saying, "I thought you ought to know. It could be important. I think it's a trail you should follow."

"But you didn't get the car's number."

"No. One doesn't tend to take car numbers, Inspector, when out walking."

"And where were you at the time? Outside Miss Lisamore's back gate?" enquired Paton innocently.

"What do you mean?" Anthony spoke sharply. "I was in Old Wood Lane. It was dark. I was simply walking back up the lane. The car turned slowly in and drove past me. It didn't put on speed." He spoke fast, word catching up on word, leaving no space where the inspector might jump in. "I thought the driver was looking for an address. If his motives were bad, seeing me he would naturally drive on, so as not to be identified. By the time he would have come abreast of Miss Lisamore's gate on the way back" – Anthony decided not to confuse the issue by suggesting that the car coming towards him a little later might have been another one – "I was in the high street."

"I belong to Beryl," said Quixote. They both turned to look at the bird. Paton had a queer feeling he knew he was alone in the world.

"You've got to believe me," said Anthony desperately.

Paton shrugged. "If you had got the number," he said, "we could trace it. I've no doubt there were dozens of cars going through the village at that hour. Do you have any idea of its size or colour?"

"Light. It could have been white. Pale, anyway. But you miss my point. It wasn't going through the village. Old Wood Lane leads off into the country. There are only two dwellings there, Cobblers and Wayside. It didn't stop at either. It didn't even hesitate. The more I think about it the more certain I am the driver was looking for this address," said Anthony with the air of a drowning man clinging to a straw and determined it shall keep him afloat.

They both looked up as Sergeant Donovan appeared in the doorway.

"I'll be going," said Anthony. "I must get back to the shop. I thought it better to slip over than to telephone." He turned in the doorway and Paton noticed with interest that he had regained a little of his poise. "I sincerely trust you will treat this information with the utmost seriousness." He nodded to both men and left. They watched him cross the lawn and round the corner of the cottage. "If he's guilty," Paton thought aloud, "he's not going to be easy to crack." He looked across at Donovan. "The field's narrowed. I've been down to the incident room. Word has come in that Paul Street was otherwise engaged that night. He was under arrest. Thinking about that poor misguided little girl, I don't know whether to be glad or sorry. She looks to be set for another shock."

"She's gone, sir. Constable Ellis told me she's gone home with her parents. If she's made it up with them, chances are she'll never know."

Paton remembered the scene in The Fox and Hounds, Goldie Montrose kissing the hands of the middle-aged couple, bringing light back into their faces. "Blimey!" he said. "Kids!" Perhaps he was better off without them.

"There's the papers, of course. She might see his photo if it appears again."

"Shouldn't think she reads papers," said Paton, but without criticism.

"That chap Sammy Smeed is about as harmless as a pitbull terrier," said Donovan. "He could've done it. Easy."

"Got the disks?"

The sergeant nodded.

"Right! Let's get on to that." He was heading for the computer when Constable Ellis appeared in the doorway.

"Mind if I come in, sir?"

"All right. What is it?" Paton spoke impatiently.

"About Mrs Tate. I went over to Pinmartin. It happens my sister is a nurse at Hamberly. I didn't have to—"

"Get to the point, Constable." He was anxious to look at the disks.

"She was there, at Hamberly, that night."

"Why didn't she say so, then? What's the mystery?"

"She had a child before she was married, sir. He's badly, what they call disadvantaged."

"Loony?" suggested Donovan, who knew Paton's views on euphemisms. "Deformed?"

"Yes. He was in the care of her parents. He wasn't expected to live, so she didn't tell her husband. But he did, and her parents died lately and she had to have him moved to Pinmartin. Her husband thinks she does a voluntary job at the local hospital canteen once a week but she only goes there once a fortnight. The other week she visits the boy. That's what the problem was. She hadn't got round to telling Mr Tate."

"Godalmighty, the things we stir up! All right, Ellis. Thanks." The constable left. Paton stood in the middle of the room, hands in pockets, his shirt sagging over his protruding stomach, rocking backwards and forwards on his heels, staring into space. "Do you ever get a conscience about your job, Donovan?"

"No." The sergeant's face split in an infectious grin.

"What about this can of worms we've opened?"

"It was here, wasn't it? We didn't put it here. Cor

blimey! Think about it." Donovan's eyes glowed. "You could write a book about what goes on in people's lives that no one knows about until somebody murders somebody. But it's not our fault, Chief Inspector, sir." He wondered why Paton was suddenly going soft. And then he wondered if he was being tested.

Paton, on his way over to the computer, turned. "Want some advice?"

Donovan looked uncertain.

"If you're going to get wedded to your work, don't get married."

Ever since meeting Goldie Montrose Donovan had been thinking about miracles. "I could get married to someone who's wedded to her work," he said. "All my generation of girls work." He knew what his superior was talking about, his wife was a weight round his neck because she didn't have a job. But that was his problem. He thought it was time Paton stopped dishing out old-fashioned advice. "Different generation," he said diffidently, and was made immediately aware by Paton's sharp scrutiny that he had gone too far. He hurriedly produced the disk.

They were a long time getting the machine started. The inspector stood by the table reading out the instructions from Belcher's Idiot Guide while Donovan put them into action. They made three false starts. "Come on, Sergeant," said Paton irritably. "Put your mind to it. I don't want to have to get Jumping George back."

"I'm trying. It beats me how these kids can work them," the sergeant gazed gloomily at the empty screen, listening to the buzzing sounds.

"They have no pre-conceived ideas of how the things should work. That's why."

"You gotta be a nerd or a child?" Donovan felt exonerated.

"I didn't say that. Look!" A column of names had suddenly flashed up on the screen.

Paton moved to stand directly behind Donovan's chair,

reading down the list. "There's one for her brother!" he exclaimed. "He said she wrote to him when their father died. Let's have a look at it."

"How do I get it?" Donovan, inept and confused, flapped his hands.

Paton turned back to his instruction sheet. "Press D for document, then type the name. Type 'NOEL' and see what happens."

Donovan hesitated, hands poised over the keyboard.

"Noel!" rasped Paton impatiently.

"Noel!" shrieked Quixote.

The two men swung round. The parrot was dancing on his perch. In the sudden silence Paton went over to the cage. Quixote remained silent. The room was very still, or seemed so. Then the bird swung on his perch, gripped the bars of his cage with his beak and claws and hung on, shrieking.

Donovan looked shaken.

"It doesn't mean a thing," said the inspector, hoping it did. "He's in the habit of repeating words if they're said loud and clear."

"She'd yell loud and clear if someone was strangling her. I would," said Donovan.

Paton strode back to the computer. "The brother's car was a sort of off-white," he said, calling the Mercedes up in his mind's eye. "Rowsell said the car he saw on Thursday night was a light colour. D for document. Come on, Mr Donovan. Then type:" He glanced at the parrot and said loudly, "NOEL."

Quixote stared beadily back at him. Donovan sat as though paralysed, staring at the keyboard. Paton gazed at the parrot. "Sorry," said Donovan. "I got the shakes."

"Come *on*," said Paton impatiently. "D for document."

Donovan pressed the key and hesitantly typed "NOEL".

They both peered at the screen. There was a letter dated March 1987. They read it swiftly. It informed Noel that their mother had died. The next one was written four years later. It was polite and dignified. "'You've got so much,' Paton read aloud, 'I wonder if you would think of sharing a little with me. Just enough to pay off the mortgage.' Nothing wrong with that," he commented. "I'd do the same myself, given the circumstances. Roll the thing up, Sergeant. There's another one below." He looked at the date and drew his breath in sharply. "Here's one written a couple of weeks ago. 'There's something I want to talk to you about privately. It concerns a fatal accident in Soho Square at 10.30 pm on the 6th of March last year.' What the hell! Roll it up, sergeant. There's another one below. Look! Look!" he exclaimed excitedly, "It's dated Thursday, the day of the murder!"

They read with growing amazement the story the man Laurie Thomas had told Beryl two years before on the Greek Island of Mykonos. And then her threat to expose her brother if he did not share what she referred to as "the family money" with her.

"He didn't get this letter," said Donovan. "Even if she posted it that day, it wouldn't arrive until after she was dead."

"No." They thought about that. "But he had time to get the earlier one. Maybe she wasn't vengeful when she wrote the first one. Maybe she wanted to find out if the story was true. Maybe if he'd responded right away . . ." Paton's voice trailed off.

"He thought about the first letter for two weeks. Nearly two weeks," Donovan said.

"Yeah. He came in answer to that first letter, all right," Paton agreed. "In the night because his wife doesn't know about the hit-and-run. Maybe he came with an open mind, hoping to say he was sorry he'd treated her badly and let's kiss and make up. If so, the poor bugger timed it wrong. He arrived when she'd been confronted by the daughter and was about to lose her reputation, found her garden was being used as a drinking club, and been roughed up by Rowsell. She wasn't in the mood to be friendly. Also, you've got to remember she'd already written the blackmail letter. Her mind was made up that she could and would get her share of the father's money."

"Maybe he offers to settle," Donovan suggested. "Why wouldn't he? Why should he kill her?"

"Maybe he came with the intention of killing her. He's got a lot to lose. If the hit-and-run can be proved he'd go to prison. Would you trust someone you'd treated badly?"

"Maybe not," Donovan agreed.

"Nobody knows he's here. He's never visited her before. He doesn't know she's got a computer because she's crying poor. He wouldn't expect her to own one. Besides, she gave him coffee in the little front room, so the chances are she took him straight there. This machine is very small. You'd have to be looking around the room in order to notice it. And the screen's gone blank. You have to be standing right in front of it to see the little standby light. Even Beryl hasn't noticed it all evening, or she'd have turned it off."

Paton straightened. It seemed as though they had the answer. "He wouldn't have wanted to park in the high street. Not with those security lights beaming out from the Post Office and his intentions uncertain. He could have been looking for a back entrance when he went down the lane and passed Rowsell."

"There's young Sammy," Donovan reminded him, "When did he come in?"

"It had to be after the murder. He's alleged to walk round the village half the night. Remember, he found the door open. She would be bound to lock up when Rowsell went. Then she would open up for the brother. When he left, if he had killed her, there's no reason why he should bother to shut the door. In fact, he'd want us to think the house had been open so a stranger could walk in.

"Now, the murder. He goes for her. She runs out into the hall."

"Maybe she gets as far as the verandah room before he catches her," said Donovan, looking expectantly at Quixote. "She shrieks—" He raised his voice to a shout, "Noel!"

"Noel! Noel!" repeated Quixote tramping frantically up and down on his perch.

"Good chap," said Paton rising from his chair. He had taken his notebook from his pocket and was looking down at the open page. "Number seven, Church Lane, Old Purford, Oxfordshire," he read. "Now, let's take a little run in the car."

Chapter 29

The inspector depressed the trip mileage recorder to 0 and looked at his watch. From a glance at the map and a quick estimate he thought there were about a hundred miles between Old Purford and Halfpenny Dun, give or take twenty. They would probably reach their destination by 4.30. That would give him plenty of time to interview the wife, visit the local police station and be back at the house to meet Noel when he returned from London.

Sergeant Donovan, sitting beside him in the passenger seat, was silent, consulting his notes.

They found Church Lane easily enough and drove slowly past the house which was a large, between the wars, white stucco villa with all the lack of character that implied. A far cry from the pretty-pretty period cottages they had left behind. More-or-less what he had expected, Paton thought. The front windows, which were decorated with horrible ruched curtains, had a permanently closed look. A narrow concrete path ran in from the road, dividing a neat lawn edged by tidy rose beds. The Mercedes was standing in the drive. Paton drove to the end of the road and turned.

"Make a note of the mileage, Sergeant."

Donovan was already writing it down. "A hundred and thirty. And it's taken us," he glanced at his watch, "nearly three hours. Take off half a hour for that hold-up at the roadworks on the M25. It wouldn't apply late at night or in the early hours."

"One and three quarters in the Merc," Paton said. He

drove back and parked in the road outside. A woman's face appeared briefly at a front window, then disappeared.

Joan met him at the door when Paton's finger was halfway to the bell. She was dressed in a pink floral blouse with a foolish little frill round the neck, and a skirt with a wide belt that accentuated her ample waistline. Her large face registered surprise. "Sorry to bother you like this," said the chief inspector. "May we come in?"

Looking disconcerted, she backed into the hall, and the two men followed.

"I want to ask you a few questions," said Paton.

"We told you all we know."

"Circumstances have changed. I'm sorry. It won't take long."

Joan reluctantly led the way across a red carpet cluttered with putty-coloured whorls and entered a spick-and-span sitting room smelling of furniture polish. A glass-topped coffee table and an enormous magazine rack stuffed with women's magazines stood primly in a circle of wide-armed, hard-looking chairs. Paton caught a glimpse of himself in the oak-framed mirror over the mantel and adjusted his expression. She did not ask them to sit down. He settled into one of the unrelenting chairs and Donovan went to stand by the window fingering his notebook, looking enviously out at the Mercedes. Joan seated herself in the big chair opposite the inspector, filling it with her square hips and large thighs.

Paton said, "You were at home, in bed, you said, when your husband returned last Thursday evening. Could you confirm that you were awake?"

She began to speak, hesitated, then looking flustered, replied, "He always comes in from his meetings about eleven. Always. Sometimes I'm asleep, sometimes I'm not. What does it matter? He always does."

Paton persisted, "Did you actually see him?"

Again, she hesitated. "Well, no. I was in bed. He doesn't always come—" she flushed, then sounding faintly defensive added, "I mean, if I was asleep, he wouldn't wake me. Why should he?"

"You sleep in separate rooms?"

She glanced aside, then nodded faintly as though the admission embarrassed her.

"So you didn't see him, and presumably didn't hear him."

She was silent, staring unhappily down at her hands.

"Mrs Lisamore."

She raised her eyes. "I think I heard him. Why do you want to know all this?" She looked upset.

"Did you hear your husband come in?" He repeated the question. "I'd like you to think carefully before you answer, Mrs Lisamore."

"I think I did," she said.

"But you're not sure?"

"The door was shut." Her eyes were frightened. Paton, feeling sorry for her, decided not to press the point.

He looked down once again at his book. "I've got a note here that he goes up to London by train. Did he go by train last Thursday?"

"Yes."

"You're quite certain of that?"

"Yes, I am." Joan sat up straight, exuding frail defiance. "The man from the local garage drove him to the station, then took the car in to have its MOT."

"Whoopee!" muttered Donovan under his breath. An MOT the day before the murder! That meant they could check the mileage.

"And how did he get it back?"

"The man left it at the station. He always does that after a service. He leaves the keys at the ticket office."

A memory surfaced in Paton's mind of a curious little pause when he had asked Noel about leaving the car at the station. He thought he had imagined the hesitation. Now he knew he hadn't. He guessed the chap had remembered about the MOT, then cast it aside as irrelevant, as indeed it was at the time. But not now. Oh no. Not at all irrelevant, in the end. "Thank you, Mrs Lisamore," he said courteously. "Could I see the MOT certificate?"

Joan looked affronted. "Don't you believe me?"

"I have to check everything." He spoke apologetically.

"Y-es. I expect it's in the car. I'm not sure whether it's locked or not. I'll get the keys. They're in the kitchen. Excuse me." She lumbered to her feet and left the room.

Donovan and Paton followed her as far as the hall then exited by the front door. "Bloody luck!" muttered Donovan, allowing his face to split into a grin as they crossed the lawn.

"Watch your expression, Sergeant."

"Yessir." He went ahead. Joan came to join them, dangling the keys from her fingers. "Try it," she said. "It might be open." Donovan turned the handle. She leaned in at the passenger's side, took the car manual from a pocket, and extricated a single sheet of paper. "This is it, isn't it?"

Paton examined the certificate, making a mental note of the mileage. Donovan looked over his shoulder. Paton handed the certificate back. "Was the car used on Friday, or Sunday?"

"No. I don't think so. Noel left it in the station car park on Friday. Sunday we stayed at home." She looked from Paton to Donovan and back. "Why are you asking me all these questions?" She looked distressed. "Surely you can't be connecting Noel with – I mean, we explained all about the fact that we had no contact. We simply didn't know Beryl."

"Yes, I understand." Paton spoke soothingly. "We have to cover every angle. Why is the car here today?"

"I was doing my weekly shop. Once a week I take Noel to the station in the morning and meet him in the evening so I can have the car for shopping."

"Yes, I see. It's a nice car, Mrs Lisamore," said the

inspector. "Do you mind if I have a look?" Without waiting for her consent he slipped into the driving seat. "Yes, very nice indeed," he added, his eyes roving over the dash, hesitating at the mileage figures, moving innocently on. He climbed out again. "If you leave a car in the drive these days," he said kindly, "it's as well to lock it. There are a great many rogues around." She was not listening, he could see.

"I don't understand why you wanted to see the MOT?" she said querulously. "Why would you think I wasn't telling the truth?"

"I didn't for one moment think you weren't telling the truth. We have to check," he said. "Thank you, Mrs Lisamore. You've been very co-operative."

She had stopped looking co-operative. She stared at him in sullen silence. Then, as he was about to speak again she asked, "Anyway, what's his MOT got to do with you? It was done in time. The insurance isn't due until next week. You're supposed to be finding Beryl's murderer."

"Just one more small matter," he said. "Do you keep any pets?"

"A cat."

"Never had a dog or bird? Budgie, or anything like that?"

"No." She seemed bewildered by the question. "No. Noel doesn't like—" She broke off. Her colour had risen. "What's – I don't understand. You're confusing me. What's this about pets? Why are you so interested in the car? What's the matter with it?"

"Nothing, Mrs Lisamore. Nothing at all. I'd like a word with your husband. What time do you expect him home?"

"His train gets in at 6.30."

"Thank you for your co-operation." Paton returned to his car. Donovan was already climbing into the passenger seat. He looked up, grinning. "Mind if I say you look like the cat that's scoffed the cream, sir?"

Paton grinned back.

"What's this about pets?"

"You're not as bright as you look, Serg," said Paton with the good humour that came when everything was falling into place. "Don't you remember that bugger offering to give Quixote a home? Sounded like a bird-lover, didn't he? If he'd had his wits about him, he'd have taken the old chap at the time of the murder and wrung his neck."

Donovan sat up with a jerk. "Hey! That's my friend you're talking about, Inspector sir."

But Paton, inserting his key into the ignition, was not listening. "Without going anywhere, and without his wife's knowledge, Noel Lisamore clocked up an extra 300 miles between Thursday and today. Let's get off to the local police station and see what we can find out there." As he turned the corner he glanced in his rear vision mirror and saw Joan still standing where he had left her, on the lawn, shoulders hunched, watching them.

Constable Fletcher said, looking over his steel rimmed spectacles at the inspector who had seated himself in the small armchair by the door, "They're very respectable people, the Lisamores. Very much involved with the community."

"Yeah. I believe he's on the local Village Hall committee. Could you tell me the names of one or two people who work round here who are on that?"

Fletcher said, "Mr Hoxton, for one. He's a local estate agent."

"Let's start with him, then. I want to know if Noel Lisamore attended the meeting last Thursday evening. See if you can get him on the phone."

While Fletcher, looking puzzled, found the number Paton stood hands in pockets gazing out of the window, whistling under his breath, feeling happier than he had felt for days. It didn't really matter whether Lisamore went to the meeting or not, with that fast car he could still get to Halfpenny Dun and back before daylight. Behind him Fletcher was asking his question.

Paton turned, waiting.

"No. Not as far as I know. Thanks, anyway." Fletcher looked up. "Lisamore was there. He left half an hour early. Said he thought he had a cold coming on and wanted to get to bed with a whisky and aspirin. He's not ill, is he?"

"Not that I know of." Paton told him of their suspicions.

Fletcher looked stunned. "Is there anything we can do?"

"Not for the moment. We're going to meet his train. We'll be in touch."

As Paton and Donovan returned to the car the inspector said, "Funny thing, this, but I'm glad Rowsell's in the clear."

"I thought you didn't like him much, sir," ventured Donovan, carefully respectful.

"Not him. No. But I like that bright little wife of his, and the kids. And the dog, and the cat," he added wistfully, wondering seriously now if he and Barbara could start again.

"I like the house," said Donovan. "How d'you like to have a house like that?"

"Envy," said Paton, affecting piety, wishing to quash the sin in himself, "is one of the seven deadlies. We've got until sixish. Let's go and see if we can find something to eat."

Chapter 30

The city commuters were streaming out of the station, hurrying to their cars, the younger ones in a frenzy to reach home, running, swinging their briefcases, urgent looking, the older ones taking their time. Joan had parked the Mercedes directly opposite the exit. She could see Noel now, looking to neither right nor left, as was his way, striding, though without speed. She moved over to the passenger seat. He opened the back door and delivered himself of his leather case, slipped behind the wheel and without greeting her reached for the ignition key.

She sensed his mood of self-absorption and was timid in her approach. "Did you have a good day?"

"No. I had a very bad day." He started the engine and waited, staring moodily through the windscreen at the stream of vehicles emerging from the car park.

Joan said, "I had a call from the police."

The car leapt forward, then stalled inches away from the bumper of a grey Rover. She waited nervously for his anger to spill. The drivers coming up behind them hooted impatiently. One pulled out and went around them to the right, another to the left. The Mercedes became an island within the two streams.

"Who came?" he asked.

"That inspector from Halfpenny Dun. Paton. And his sergeant. He wanted to go over what we said about Thursday night. And he wanted to see your MOT certificate."

"MOT? Why?"

"I don't know."

Noel once again switched on the ignition. The last car turned out of the station entrance and disappeared in the main thoroughfare. Noel followed. Paton and Donovan, in the Ford Cortina, moved out of the car park, waited until the Mercedes had turned into the road, then cautiously followed.

The Mercedes crept forward. Noel was staring straight ahead, driving too slowly. Someone honked his horn then two cars fled past, both drivers giving the thumbs down sign.

"They asked what time you would be home. What's the matter?" asked Joan nervously. "Is there something wrong with the car? Why are you going so slowly?"

Noel turned into Belvedere Drive, which would lead eventually into Church Road, though by a circuitous route. The Cortina hesitated at the turn. Paton was endeavouring to keep out of sight.

The Mercedes was nearing the end of Belvedere Drive. The next right turn would take them into a curved lane that ran round the back of the council houses and bring them back into Church Road. Noel swung the wheel and the car turned left.

"Where are you going?" She sat forward in her seat, looking up at him, disconcerted.

He kept the car moving slowly, going in the direction of the motorway. "Did you tell them what time I would be home?"

She said in a flurry, "I don't remember. Yes, I think I did. Noel, where are you going?"

He pulled over to the grass verge and braked to a stop. "You had better get out," he said.

"What do you mean?" Her voice rose. "What do you want me to get out here for? Noel! What on earth is the matter with you?"

"Get out."

"And walk home? From here?" She was outraged.

He spoke to her as though pronouncing an ultimatum,

"Do you want to get out?" For the first time, he looked at her, and she saw the darkness in his face.

"You've done something, haven't you?" Her voice was scarcely audible.

In the wing mirror he saw the Cortina. "What sort of car did they come in?"

"I don't know. Blue."

The Mercedes leapt forward, swung left, put on speed. Ahead now were the motorway signs. "What have you done, Noel?" She kept her mind blank, waiting for the answer, dreading it, in one part of her, knowing.

Noel, watching the rear-vision mirror, saw the Cortina coming up fast behind. "If I'd thought you would be in any way sympathetic, I'd have told you before." He turned left again and shot up the slip road to enter the motorway. Joan watched the speedometer – 50, 60, 70, 80, 90. "Noel! Where are you going?" She began to cry helplessly.

"I'm not going anywhere." He sounded calmer now, as though the speed had eased some of the tension. They left the cars in the slow lane behind, moved right into the fast one. The needle crept higher – 95, 98. "I'd have told you if I had thought you would be even the smallest bit on my side," Noel said bitterly. "But you never are."

A hundred, 105. He had lost the police car, now. "I'm always on your side," Joan cried, though knowing she had not been. Not since his father's death when she had seen him clearly for the first time. "What would you have told me? What had you to tell?"

"Beryl wrote to me after Father's death, asking for money."

"Did you send her some?" She knew he had not, never would have.

"Why should I?" he demanded angrily.

"You should." She was suddenly passionate, forgetting about the car's speed, letting loose all the stored up ill-feeling and disappointment that had been with her for so long. "You know you should. Your father was wrong, to leave all that money to you. Wicked and cruel and vindictive. I tried to tell you it wasn't fair. You could have shared so easily," said Joan, yearning after the lost happiness that could have come from inviting Beryl into their lives. "We have so much."

"Beryl was an immoral bitch. She ruined my life."

"She didn't!" cried Joan, unknowingly sealing her fate. "We could have been so happy, if only you had let her in. It was that awful father of yours who ruined your life. And you didn't have to let him, either." Even knowing it was too late to say this, she rushed on, "We didn't need the money. You've got a good job. Everything could have been so different. You ruined it yourself. You must know that. You ruined your life yourself, Noel. And mine."

He took his startled eyes off the road and saw the truth in her honest, unhappy face; saw his ultimate humiliation in her rejection of him. In a final act of vengeance he swung the wheel.

As the car swerved she knew, though on another level she had known for hours, all day, it seemed, there was nothing to be done. She felt her soul flying with the racing cars that were coming now from every direction, streaking past and around, horns screaming, brakes screeching. She felt herself weightless, rising in the air, floating, looking down. She saw Noel, spreadeagled against the crash barrier, his face upturned, his eyes wide. He was looking at her. She heard his voice, speaking from somewhere in the back of her head, "It wasn't my fault," and felt eerily sad, yet at the same time thinking that it didn't matter, any more.

Noel groaned. His shoulder hurt. Beneath a flattened piece of metal less than a yard away he could see the pink material of Joan's frilly blouse, and a lot of blood. He tried to stagger to his feet, and fell back. He could hear the screaming, and the shouting and running. Somewhere amidst the carnage there were flames. There was an explosion that seemed to go right through him. Panicking, he tried again to rise. He was aware of not dying; of not wanting to die, after all, yet at the same time being terrified of the living that he had tried to end.

A voice asked, "Is he alive?"

"Yes. He seems to be trying to say something." The man bent his head, listening. "What's the problem, old chap?" He straightened and spoke to someone beside him. "He's saying, 'It wasn't my fault.'" The other man leaned over, looking into his face. "It was," he said with feeling. "That's the bastard who was driving the Merc. If he didn't cause it, I don't know who did." He looked down at the still form, crumpled at their feet. "Keep it for the courts, son," he said bleakly. "You're for it. I hope."

In the distance a police siren wailed.

It was eleven o'clock when they set out for home, using the A40 because the motorway was still blocked with the debris of smashed cars. Twelve people dead and 37 injured. Paton remembered the Mercedes stopping not far from the station and thought if he had raced ahead then and blocked it, all those lives would have been saved and the injured would be home now, safe in their beds. Hindsight! It was always there to haunt a man. If I'd done this. If I'd done that. He drove slowly for it was raining hard, the water flooding across the windscreen, the wipers whining, traffic that had been fed in from the motorway building up. He felt sorry for those who had to clear the broken glass and smashed vehicles. It was going to take them a long time, and the rain wouldn't help.

Donovan was silent, thinking about his parrot.

And Rowsell was innocent, Paton thought warmly. Why did he care? There hadn't been time to analyse this feeling he had about Rowsell, his house, his animals and his children. Now he tried to focus his thoughts on them, but they shied away, as though it were too personal a matter to be looked at, even in the privacy of his own mind.

He thought of Mrs Tate with regret. He thought of Mrs Grey of the sexy hips, placing her as one of life's survivors. Penn, the unspeakable vicar. He told himself that exposing Penn balanced out what had regrettably been done to the Tates. It was par for the course, as his father-in-law would say, that some would become innocent victims of other people's sins.

Thinking of his father-in-law brought him to Barbara. He wondered how she would feel about going to New Zealand when he retired. He wondered if that woman's hair would grow again. Innocent victim? Not so innocent, that one, he decided, and remembered Donovan saying you could write a book about his life in his job. Maybe he would.

He remembered thinking as he walked round Crumford Place park that Barbara would fit in nicely in a village like Halfpenny Dun, baking apple pies for the Harvest Festival, making jam to be judged at the Horticultural Society's annual show. Why had he been so adamant that they must live in London? He could imagine her, the Colonel's daughter, chatting up people like Rowsell and Ashenden and Grey. A kind of euphoria, familiar enough to him in the immediate aftermath of a job brought to its successful conclusion, made everything seem possible.

The rain had virtually stopped by the time they reached Wandsworth where he dropped Donovan off. He drove back over Putney Bridge to Fulham. The houses in Donkey Lane were mainly in darkness. No doubt Barbara was in bed. He looked up at the bedroom window. There was no light showing through the curtains. And then he saw that the curtains had not been drawn, and wondered vaguely why. He hoped she wasn't asleep. "I've got news for you," he would say.

He locked the car, went up the path with a jaunty tread, put the key in the door, pushed it open and switched on the light. He would have put his keys on the little antique table Barbara's parents had given them, except that it was not there. The telephone had been placed neatly on the floor against the wall. He stared at it without comprehension, put the keys back in his pocket and went upstairs. The light from the hall showed the bedroom to be empty. Barbara's wardrobe door was open. The contents, even the hangers, were gone. He turned on the light. The bed was neatly made up. The dressing table was bare.

He came slowly back downstairs and went into the sitting room. It looked somehow different. He sat down in a chair waiting for reality. There was an unfamiliar space on the wall opposite, where a picture had been. He looked round the room. The mantelpiece, normally cluttered with photographs of Barbara's family, postcards and ornaments, was bare. There were other things missing. A lamp. Potted plants.

The telephone rang. He staggered to his feet, hurried into the hall and bent down to pick up the receiver. "Hello."

"Chubby." It was Barbara's voice. "I've been trying to get you since—"

"Where are you?" The bewilderment went but alarm bells were sounding in his head. Had he forgotten he was to pick her up, again?

"I'm all right," she said. "I'm with someone who is looking after me very well."

"Oh!" he said, then uncertainly, "When will you be home?"

"I am home," she said. "I've taken my things. Those that are personal to me. We can sort the rest out later. You hadn't noticed, had you?" Was she laughing, or crying? He could not be sure. Then the line went dead.

He stood there in the empty hall with the receiver in his hand, waiting for his mind to assimilate what had happened. After a while he went back to the chair in the sitting room and sat staring at the space on the wall opposite, waiting to be hit by desolation and despair.

It was anti-climax that came. Only that.

He knew why he had dug in his heels and refused to move out of the London that Barbara so disliked. It was because the differences between ill-assorted couples were honed down in big cities where nobody cared much who was who. It would not be like that in his pie-in-the-sky village that he had carelessly invented with nine-tenths of his mind on his job. Take the discomfort he felt in Barbara's parents' house and multiply it by 365 days, add Barbara's resentment at not being included in the social band where she belonged because she was married to a man who didn't fit . . .

Suddenly he knew what it was about Rowsell and his family that had disturbed him. "Lovely family. Lovely," as Mrs Dodson at the Post Office Stores had said. Envy and regret for what might have been had he started out along the right track, with the right girl. This evening he had been following the biggest red herring of them all, superimposing the triumph of a job well done on to the broken shards of his marriage, willing it to hold together until another excitement whirled him away. He didn't blame her for going. He hoped she had found someone suitable. He felt sure she had. She wouldn't be so silly a second time.

The cat entered through the cat flap and looked up at him, mewing. He poured a saucer of milk, watched her drink it, then turned out the light and wearily climbed the stairs.

Boyd County Public Library